AMONG THE
WICKED

AMONG THE
WICKED

Linda Castillo

MINOTAUR BOOKS ⚹ NEW YORK

AMONG THE WICKED. Copyright © 2016 by Linda Castillo. All rights reserved. Printed in the United States of America. For information, address St. Martin's Press, 175 Fifth Avenue, New York, N.Y. 10010.

www.minotaurbooks.com

Designed by Omar Chapa

Library of Congress Cataloging-in-Publication Data

Names: Castillo, Linda, author.
Title: Among the wicked: a Kate Burkholder novel / Linda Castillo.
Description: First edition. | New York: Minotaur Books, 2016. | Series: Kate Burkholder; 8
Identifiers: LCCN 2016001434| ISBN 9781250061577 (hardcover) | ISBN 9781466867277 (ebook)
Subjects: LCSH: Burkholder, Kate (Fictitious character)—Fiction. | Women police chiefs—Ohio—Fiction. | Amish—New York (State)—Fiction. | Murder—Investigation—Fiction. | Undercover operations—Fiction. | BISAC: FICTION / Mystery & Detective / Police Procedural. | GSAFD: Suspense fiction. | Mystery fiction.
Classification: LCC PS3603.A8758 A83 2016 | DDC 813/.6—dc23
LC record available at http://lccn.loc.gov/2016001434

Our books may be purchased in bulk for promotional, educational, or business use. Please contact your local bookseller or the Macmillan Corporate and Premium Sales Department at 1-800-221-7945, extension 5442, or by e-mail at MacmillanSpecialMarkets@macmillan.com.

First Edition: July 2016

10 9 8 7 6 5 4 3 2 1

For my readers

Acknowledgments

One of the highlights of being an author is having the opportunity to get out and meet readers. Every summer I travel to Ohio's Amish Country and beyond for a book tour. I'd like to take this opportunity to thank all the wonderful librarians, booksellers, and others who make it possible: Jim Gill at the Dover Public Library; Dawn Groves at the Massillon Public Library; Jodie Hawkins at the Stark County District Library, Lake Community and Perry Sippo Branches; Pam DeFino at the Cuyahoga County Public Library, Berea Branch; Holly Camino at the Medina County District Library; Sharon Kelly Roth at Books & Co. in Dayton, Ohio; Barbara Peters at the Poisoned Pen in Scottsdale, Arizona; Jill Miner at Saturn Books in Gaylord, Michigan; Robin Agnew at Aunt Agatha's in Ann Arbor, Michigan; John Kwiatkowski at Murder by the Book in Houston, Texas; all the fine members of the Dover Rotary Club (and those great lunches!); and of course I would be remiss not to mention radio personality and all-around fun guy Bob Scanlon at WJER Radio in Dover for those fun-filled mornings at Williams Furniture. Thank you so much for supporting me and the books, for making every event such a success, for spending time and sharing stories with me, and for making all of it so very enjoyable.

I also owe much gratitude to the brilliant and dedicated publishing pros at Minotaur Books: Charles Spicer, Sally Richardson, Andrew Martin, Jennifer Enderlin, Sarah Melnyk, Jeanne-Marie Hudson, Kerry Nordling, Paul Hochman, Kelley Ragland, Marta Ficke, April Osborn, David Rotstein, and Melissa Hastings. Many heartfelt thanks for all you do to bring the books to life. (And for always showing me such a fabulous time when I'm in New York!)

I also wish to thank my friend and agent, Nancy Yost. For everything—thank you!

Blessed is the one who does not walk in step with the wicked.

                                   —Holy Bible, Psalm 1:1

AMONG THE
WICKED

PROLOGUE

She waited until three A.M. She'd tried to sleep, but it was a fruitless endeavor. Instead, she spent five hours twisting in sheets damp with fear sweat, heart pounding, her mind running the gauntlet of the myriad things that could go wrong. Finally, too wired to lie still a moment longer, she tossed the covers aside, rose, and stripped off her nightgown.

Kneeling, she pulled the neatly folded clothes from beneath the bed where she'd hidden them: Long underwear. Blue jeans. Sweater. Two pairs of socks. Insulated gloves. Wool hat. It had taken her weeks to amass those few simple necessities; she'd been forced to delay her escape twice. She'd stolen for the first time in her life. Lied to people she loved. But she'd finally collected enough cold weather gear to get her through. The rest was up to God.

Shivering in the darkness, she pulled on her clothes and tucked the gloves into her pocket. She listened for signs that someone else was awake, but the only sounds were the hiss of cotton against her bare skin and the quick in and out of her breaths. She'd wanted insulated boots, preferably with some tread, but she hadn't been able to afford them, and they were too unwieldy to steal. Her muck boots were going to have to do.

Fully dressed, she slid the cell phone from beneath the mattress. She never risked leaving it on; cell phones were strictly forbidden by the *Ordnung*. The punishment for such a transgression would be brutal and swift. Hopefully, she had enough battery left for the only call she needed to make.

Shoving the phone into the rear pocket of her jeans, she padded in stocking feet to the bedroom door. A smile came to her face when it glided open without so much as a squeak. Amazing what a little lard did to an old hinge. And she reminded herself it was the inattention to details that got you caught. That, she thought, and trusting the wrong people.

Not her. She didn't trust anyone. Hadn't for a long time. Sometimes she didn't even trust herself.

She'd planned this excursion for weeks. She'd run through every detail a thousand times. Envisioned the hundreds of things that could go wrong, and adjusted her plan accordingly. She'd visualized success, too. And she'd never lost sight of what it would mean to her life. It was the one thing that kept her moving forward when everything else was lost.

Freedom.

Silently, she crept into the hall, where scant feet away, the doors to three other bedrooms held the threat of discovery. There were no windows in the hall, no light of any kind, but she'd anticipated the darkness. She'd memorized every step and knew her route as intimately as she knew her own face. Three strides and she reached the stairs. Hand on the banister, the wood hard and slick beneath her palm. She knew not to touch the wall, or risk knocking the picture off its hook. Senses heightened to a fever pitch, she crept down the steps, skirting the fourth one to avoid the squeak of the nail against wood.

At the base of the stairs she paused again to listen, but all she heard was the buzz of the kerosene refrigerator in the kitchen and the tick of the clock above the stove. The sounds were nearly eclipsed by the roar of fear in her head. She could feel her knees shaking; her hands were unsteady, her palms wet with sweat. She couldn't afford to be afraid; fear was a distraction that led to mistakes, and dear God, she would not screw this up. She tried to calm herself—a deep breath slowly and silently released—but it was no use. Terror was a dark presence, its breath hot on the back of her neck.

The faint rectangle of the kitchen doorway beckoned. No flicker of the lantern. No one awake at this hour. To her right, the muddy light from the front window seeped into the living room. The three-quarter moon was another detail she'd meticulously planned for. What she hadn't counted on was the cloud cover. It wasn't going to stop her.

She moved across the plank floor as soundlessly as a ghost. Through the kitchen, linoleum cold against her feet even through two pairs of socks. Then she was in the mudroom. Colder there. No heat. A draft blasting in beneath the exterior door. Coat on the hook. Not heavy enough, but it would have to do. Her boots were next to the rug where she'd left them after mucking stalls earlier, still smelling of horse manure. She shoved her feet into the boots. Pulled on the coat. Buttoned it with shaking fingers. She tugged the gloves from her pockets, jammed her hands into them. Sweating now beneath the coat. Breaths coming short and fast. Fear mocking her as she reached for the knob, telling her she couldn't do this. She didn't smile this time when the door glided noiselessly open.

Outside, snow coming down hard. A quick shot of dismay. She should have anticipated it. For an instant she worried about leaving tracks. But as she made her way down the porch steps, she realized it was snowing hard enough to cover any trace that she'd been there. The low visibility would work to her advantage, too. If someone happened to wake up and look out the window, they wouldn't see her. Another gift from God.

A hysterical titter squeezed from her throat as she sprinted across the yard. Awkward in the muck boots. Feet silent against the snow. Breaths puffing out in front of her. Snowflakes pecking at her face like sharp little beaks. She ran past the shed. Ducked beneath the clothesline. She could just make out the hulking shape of the barn twenty yards to her left. Remembering to avoid the horses lest they whinny in anticipation of hay, she veered right. Past the T-post demarcating the garden. The maple tree in the side yard.

She reached the rail fence, scaled it with the ease of a gymnast, landed on her feet on the other side. Through the veil of white, the mottled wall of trees beckoned. A profound sense of liberation engulfed her as she raced across the pasture. Boots crunching over tufts of frozen grass. The wind whipped at her face, yanked at her coat and hat. Snow stung her eyes. But she knew exactly where to find the mouth of the path cut into the woods. A deer trail she'd been widening and clearing for weeks now. The sons of bitches should have paid closer attention to how she spent her afternoons. . . .

The woods swallowed her, taking her in. The wind chased her for several yards and then tapered off, unable to penetrate the trees. Otherworldly silence all around. The tinkle of snow pellets. She ran for a hundred yards, careful to avoid the fallen log that had been too heavy for her to move. Stooping to avoid the low branch that had been too thick to break.

She stopped in the clearing, bent at the hip and set her hands on her knees. A minute to catch her breath. She had time. Only two miles to go. Past the lake ahead. A right turn at the deer blind. From there, another mile to the road. The most dangerous part of her plan was done.

Giddiness rose inside her. She choked out another laugh, a maniacal sound in the dark and the snow. "I did it," she panted. "I did it. I *did* it."

Straightening, she wiped a runny nose and glanced behind her. Another layer of relief rippled through her when she found the trail empty.

"I beat you," she whispered. "Bastards."

She started down the trail at a jog, finding her rhythm, settling into it. Snow stinging her cheeks, making her eyes tear, but she didn't care. Trees swept by. Elation pushed her forward. So close now she could smell the sweet scent of freedom. A new life. A future.

She reached the lake, a low plane of white to her right. For fifty yards the path ran parallel with the bank. The snow sparkled like diamonds on the ice. On the other side, another line of trees. Muscles screaming, lungs burning, she picked up the pace. One foot in front of the other. Faster now. Comfortable with the pain. Bring it on.

The sight of the footprint stopped her dead. Panting, she stared, confusion and disbelief pummeling her like fists. Alarm knocking at her brain. Terror breathing hot down the back of her neck.

Not possible, she thought.

Her eyes tracked the prints left, into the woods. Not yet covered by snow. *Fresh*. But who would be out here in the middle of the night? Even as her brain posed the question, another part of her already knew, and the knowledge sent a lightning strike of adrenaline burning through her.

A dozen scenarios played in her mind's eye. Continue down the trail at a faster pace, outrun them. Abandon the trail and flee into the woods, lose them in the trees. Or set out across the lake and escape into the forest on the other side. But she knew that wasn't a good idea. While it was bitterly cold tonight, the highs last week had hovered near fifty degrees. She wasn't sure the ice was thick enough to support her weight.

A figure materialized from the woods and stepped onto the trail ahead. A white phantom with dark holes for eyes. Hat and canvas coat caked with snow. Recognition flashed. She tried to be relieved, but her heart didn't slow, her legs didn't stop shaking.

"You scared the shit out of me!" she exclaimed.

A familiar grin. "Sorry."

"What are you doing here?"

"I couldn't sleep." Eyes skittered away from hers. "I couldn't let you leave without saying good-bye." A step closer.

Instinct screamed for her to maintain a safe distance, but she ignored it. No danger here, she reminded herself. Just the paranoia playing tricks on her. "I told you I'd call."

"We both know you won't."

She wanted to argue, but there was no time. She tried to ignore the uneasiness slinking over her, grappled for the last remnants of a trust that had been shattered time and time again. But there was something in those familiar eyes that hadn't been there before.

"I have to go," she whispered. "I'm sorry."

"I love you." Another step. Close enough to touch. *Too close.* "Please don't go."

A flash of resolve. A stab of regret. Spinning, she skidded down the bank, launched herself into a dead run across the lake.

"Wait!"

She didn't dare slow down. A few yards out, she slipped, fell hard on her belly. Snow against her face, in her mouth. Ice groaning from the impact. A split second and she was back on her feet. She ran for fifty yards. Arms pumping. Boots sliding. Eyes flicking toward the bank behind her. No one there. But where?

She continued across the lake. Slower now. Ice creaking beneath her feet. Nearly to the center. Not much farther.

A sickening *crack!* reverberated across the ice. Water sloshed over the tops of her boots. Slush beneath her feet. The realization of a mistake. Another step and the ice crumbled. A trapdoor swallowing her feet first and sucking her down. The shock of cold burned like fire against her skin. She spread her arms, hands slapping against the ice. But the momentum dragged her down, plunging her into freezing blackness. Water closed over her face. Cold ripped the breath from her lungs.

Darkness and panic and underwater silence. On instinct, she kicked her feet. Paddled with her hands. She was a strong swimmer, had swam the length of this lake a dozen times last summer. Her face broke the surface. She sucked in a single breath. Chest too tight. Bottomless cold beneath her.

Sputtering, she reached for the jagged edge of the ice, gripped it with gloved hands and tried to pull herself out of the water. Her shoulders cleared, but the ice broke off in her hands, plunging her back in. Her boots were filled with water. Using her right foot, she toed off the left boot. One foot bare. Body quaking with cold. She could still make it . . .

Kicking hard, she grabbed the edge of the ice, tried to heave her body from the water. Again, the ice crumbled, sending her back into the water. *No,* she thought. *No!* Another wild grab. The ice was solid this time. A scream tore from her throat as she heaved herself upward, but her coat was waterlogged. She wasn't strong enough to pull herself out.

"No . . ." She'd intended to scream, but the word was little more than a kitten's mewl.

For the first time it occurred to her that she might have to abandon her plan. The thought of failure outraged her. After all the preparation, the hope and planning, after seeing to every detail, she was going to drown in this stinking fucking lake like some dumb animal that had wandered onto thin ice.

"*No!*" She tried to slam her fist down on the ice, but her arm flailed weakly. Instead, she reached out and clung to the frozen edge. Shivering. Teeth chattering uncontrollably. Strength dwindling with astounding speed.

Through the driving snow, she caught sight of the figure. Twenty feet away, watching her. She tried to speak, but her mouth refused to move. She raised her hand, a frozen claw against the night sky. She couldn't believe this was happening. That her life would end this way. After everything she'd been through. So close, and now no one would ever know . . .

Exhaustion tugged at her, promising her a place that was warm and soft and comforting. It would be so easy to let go of the ice and give in. End the nightmare once and for all.

Her fingers slipped. Her face dipped beneath the surface. Water in her mouth. In her nose. Body convulsing. Too weak to fight. She broke the surface, coughing and spitting, the taste of mud in her mouth. She looked at the figure, no longer a threat, but her only chance to live.

"Help," she whispered.

The figure lay bellydown on the ice. A branch scraped across the snow-covered surface. "Grab on," the voice told her. "Take it and hold tight."

Hope flickered inside her. A candle fighting to stay lit in a gale. She reached for the branch with hands no longer her own. She couldn't feel them, but watched as her gloved fingers closed around the base.

Ice scraped her coat as she was pulled out, breaking beneath her weight at first, then holding. Closing her eyes, she clung to the stick. Then she was laid out on the ice, still gripping the branch, unable to release it. Violent tremors racking her body. Cold tearing into her flesh like cannibal teeth. Her hair was already beginning to freeze, sticking to her face like strips of cloth.

She was aware of movement, booted feet in the snow. Then she was being dragged toward shore. When she opened her eyes, she saw the black skeletons of the tree branches against the night sky. Strong hands beneath her arms.

She looked up at the sky. Snow slanting down. Her feet leaving furrows in the snow. And she wondered: *How will I run without my boot?*

CHAPTER 1

Dusk arrives early and without fanfare in northeastern Ohio in late January. It's not yet five P.M. and already the woods on the north side of Hogpath Road are alive with shadows. I'm behind the wheel of my city-issue Explorer, listening to the nearly nonexistent activity on my police radio, uncharacteristically anxious for my shift to end. In the field to my left, the falling snow has transformed the cut cornstalks to an army of miniature skeletal snowmen. It's the first snow of what has been a mild season so far, but with a low-pressure system barreling down from Canada, the situation is about to change. By morning, my small police department and I will undoubtedly be dealing with a slew of accidents, hopefully none too serious.

My name is Kate Burkholder and I'm the chief of police of Painters Mill, Ohio, a township of just over 5,300 souls, half of whom are Amish, including my own family. I left the fold when I was eighteen, not an easy feat when all I'd ever known was the plain life. After a disastrous first year on my own in nearby Columbus, I earned my GED and landed an unlikely part-time job: answering phones at a police substation. I spent my evenings at the local community college, eventually earning an associate's degree in criminal justice. A year later, I graduated from the police academy and became a patrol officer.

Over the next six years, I worked my way up to homicide detective and became the youngest female to make the cut.

When my *mamm* passed away a couple years later, I returned to Painters Mill, my past, and my estranged Amish family. The police chief had recently retired and the town council and mayor—citing my law enforcement experience and my knowledge of the Amish culture—asked me to fill the position. They'd been looking for a candidate who could bridge a cultural gap that directly affected the local economy. My roots had been calling to me for quite some time, and after weeks of soul-searching, I accepted the position and never looked back.

Most of the Amish have forgiven me the transgressions of my youth. I may be an *Englischer* now, but when I smile or wave, most return the gesture. A few of the Old Order and Swartzentruber families still won't speak to me. When I greet them—even in my first language of *Pennsilfaanisch Deitsch*—they turn away or pretend they didn't notice. I don't take it personally. I like to call that part of my repatriation a work in progress.

My own family wasn't much different at first. Early on, my sister and brother would barely speak to me. In keeping with the Anabaptist tenet of excluding the wicked from the group, they'd effectively excommunicated me. We're still not as close as we once were; chances are we'll never again find the special bond we shared as children. But we've made headway. My siblings invite me into their homes and take meals with me. It's a trend I hope will continue.

I'm anticipating the evening ahead—a quiet dinner at the farm where I live with my lover, John Tomasetti. He's also in law enforcement—an agent with the Ohio Bureau of Criminal Investigation. I love him, and I'm pretty sure the feeling is mutual. Like any couple, we've encountered a few bumps along the way, mostly because of our pasts—both of which are slightly checkered. But he's the best thing that's ever happened to me, and when I think of the future, it makes me happy to know he's part of it.

I'm doing fifty, headlights on, wipers making a valiant attempt to keep the snow at bay. I've just crested the hill at the intersection of County Road 13 when the buggy materializes out of nowhere. I cut the wheel hard to the left and stomp the brake. The Explorer fishtails, but I steer into the skid. For an instant, I think I'm going to plow into the back of the buggy. Then the tires catch asphalt and my vehicle comes to an abrupt halt on the gravel shoulder on the opposite side of the road.

I sit there for a moment, gripping the wheel, waiting for the adrenaline to subside. Several thoughts strike my brain at once. I didn't see the buggy until I was nearly upon it. The accident would have been my fault. Everyone on board probably would have been injured—or worse.

Through the passenger side window, I see the horse come to a stop. Flipping on my overhead emergency lights, I back up so that I'm behind the buggy to protect it from oncoming traffic. I grab my Maglite from the seat pocket and get out, noticing immediately that there's no lantern or reflective signage anywhere on the buggy.

The driver exits as I approach. I keep my beam low to avoid blinding him as I take his measure. Male. Six feet tall. Mid-thirties. Black jacket. Black, flat-brimmed hat. Matching steel-wool beard that hangs to his belly. His clothes, along with the fact that the buggy is without a windshield, tell me he's Swartzentruber. I've seen him around town, but I've never spoken to him. I don't know his name.

"*Guder Ohvet*," I begin. Good evening.

He blinks, surprised that I speak Pennsylvania Dutch, and responds in kind.

Leaning forward slightly, I shine my beam into the buggy. A thirtyish Amish woman, also clad in black, and six children ranging in age from infant to preteen are huddled in the rear, their legs covered with two knitted afghans. The woman is holding a baby. Dismay swirls in my gut when I'm reminded how this could have turned out.

"*And Wie bischt du heit?*" I ask the woman. How are you today?

She averts her gaze.

"*Miah bin zimmlich gut*," comes the man's voice from the front. We are good.

When dealing with the Amish in an official capacity, particularly the Old Order or Swartzentruber, I always make an effort to put them at ease before getting down to police business. Smiling at the woman, I lean back and address the man. "*Sis kald heit.*" It's cold today.

"*Ja.*"

"What's your name, sir?"

"Elam Shetler."

"Do you have an ID card, Mr. Shetler?"

He shakes his head. "We are Swartzentruber," he tells me, as if that explains everything.

To me, it does. The Amish don't drive; if they need to travel a long distance, they hire a driver. Most do not have driver's licenses, but apply for DMV-issued ID cards. Not so with the Swartzentruber, whose belief system prevents them from having their photographs taken.

"Mr. Shetler, I came over that hill and didn't see your buggy." I motion toward the vehicle in question. "I couldn't help but notice you don't have a lantern or reflective signage."

"Ornamentation," he mutters in Pennsylvania Dutch.

"I nearly struck your buggy." I nod toward his wife and children. "Someone could have been seriously injured."

"I trust in God, not some *Englischer* symbol."

"*Ich fashtay.*" I understand. "But it's the law, Mr. Shetler."

"God will take care of us."

"Or maybe He'd prefer you put a slow-moving vehicle sign on your buggy so you and your family live long, happy lives."

For an instant he's not sure how to respond. Then he barks out a laugh. "*Sell is nix as baeffzes.*" That is nothing but trifling talk.

"The Revised Ohio Code requires reflective signage on all slow-moving vehicles." I lower my voice. "I was there the night Paul Borntrager and his children were killed, Mr. Shetler. It was a terrible thing to behold. I don't want that to happen to you or your family."

I can tell by the Amish man's expression that my words are falling on deaf ears. His mind is made up, and he won't change it for me or anyone else. I'm trying to decide whether to cite him when my phone vibrates against my hip. I glance down to see Tomasetti's number on the display.

Opting to call him back, I return my attention to Shetler. "Next time I see you on the road without the proper signage," I tell him, "I will cite you. You will pay a fine. Do you understand?"

"I believe we are finished here." Turning away, he climbs back into the buggy.

I stand on the shoulder, listening to the jingle of the horse's harness and the *clip-clop* of shod hooves as he guides the buggy back onto the asphalt and drives away.

Snow falls softly on my shoulders. The cut cornstalks whisper at me to let it go. "Jackass," I mutter.

I'm sliding behind the wheel when my radio cracks. "Chief?" comes the voice of my second-shift dispatcher.

I pick up my mike. "What's up, Jodie?"

"You've got visitors here at the station."

"Visitors?" For an instant I envision my sister or brother sitting in the reception area, feeling out of place while they wait for me to show. "Who is it?"

"Agent Tomasetti, some suit from BCI, and an agent from New York."

My memory pings. Tomasetti had mentioned a few days ago that the deputy superintendent wanted to talk to me about an investigation. But the meeting hadn't yet been scheduled and he didn't have any details. Odd that they would drop by after hours on a snowy afternoon without giving me a heads-up. Even more unusual that one of the men is from New York.

"Any idea what they want?" I ask.

"I don't know, but they look kind of serious, Chief." She lowers her voice to a whisper. "Like there might be something big going on."

"Tell them I'll be there in ten minutes." Perplexed, trying not to be aggravated, I put the Explorer in gear and start toward the station, hoping Elam Shetler and his family make it home safely.

I arrive at the station to find Tomasetti's Tahoe and an unmarked brown Crown Vic with New York plates parked next to my reserved spot. There's already a dusting of snow on the vehicles. I park and hightail it inside. When I enter reception, I find my second-shift dispatcher, Jodie, sitting at her desk, eyes closed, drumming her palms against her desktop to Adele's "Rolling in the Deep."

Usually, her workaday antics are a source of entertainment for all of us. Since we have official visitors this afternoon, I'm not quite as amused. I'm midway to her desk when she opens her eyes. She starts at the sight of me, then quickly turns off the radio. "Hey, Chief."

I pluck messages from my slot. "Any idea where our visitors are?"

"Agent Tomasetti's showing them the jail in the base—"

"Right here, Chief," comes Tomasetti's voice from the hall.

He's still clad in the charcoal suit and lavender tie he put on at seven this morning. He's wearing his professional face, no smile for me, and I know this isn't a happenstance visit. The two men coming down the hall behind him aren't here for a tour of my single-cell basement jail.

"Hi . . . Agent Tomasetti." It's a ridiculously formal greeting considering we've been living together for over a year.

"Hi." Two strides and he extends his hand. "Sorry for the last-minute notice."

"No problem. I was on my way here anyway."

"Heavy weather in store for New York tomorrow," he explains. "Investigator Betancourt wants to drive back tonight, before the roads get too bad."

"Long drive." I turn my attention to the two men coming up beside Tomasetti. I don't recognize either of them, but I can tell by their demeanors that they're law enforcement. Overly direct gazes. Suits off the rack. Taking my measure with a little too much intensity. Grim expressions that relay nothing in terms of emotion or mood. That cop attitude I know so well. I catch a glimpse of a leather shoulder holster peeking out from beneath the taller man's jacket.

Tomasetti makes introductions. "This is Deputy Superintendent Lawrence Bates with BCI." He motions to a tall, lanky man with an angular face and skin that's deeply lined, probably from years on the golf course. Blue eyes behind square-rimmed glasses. Hairline just beginning to recede. The slight odor of cigarettes he tried to mask with chewing gum and cologne.

I extend my hand. "Nice to meet you, Deputy Superintendent Bates."

He brushes off the formal title with a grin that belies an otherwise serious demeanor. "Larry, please." He has a firm grip. Dry palm. Quick release. "I patently deny whatever Tomasetti has told you about me."

I return the grin. "I hope so."

Tomasetti motions to the other man. I guess him to be about the same age as Bates. Conservatively dressed in a gray suit, white shirt, red tie, he looks more like a fed than a statie. He's not much taller than me, but he's built like a bulldog and has a face to match. Dark, heavy-lidded eyes just starting to go bloodshot. Five o'clock shadow. He's got *long day* written all over him.

"This is Frank Betancourt, senior investigator with the BCI division of the New York State Police."

I detect calluses on his hand when we shake, telling me he spends a good bit of his time at the gym lifting weights. His eyes are direct, and when I look at him, he holds my gaze.

"You're a long way from home," I tell him.

"That's not such a bad thing this time of year." His smile is an afterthought, his jowls dropping quickly back into a frown.

A pause ensues. An awkward moment when no one says anything. And I realize that with the niceties out of the way, they're anxious to get down to business.

Bates rubs his hands together. "Can we have a few minutes of your time, Chief Burkholder? We've got a developing situation in upstate New York we'd like to discuss with you."

Out of the corner of my eye, I see Tomasetti scowl.

"We can talk in my office." I motion toward the door and lead the way inside. "Anyone want coffee?"

All three men decline, telling me they're seasoned enough to know that police stations and decent coffee is an oxymoron. Tomasetti and Bates settle into the visitor chairs adjacent to my desk. Betancourt chooses to stand and claims his place near the door.

I remove my coat, hang it on the rack next to the window, and slide into my chair. "It's not often that we have visitors from BCI or the New York State Police," I begin.

"Tomasetti tells me you used to be Amish," Bates says.

"I was. I was born here in Painters Mill to Amish parents, but I left when I was eighteen."

"You speak German?"

"Yes, I'm fluent in Pennsylvania Dutch." For the first time, a tinge of annoyance nips at me. I feel as if I'm being held in suspense; they want something but they're being coy about tipping me off because they suspect I may refuse. I wish they'd stop beating around the bush and get to the point. "What exactly can I do for you?"

Bates looks at me over the tops of his glasses. "A couple months ago, the sheriff up in St. Lawrence County—Jim Walker—contacted the state police for help with a developing situation inside an Amish community." He motions to Betancourt. "Frank was assigned the case and had been working with Jim. Two weeks ago, Jim suffered a heart attack. He's on leave and everything was sort of put on a back burner. Things heated back up three days ago when an Amish girl was found frozen to death in the woods a few miles from her home.

"This Amish settlement straddles two counties, St. Lawrence and Franklin, so we contacted the Franklin County Sheriff's Department and brought in Sheriff Dan Suggs. It didn't take them long to realize neither agency had the resources to see this thing through."

The state police usually have a pretty decent budget and resources galore with which to assist small-town law enforcement. In this case, however, the police lab and databases are not the kinds of investigative tools the sheriff needs. And for the first time I know what they want from me.

"We're familiar with some of the cases you've worked here in

Painters Mill, Chief Burkholder," Bates tells me. "You've done some impressive police work." He slants a nod at Tomasetti. "I talked to John about your particular skill set, and I thought you might be able to assist with this case."

Bates motions to Betancourt. "Since Tomasetti and I are pretty much window dressing, I'll turn it over to Frank."

Betancourt comes to life. "On January twenty-first, a couple of hunters found the body of fifteen-year-old Rachel Esh in the woods a few miles from where she lived."

His style differs greatly from Bates's, who seems more politician than cop, preferring to ease into a conversation with a joke and small talk. Not so with the senior investigator. While Bates is laid-back, Betancourt is intense and jumps into the discussion feetfirst. I get the impression he's not shy about ruffling feathers, either.

"What was the cause of death?" I ask.

"The autopsy showed she died of hypothermia due to exposure. There was a snowstorm. For some reason she was out in it and froze to death. ME ran a tox, which showed she had traces of OxyContin in her bloodstream at the time of her death."

"Odd for an Amish girl that age to have drugs in her system," I say. "Does the sheriff suspect foul play?"

"She got the drugs somewhere." Betancourt leans closer. "But even more perplexing is the fact that she'd recently been pregnant."

"Recently pregnant?" I look from man to man. "What do you mean?"

"During the autopsy, the ME found evidence that she'd recently lost a baby. Some fetal material had been left behind."

"Miscarriage?" I ask.

"ME thinks she had an abortion."

"Is parental consent required in New York?" I say.

Betancourt shakes his head. "Nope."

19

"Is there a boyfriend?" Tomasetti asks. "Anyone talk to him?"

"We talked to a lot of people, including her parents, and no one knows who she'd been seeing. We couldn't come up with a single name," Betancourt growls. "No one had ever seen her with a guy. She never talked about him. The family she was living with claimed she didn't have a boyfriend."

"So she wasn't living with *her* family?" I ask.

Betancourt shakes his head. "Evidently, she had some problems with her parents. She moved in with another family, who are also Amish. Basically, no one seemed to know shit about what might've been going on in this girl's life."

"Or else they're not talking." I think about that for a moment. "Had she been reported missing?"

Betancourt shakes his head. "The family she was living with figured she'd run away, gone back to live with her parents. Apparently, she'd done it before. No one checked."

"Sometimes the Amish prefer to take care of their own problems," I tell him. "If they can avoid involving outsiders—including law enforcement—they will, for better or for worse."

"This time it was for worse," Bates mutters.

"Interestingly," Betancourt says, "this girl wasn't dressed in Amish clothes."

"That may or may not be relevant." He gives me a puzzled look so I expand. "At fifteen, she may have been starting *Rumspringa*, which is a teenage ritual, so to speak, in which Amish youths don't have to follow the rules in the years leading up to their baptism. The adults pretty much look the other way." I consider this before continuing. "What was she doing in the woods in that kind of weather?"

"No one knows if she was there of her own accord or if someone took her there and dumped her," Betancourt replies.

"Sheriff Suggs tells us the Amish up there aren't very forthcoming," Bates says. "He's not getting much in terms of cooperation."

"How did the ME rule on manner of death?" Tomasetti asks.

"Undetermined," Bates replies.

Betancourt nods. "That didn't sit well with Jim. Frankly, doesn't sit well with me, either. I mean, we have a dead fifteen-year-old kid who'd ingested OxyContin. Gotten herself pregnant. Had an abortion. Froze to death in the woods. And no one will tell us shit."

"What's the age of consent in New York?" I ask.

"Seventeen," Betancourt says. "There's a Romeo and Juliet law, but if the guy who got her pregnant is more than four years older than our girl, we got him on statutory rape."

"Do the parents know about the abortion?" I ask.

"Didn't even know she was pregnant."

Tomasetti shrugs. "You check with local clinics? Area doctors?"

Betancourt and Bates exchange a look. "ME thinks maybe the abortion wasn't done at a clinic."

"Home abortion?" I ask.

"Probably," Bates replies. "No sign of infection or anything like that, but—and I'm speaking in layman's terms here—I guess there was some internal damage. Not life-threatening, but present nonetheless." Sighing, he motions toward his counterpart. "So we got all of this and then the sheriff gets a visit from a neighbor."

All eyes fall on Betancourt. Expression intense, he leans closer. "A few days after the girl was found, a neighbor, who'd heard about the girl's death, called Jim Walker at home and informed him that a few weeks before her death, Rachel told her there were 'bad goings-on' out at that Amish settlement."

"What kind of goings-on?" I ask.

"According to the neighbor, the girl clammed up, wouldn't get into details. But she thought the girl might've been referring to some kind of abuse and afraid to talk about it. Apparently, there are a lot of rumors flying around."

Tomasetti shifts in his chair. "What kind of rumors?"

"The kind that'll put a chill in your fucking spine." Betancourt tugs a smartphone from the inside pocket of his jacket. "Sheriff Suggs knows a lot more about the situation than I do. You mind if I put him on speaker?" He doesn't wait for anyone to respond and scrolls through his phone. "Dan wanted to drive down here with me but couldn't get away. I got him standing by."

"Sure." I slide a couple of files aside to make room for his phone. He sets it on my desktop.

The sheriff answers on the fourth ring with a stern "Yeah."

"You're on speaker, Dan. I'm here in Painters Mill, Ohio, and I got Chief Kate Burkholder with me." A quick nod at me and he identifies Tomasetti and Bates. "I briefed them on the situation up there in Roaring Springs. We're wondering if you can give us the particulars."

"All I got is rumors mostly." A scraping sound as the sheriff shifts the phone. "Let me give you guys some background first to help fill in some of the blanks and put all this into perspective. About twelve years ago, several Amish families moved from Geauga County, Ohio to a rural area outside Roaring Springs."

"Geauga County isn't far from Painters Mill," I tell him.

"We're located in upstate New York, by the way, about twenty miles from the Canadian border, not far from Malone." He sighs. "Anyway, over the years, these Amish families established a solid settlement and integrated into the community. They were good citizens, good neighbors, and their presence here was, frankly, good for the town. Some of the local merchants started doing business with the Amish, selling everything from eggs to quilts to furniture. Folks started coming into

Roaring Springs from miles around to buy things. Tourists started showing up. Everything changed three years ago when the bishop passed away and the congregation nominated an Amish preacher by the name of Eli Schrock."

"Name's not familiar," I tell him.

"Rumor has it that Schrock—and a few of his followers—felt the previous bishop had been too lenient with the rules, so Schrock tightened the screws. I've heard he's big into the separation thing. Most of the Amish stopped coming into town, stopped selling their trinkets, and basically stayed away." He huffs a short laugh. "Mayor didn't like it much; he was banking on Roaring Springs being the next Lancaster County. Of course, the Amish weren't breaking any laws and they're certainly entitled to stay separate if that's what they want.

"Once Schrock took over, the Amish community just kind of faded away. We saw their buggies and hay wagons around on occasion, but they were quiet and law enforcement never had a problem with them. No neighbor disputes or anything like that. Honestly, no one paid much attention to them until this dead girl showed up."

"Where was the girl living?" I ask.

Papers rattle on the other end. "With Abe and Mary Gingerich."

"What's your take on them?"

"Talked to them at length after the girl was found. They're decent. Religious. Quiet. They were pretty broken up about the girl, but I got the impression they don't care much for us non-Amishers."

"Do you have a sense of what might be going on, Sheriff Suggs?" I ask.

"I've been sheriff of Franklin County for more than sixteen years. I know this county like the back of my hand. But honestly, Chief, I don't know shit about what goes on up there in that Amish settlement." He sighs heavily. "Look, I don't judge people because of how they dress or what they believe. I sure don't have anything against the Amish. But it's sort of common knowledge around here that some of those people are odd."

"Anything specific?" Tomasetti asks.

"Last summer, there was this Amish kid, ten or so years old, came into town with his mom. The cashier at the grocery noticed he had bruises all over his legs. She called us, claiming they looked like whip marks. One of my deputies drove out there. No one would talk to him—not a soul stepped forward. So we involved Child Protective Services. They investigated but were unable to locate the boy or the family.

"In addition to that, we've had a couple of phone calls in the last year. Anonymous. One female claimed people were being held against their will. We were able to trace both calls to the Amish pay phone a mile or so down the road from the settlement. I went out there myself, but as was the case with the boy, no one would talk to me and I was never able to locate the woman who'd made the call or anyone who would substantiate her allegations."

Betancourt makes a sound of disapproval. "Tell them about Schrock."

"Eli Schrock is the bishop out there. He's a charismatic guy. Smart. Well spoken. Devout. Respected by the community. Followers are loyal. I mean these people are *devoted* to him." He pauses. "All that said, there are rumors flying around that some of his followers are scared of him and afraid to speak out. That he's been known to punish people who don't follow the rules."

"What kind of punishments?" Tomasetti inquires.

"Allegedly, he locked one guy in a chicken coop. Held him there for two or three days without food. I heard secondhand that a young man took a few lashes from a buggy whip. One of my deputies says he was told of at least one family that fled in the middle of the night, leaving everything they couldn't carry behind, lest they be stopped by Schrock or one of his followers."

"Any charges filed?" Tomasetti asks.

"Again, no one will talk to us. No one will come forward," Suggs tells him. "Not a damn soul. I spent some time out there after the Esh girl was found. Had a couple of deputies with me, and we couldn't get anyone to answer a single question."

"What's the settlement like?" I ask.

"Eight hundred acres of farmland and forest. River cuts through, so there are some ravines, too. It's pretty isolated. Rugged in places. Pretty as hell in summer. Schrock bought it at a rock-bottom price when he first arrived twelve years ago. Moved into the old farm-house. Lived quietly up until the previous bishop passed away."

"How many people live there?" Bates asks.

"I'd say there are a dozen or so families. The Amish built some nice homes. No electricity, of course. They built barns, too. Got some cattle and horses. A few hogs. They farm the land. Corn and wheat. Hay. Had a couple trailer homes brought in, too. Most of the families have their own land. Only way I know all this is property tax records. Solid information is tough to come by because the community's interaction with the rest of the town is pretty much nonexistent."

Betancourt looks from Tomasetti to Bates, his eyes finally landing on me. "Sheriff's department is worried about the kids out there."

"Especially after this girl showed up dead," Suggs says.

"How many kids?" I ask.

"There are at least forty children under the age of eighteen living inside the settlement. After the Esh girl was found, we sent two social

workers from Child Protective Services out there. There's no indication of abuse, neglect, or maltreatment. But frankly, I don't think CPS
got the whole story."

Tomasetti eyes Betancourt; his expression isn't friendly. "What do
you want with Chief Burkholder?"

Betancourt stares back, unmoved. Tension clamps bony fingers
around the back of my neck.

"I think those kids are at risk," the investigator says. "I think Schrock
is abusing his followers. I think people are afraid to come forward, and
if we don't get someone in there to figure out what the hell's going on,
someone else is going to show up dead, or just disappear and no one
will be the wiser. Someone in law enforcement needs to get in there and
get to the bottom of things."

"Undercover?" Tomasetti asks.

"That would be ideal," Suggs tells him. "Problem is, we have no one
who meets that particular criteria."

"You need someone who understands the culture, has some insights
into the religion; someone who knows the language," Bates adds.

"So whoever goes in," I say slowly, "would need to pose as an Amish
person and become part of the community."

"Exactly," Suggs replies.

A beat of silence ensues.

"You mean me," I say.

"I know it sounds kind of extreme . . ." Betancourt begins.

Tomasetti cuts him off. "Not to mention dangerous. Especially if
Schrock is unstable or fanatical or both."

Betancourt takes the comment in stride. "We would create an identity for you. Set up some form of communication. And of course, we'd
pay for travel, housing . . . whatever supplies and clothing you'd need."

"The county will pay your salary while you're there," Suggs adds.

"You'll be officially deputized and work on a contract basis with Franklin County."

"You've got the background and the experience, Chief Burkholder." Bates offers a full-fledged smile. "Besides, you're the only cop we could find in the country who's fluent in Pennsylvania Dutch."

CHAPTER 2

By the time the three men leave my office, it's after six P.M. I'd expected Tomasetti to stick around, but he had to drop Bates off at the BCI field office in Richfield, since Betancourt was leaving directly for New York. I know the conversation we began here will continue once I get home.

He's got a good poker face, but I know he's not pleased at the prospect of my going into a suspect community nearly six hundred miles away for an unspecified period of time. Of course there wasn't much he could say about it with two of his peers present. I'd assumed Bates knows, or at least suspects, that Tomasetti and I are involved. Now I'm not so sure. If Bates had any inkling that we're together, Tomasetti would have been excluded from the meeting. In fact, once Bates got wind of us living together, Tomasetti would be transferred so that Painters Mill no longer fell within his region. Like most law enforcement agencies—my own small department included—BCI has strict rules about fraternization. Another complication piled on top of an already complicated situation.

I rush through my end-of-shift reports, but my mind isn't on the stops I made in the course of my day. The part of me that is a cop is flattered, even a little tantalized, at the prospect of an undercover assignment. I have a respectable amount of law enforcement experience under my belt. I spent nearly seven years as a patrol officer in Columbus. Two years in homicide. That's not to mention the four years I've been chief. But I've been around long enough to know that no amount of law enforcement experience automatically qualifies you for undercover work.

That type of environment takes a certain breed of cop with a specific set of personality traits, not all of which I possess. I've known several undercover cops over the years, most of whom worked in narcotics. It's dangerous, intense work that involves weeks or months of assuming an identity, infiltrating a sometimes-hostile organization or group, and earning the trust of those in the know. You're isolated, cut off from friends and family, and most often surrounded by individuals you can't trust and don't necessarily like.

Most cops who take on the challenge are young and male. Adrenaline junkies who like being in the thick of things. Extroverts. Good liars. High-energy. Most important, they have an innate ability to transform themselves and take on another persona. They'd never admit it, but a lot of them think they're bulletproof. A few of the narcs I've known have gotten in too deep and ended up in rehab afterward.

I'm none of those things. A few years ago, I might have jumped at the opportunity, if only to prove to myself that I was capable. But I've reached an age where I'm secure in my job. I'm comfortable in my own skin and content with my accomplishments. I like my life the way it is: stable and predictable. While I still like a challenge, I have nothing to prove to anyone. And I'm sure as hell not bulletproof.

That's not to mention Tomasetti. He knows, more than anyone, that no one is impervious to tragedy, especially loved ones. I have to take his feelings into consideration. If I decide to move forward, it won't be easy for him. Five years ago when he was a detective with the Cleveland

Division of Police, a career criminal by the name of Conn Vespian targeted Tomasetti's wife and two children and murdered them in cold blood. Tomasetti is a strong man, but no one recovers from that kind of loss; not unscathed, at least. As a result, he's overprotective and can be overbearing. He's a good cop; I value his opinion and I care about what he thinks, but I know even before discussing this with him that he will not give his blessing.

I'm out the door by eight P.M. The roads are slick with an inch or so of snow, and it takes me forty-five minutes to reach the farm in Wooster. As I drive up the lane, the windows of the old farmhouse glow yellow. Tomasetti has left the porch light on for me. I park next to his Tahoe and enter through the back door. The kitchen is warm and filled with the aroma of the beef stew I tossed into the Crock-Pot this morning. A bottle of Pinot Noir and two glasses sit on the counter. I've taken off my boots and am in the process of hanging my coat on the rack when he appears at the kitchen door. He's fresh out of the shower in faded jeans, a flannel shirt over a waffle henley, white socks on his feet. He doesn't smile, but I can tell by the appreciative way his eyes sweep over me that he's glad to see me.

"Sorry we waylaid you like that earlier," he begins. "Betancourt wanted to beat the bad weather moving in."

"Sounds like an interesting case." I cross to the counter and lift the lid off the Crock-Pot. I stir the stew, but my attention is riveted to the man standing a few feet away. "Does Bates know we're living together?"

"No." He comes up beside me and pours two glasses of wine. "If he'd known, I wouldn't have been in that meeting today."

"Thought that might be the case." I give the pot another stir and replace the lid. "Is your not telling him by design?"

"Never came up." He hands me a glass. "I didn't think it would be an issue."

"It is now," I tell him.

He sips his wine, looks at me over the rim of the glass. "I guess that means you're thinking about taking the assignment?"

"Considering it."

Nodding, he sets down the glass, opens the cabinet and pulls out two bowls, sets them on the counter. "You ever do any undercover work?"

I shake my head. "No."

"I don't have to tell you it can be dangerous."

"I have no such illusions."

Taking the glass of wine from my hands, he turns to me and wraps his fingers around my biceps. He doesn't speak until I raise my gaze to his. "Kate, you're an experienced cop. You're good at what you do. I know that."

"I sense a 'but' coming."

He stares at me with such intensity that I feel stripped bare, as if he can see all the doubts, the fear, the knowledge of what we both know is coming next. "I'm not going to beat around the bush," he says. "This is your decision, not mine. That doesn't mean I'm going to shove my concerns aside, pat you on the back, and tell you to go for it. I'm sure as hell not going to congratulate you. I don't want you to do it for a number of reasons, all of which I'm sure you're aware."

"I know it won't be an easy assignment."

"Easy is not the right word, Kate."

"Tomasetti, I'm not some foolhardy rookie."

"No one said you are." He gives my arms a gentle squeeze. "But you'll be on your own, in a rural area. A *remote* area. You'll be isolated. No backup. You may not have a reliable mode of communication or transportation. And there's no way for you to know what you might be walking into."

"We're talking about an Amish community, not some drug cartel."

"We both know the kinds of things that can happen in an Amish community, though, don't we?"

I ease away from him and pick up my wine. I sip, but I don't taste. "Tomasetti, there are forty kids in that settlement. A dead fifteen-year-old girl—"

"And you're the only one who can save them, right?" He shows his teeth in a poor imitation of a smile.

"This is not about ego."

"Then let someone else handle it."

"There is no one else."

"They can put someone in there with undercover experience. Have him pose as some schmuck who saw God and wants to join the church."

"I'm sure that wouldn't arouse suspicion," I say dryly.

"Not if he's good, and most of these guys are."

"I didn't ask for this," I point out. "They came to me. Betancourt drove all the way from New York to ask for my help."

"You can say no. You don't owe them anything."

"I know that. But Tomasetti, they're right. I'm the best person for the job. I know the Amish. I know the culture. The language. The religion. I know the dress and traditions. I can get in there. I can blend and do what needs to be done. And get out."

"Kate, what exactly do you hope to prove? What's your goal here?"

"Did it cross your mind that maybe I care? That I want to help?"

"If you're looking for a spot with BCI, I can put in a good word for you."

"I was hoping we could discuss this like adults."

"You should know by now I don't make nice. I don't play fair."

"Stop trying to manipulate me. It's not going to work. I have my own mind and I'm capable of making my own decisions."

"I know that. But I'm saying what needs to be said. In case you haven't noticed, I love you. I love our life together, what we've built. I don't want you taking on a dangerous assignment."

His words deflate the anger burgeoning inside me. For a moment, the only sound is the tinkle of snow against the kitchen window and the thrum of my own heart. I watch Tomasetti pull himself back, reel in his temper. Stepping away from me, he goes to the cabinet and pulls out two water glasses.

"I want to do it," I hear myself say.

"Yeah, I got that."

I scramble for the right words, but they elude me. "I don't know how to make this easier for you."

"Say no."

"I can't. I'm sorry."

He offers an unhappy smile as he drops ice cubes into each glass. "So your mind is made up?"

"Yes."

Setting the glasses on the counter, he turns to me, gives me his full attention. "Look, I don't like the idea, but if you want to do it, I'll respect your decision."

"Thank you."

Two steps and I go into his arms. I press my mouth against his. He dives into the kiss without hesitation, and not for the first time I'm astounded that he can still move me so profoundly.

"Maybe we ought to sleep on it," he whispers.

I start to speak, but he silences me with a kiss.

CHAPTER 3

It's nearly eight A.M. and I'm in my office at the station, my phone pressed to my ear, listening to a bad rendition of Journey's "Wheel in the Sky." From the reception area, I hear Mona arguing with a caller about a snow plow that blocked her driveway with snow. So far Mona's winning the argument.

I didn't get much sleep last night. Not because I didn't make good with Tomasetti. I did. But I couldn't stop thinking about the assignment. I couldn't stop anticipating all the things that could go wrong or wondering if I have what it will take to pull it off. Maybe Tomasetti was right. Maybe I'd get up there and find myself in over my head. Then I thought of the dead fifteen-year-old Amish girl, the forty children at risk, and an Amish community that has fallen under suspicion, and I realized I didn't have a choice. All I can do is my best. It's all any of us can offer. I hope it's enough.

I rose early and left while Tomasetti was in the shower. I called Betancourt on my way to the station. He must have driven through the night because he was back in New York and already at his office.

"How soon do you need someone up there?" I begin without preamble.

"How fast can you get here?"

"I have a few things I need to tie up." In the back of my mind, I'm already thinking about how the mayor and town council will react to a request for leave. "If you could e-mail me an official request, I'll present it to the mayor."

"Whatever you need, Chief. We appreciate your agreeing to come up here and lend us a hand. I know it's a sacrifice to be away from home and your family and your own jurisdiction."

"What kind of time frame are we looking at?" I ask.

"It's hard to say. It's going to depend on how quickly you can get in there and figure out what's going on. Could be a week or a month." He chuckles. "Hell, might be that there's *nothing* going on."

Neither of us believe it.

"I'm going to need an identity," I tell him. "Social Security number. Address. In Ohio, most of the Amish carry ID cards. Tomasetti or Bates can probably help me get one under an assumed name."

"You'll need a work history," he says, thinking aloud, and I'm reminded of Tomasetti telling me that neither Betancourt nor Suggs have thought this thing through. . . .

"Might be better if I did domestic work in the past," I tell him. "I cleaned houses for people. Got paid in cash."

"That's good," he says. "Nothing to trace."

"Amish names are pretty specific, too."

"Ah . . . that's a little out of my area of expertise. You got a name in mind?"

I think about it a moment. "I'll go by Kate Miller. That's a common Amish surname here in Ohio. Thirty-five years old. Born August nineteenth." I rattle off the address of a recently abandoned house on the outskirts of Millersburg. "I rented a farmhouse outside of Millersburg."

"Did you stay up all night thinking about this stuff?"

"Actually, I did."

"A lot of lies to keep straight."

"I'd better get used to it." We laugh, but my nerves are zinging.

"The closer to the truth, the better," he says.

"Okay."

"Suggs and I will brief you when you get up here."

"In the interim, I'll e-mail you everything I'll need in terms of my background and things I'll need once I arrive."

"Great."

"I'm obviously going to need to rent a place while I'm there. As close as possible to the Amish community. If you could look into that."

"Sure thing."

"A lot of Amish homes don't have electricity. I'd appreciate it if you could find me a place that at least has electricity. At the very least I'll need to charge my phone."

"Of course. I'll get right on it."

"I'll be driving my official vehicle to New York. I'll need a secure place that's out of sight from the public to park it while I'm there. I'm sure it's overkill, but I don't want anyone to see Ohio plates parked at the sheriff's department."

"I thought of that, actually. We got an impound garage."

"That'll work." I think about transportation and not for the first time I'm reminded of just how complicated the assignment is going to be. "The Amish use drivers when they need to travel long distances. Here in Ohio we call them Yoder Toters. If you can manage it, I'm going to need to make contact with someone who regularly drives the Amish."

"Shit, Chief, I don't know anything about the Amish there in Roaring Springs, but I'll get with Suggs. I'm sure he'll get us what we need."

"I'll have two firearms with me. I'm assuming that won't be a problem."

"We'll get all the official paperwork handled when you arrive. Might be a few forms for you to sign."

"In the meantime, I'll continue working on my story. My background. My family situation. Why I've relocated to Roaring Springs at this point in my life. Why I'm not married."

"Maybe you're a widow? Husband killed in a buggy accident, or something?"

"I like the widow part, but my dearly departed husband probably shouldn't have met his demise in any way that would have hit the newspapers. Chances are, no one will be checking out my story, but if they do, it has to be something believable and untraceable. An illness would be better. Cancer or something."

"Gotcha."

"I'll figure out the details before I get there, put everything on paper for you and Sheriff Suggs."

We fall silent, everything that's been said ringing over the line. "Do the Amish in that part of New York have a newspaper of any sort?" I ask after a moment.

"As a matter of fact, they do. *The Bridge* is printed every other week right in Roaring Springs."

"I'd appreciate it if you'd pick up a copy for me."

"No problem."

"I'm going to get things rolling here," I tell him. "Hopefully, I'll be there in a day or two."

"I'll call Suggs and let him know. He'll be glad to hear it. In the meantime, Chief Burkholder, if there's anything you need to get things moving, give me a call and I'll make it happen."

I thank him, but in the back of my mind, I know the most difficult part of the assignment has yet to begin, and it has nothing to do with Agent Betancourt.

An hour later, I'm in the City Building sitting across from Mayor Auggie Brock. He's a portly man with hound dog jowls and the smile of a born politician. This morning, he looks as if he just lost the election.

"How long are you going to be gone?" he asks.

"I'm not sure, Auggie. I basically have to get inside this community, make contact with the right people, and try to find out what—if anything—is going on." I shrug. "It could take a week, or a month."

I cringe inwardly at the thought of the assignment taking that long. Even as I sit here across from the mayor, laying out the digest version of the case, it's Tomasetti I'm thinking of, not the mayor or the town council or even my position as chief.

He sits back in his chair, looking at me as if I've somehow betrayed him. "A *month*? Seriously? Who's going to run your department while you're away?" he asks in exasperation.

"Glock is more than qualified. He's got the experience. The team respects him. He can handle it."

He picks up the letter from Betancourt and reads it for a third time, his eyes darting left to right, his mouth twisted into a frown. "You know we can't pay you if you're going to be contracting with another agency."

"The sheriff's department is going to match my salary."

The news calms him down a little, but he's still not happy with me. "You're going to have to use vacation days. You know that, right?"

I'd been hoping the township would let me take the time off without burning through my precious vacation days. Tomasetti and I had been planning a trip to the Caribbean in the spring. I'll probably regret it later, but I don't argue. "That's fine."

"If something goes wrong here, will we be able to reach you?"

"I'm going to New York, not Mars. I'll have my phone with me."

I've known Auggie for nearly five years. While we've never been friends, he has been a professional and political ally. He's been fair and supportive—albeit tight with my budget—even when the town council was not. It's disheartening to realize that while this assignment will be an inconvenience for him, it could be potentially dangerous for me and he has yet to acknowledge that.

"So is this a dicey gig you're walking into?" he asks.

I smile. "You know how dangerous those Amish are. . . ."

His eyes widen.

I laugh. "Auggie, I'm kidding."

He actually blushes, and I'm reminded why I like him. "Well, it *is* undercover," he mutters.

"Sheriff Suggs is concerned about the children," I tell him. "I'll need to be on my toes, but I don't believe the assignment is dangerous." I offer another smile. "But I'm glad you asked."

"Oh . . . well. I'm relieved you won't be in any danger. We want you back here in one piece."

"Thanks, Auggie." We rise simultaneously.

I motion to the letter. "I'd appreciate if you kept everything we talked about confidential."

"I may need an explanation for the town council, Kate."

"The council members are fine. And of course, I'll fill in everyone in my department. But the fewer people who know where I am and what I'm doing, the better."

"Sure."

I extend my hand for a shake. "And if you could mention my vacation to the town council, I'd appreciate it."

"I can't make any promises, but I'll see what I can do."

CHAPTER 4

I spent a good part of the morning with my sister, Sarah. To say she was surprised that I wanted to borrow Amish dresses from her was an understatement. A small stab of pain caught in my chest when I saw the flash of hope in her eyes. I knew what she was thinking: that I'd come to my senses and decided to return to the plain life. I didn't go into detail, but explained to her that I needed the clothes for an assignment.

"Your least favorites," I told her. "I'm not particular, but the plainer, the better."

"I've more bosom than you, Katie." She patted her belly. "The baby, you know. I'll need to take them in."

"They don't have to fit well, Sarah. Besides, there's no time for you to alter them."

"That's my Katie, always in a hurry." But she tempered the statement with a smile.

Remembering I'd be joining the church district in New York as a relatively new widow, I added, "And black, if you have them."

"Black?" She tossed me a quizzical look, and not for the first time I'm reminded of the stark contrast between my life and hers.

"I can't get into why," I told her, relieved when she didn't press.

An hour later, I walked away with five plain dresses. Three black, one navy, and one dark gray. Five aprons. An organdy *kapp* and a black winter bonnet. A quick stop at the Walmart in Millersburg, and I own two pairs of plain black sneakers. An insulated black barn coat that comes nearly down to my knees. Several pair of black cotton tights for warmth. Rubber boots for getting around in the snow. Betancourt warned me upstate New York is frigid, with plenty of lake effect snow in late January.

Next, I swing by *En Schtich in Zeit*, A Stitch in Time. It's an Amish quilt and sewing shop on Main Street just two blocks from the police station. Twenty minutes later, I walk out with four crib quilts and half a dozen potholders—all by the same quilter so that the stitching and workmanship are consistent. I also purchased a used sewing kit—the kind any Amish woman might have in her home for mending clothes. All of it cost me a month's salary—which will hopefully be reimbursed by the sheriff's department—but I figure I'll need an Amish-related vocation while I'm there. A profession that serves double-duty, because I'm pretty sure I'll be able to use it to my advantage when it comes to meeting people and, hopefully, infiltrating the community.

I'd texted Mona earlier and asked her to call everyone in the department for a short meeting. I called Glock personally and asked him to meet me beforehand. I know he'll be happy to fill in while I'm away, but I don't want to blindside him in front of his peers.

When I pull in to my reserved parking spot, I notice every slot is filled and Glock's F-150 is already there. I walk inside to find all three of my dispatchers—Mona, Lois, and Jodie—standing at the dispatch station. I can tell by their expressions that they're wondering why I've called a meeting. They know something's up and speculation is running rampant.

"In case you're wondering," I say as I pluck messages from my slot, "I'm not leaving the department."

"That's a relief," Lois says with a sigh.

Mona elbows her. "Told you."

"And you're not pregnant?" Jodie blurts.

"Not lately." I try not to let them see my smile as I continue toward my office. "Send Glock in, will you?"

"You owe me five bucks," Mona whispers behind me, and the three women break into laughter.

I've just let myself into my office and turned on my computer when Glock appears at my door. "You wanted to see me, Chief?"

"Hey." I motion to the visitor chair. "Have a seat and close the door."

Rupert "Glock" Maddox is a former Marine with two tours in Afghanistan on his résumé. Not yet forty years of age, he's a good cop with an easygoing personality, solid judgment, and a wicked sense of humor I enjoy a little too much. He's my most experienced officer, respected by his peers and the community alike—and the first African American to grace the ranks of the department.

"I feel like I've been called into the principal's office," he says, but he's grinning as he takes the chair.

I smile back. "You have."

"Skid did it, Chief. I swear."

I laugh outright. Chuck "Skid" Skidmore is one of my other officers. His sense of humor rivals Glock's, and not for the first time I'm reminded how lucky I am to have these young officers working for me.

"I'm going to be gone for a few weeks, and I'm putting you in charge while I'm away."

His eyes sharpen on mine. "Everything okay?"

"Everything's fine. I'm going to do some contract work for Franklin County in upstate New York."

"I saw those BCI guys in your office yesterday." He raises his brows. "New York?"

I tell him about the assignment. He's the one officer on my team I know does not have a penchant for gossip. "I think it's going to be a quick in and out, probably two or three weeks."

He doesn't look as convinced as I want him to be. "Undercover work can get kind of dicey. . . ."

"You sound like Tomasetti." Glock is one of the few who knows Tomasetti and I are living together.

"He's got a point."

"We're talking about an Amish community, so I don't expect any problems. Still, with regard to the department, and for simplicity's sake, I've decided to keep it vague."

"Probably a good idea." He looks at me as if seeing me in a whole new light. "Anything special you want done here while you're gone?"

"I think business as usual would be our best bet."

"You got it, Chief." I'm a little more touched than I should be when he extends his hand to me for a squeeze and a shake. "Will you do me a favor?"

"Name it."

"Call if you need anything."

I give his hand a reciprocal squeeze. "Bet on it."

Ten minutes later, I'm standing at the half podium in our storage closet–turned–meeting room. Everyone on staff at the Painters Mill PD is here, including Pickles, who just turned seventy-five. As usual, he's in full uniform, including his trademark Lucchese boots, which are polished to a high sheen. He's down to about ten hours a week now, which includes the elementary school crosswalk and the occasional jaunt down Main Street to ticket folks who don't put a quarter in their parking meter.

"Looking sharp, Pickles." Sitting next to him, Skid nurses an extra large cup of coffee from LaDonna's Diner. He's the resident practical joker and all-around smartass, both of which are endearing traits—most of the time, anyway.

"That's what your wife told me this morning," the old man replies.

T.J. Banks, my youngest officer and the only rookie, coughs out a laugh.

For the first time it occurs to me that I won't have my team around to support me. To make me laugh. To back me up. I'm not married to my job, but I enjoy my work. I love the people I work with. They are my family, and the department is the one place, it seems, where I fit in.

I tap the mike, realize I don't need it, and flip it off. "I just wanted to let all of you know I'm going to be away to consult on a case out of state for a couple of weeks. Glock will be acting chief in my stead. Business as usual here at the station."

"Which are code words for behave yourselves," Pickles mutters.

I spend twenty minutes going over assignments and another half an hour as each of my officers reports on things they encountered during patrol since our last meeting. As I wrap things up and watch my team shuffle from the room, I experience an oddly emotional moment and an overwhelming need to call them back. I know it's silly, but in that instant, it feels as if I've bid them farewell and may never see them again.

I'm sitting at the table in the warmth of our farmhouse kitchen. Rain taps like gentle fingers against the window above the sink. A candle flickers in the center of the table, the scent of warm vanilla wafting up to mingle with the aromas of basil and tomato from the soup simmering on the stove. Tomasetti stands at the sink, rinsing our wineglasses, a dish towel slung over his shoulder. From the living room, Harry Connick Jr.'s smooth-as-silk voice floats on the air like smoke.

It should be one of those rare slices of time when everything is right in the world and I'm reminded of all the things that are settled and good in my life. All the things I have to be thankful for. I'm with the man I love, and confident in the knowledge that I'm loved as fiercely in return. I should be relaxed and happy because I'm ensconced in the warmth and comfort and familiarity of my home. But I'm none of those things. I'm antsy and edgy, and though I should be content, some small part of me is already gone.

The clock on the wall ticks, a metronome that never stops. Another minute gone that can't be gotten back. I want to reach out and stop those black hands.

At the stove, Tomasetti still has his back to me. He's putting up a good front, but I know he's angry with me for agreeing to the assignment. We both know that if he turns, I'll see what he's thinking, and this perfect slice of time will no longer be perfect. I don't know how to make any of it right.

"You're quiet," I say when I can stand the silence no longer.

"I'm not the only one." He looks at me over his shoulder. "I suppose I'm just thinking."

"About my leaving?"

"About the soup." But he grins. "Needs a little more cayenne."

I laugh and some of the tension leaches from my shoulders. "I miss you already."

"Not too late to pull out."

I watch as he taps red pepper into the soup. "I can't. I'm sorry."

"I know. I shouldn't have said that."

"But there it is."

He ladles the soup into bowls and brings them to the table, sits across from me. "When are you leaving?"

"Tomorrow morning. Early."

"You packed?"

"Yep." I tell him about the dresses I borrowed from my sister, and he groans.

"Any idea how long you'll be gone?" he asks.

"I can't imagine it taking any longer than a couple of weeks. Three, max."

"Three weeks can seem like an eternity when you're working undercover."

"I know."

"You sure you're up to it?"

"I don't expect it to be easy, but I can handle it."

He's looking everywhere except at me. I know it's because he doesn't want me to see what's in his eyes. John Tomasetti might have a good poker face, but there are certain things he can't hide—not from me. I know him too well. I know anger is one of them.

I'm not hungry, but I pick up my spoon and eat some of the soup anyway. It's good, but too spicy. "Tomasetti."

Finally, he looks at me. Dark eyes level. Resentment simmering just beneath the surface, hidden by a thin film of civility.

"I know you don't want me to do this," I tell him. "I get that."

"You're right. I don't know what else to say."

"You could give me your blessing." I set down my spoon. "You could trust my judgment. My capabilities."

"I do," he snaps. "What I don't trust is this group you're going into."

"They're—"

He cuts me off. "I know. They're Amish. You keep reminding me of that like they're a bunch of fucking angels. But guess what, Kate? Somehow a fifteen-year-old girl ended up dead. She got pregnant. Had an abortion. Her body was pumped full of a dangerous narcotic. And she froze to death out in the fucking woods. That's not to mention the rumors flying about that strange son of a bitch running things."

"I guess you've been doing homework."

"What do you expect?" he asks, his voice a scant inch away from nasty. "Undercover work is dangerous no matter how you cut it."

"I'm not worried—"

"Maybe that's the problem, Kate. You're not worried. You're not afraid to put yourself out there. You're not afraid to lay it on the line. Maybe you should rethink that."

I stare at him, my heart beating hard in my chest. Temper and uncertainty pull me in opposite directions. "I have to do this," I tell him.

"Why?"

"Because I'm a cop. Because I'm the best person for the job. Because I'm good at what I do. Because she doesn't have anyone else to speak for her."

I'm not exactly sure where that last line came from. A place inside me that remembers what it was like to be a fifteen-year-old Amish girl and not have anyone to turn to when my life was shredded by an act of violence. When everyone—my own family included—swept it under the rug and pretended it never happened. I'm lucky because I survived. Rachel Esh did not.

"I need you behind me on this," I say, surprised that my voice is shaking. "I don't want to leave with things unsettled between us."

"Things are not unsettled."

"It doesn't feel that way."

Frowning, he gets to his feet and rounds the table, pulls me to my feet. "I love you. That's not going to change. You got that?"

I don't trust my voice, so I reply with a nod.

"I wouldn't be doing my due diligence if I didn't give you shit about this."

"I got the message," I tell him.

"When you love a cop, worrying sort of comes with the territory."

"Same goes."

"With you"—growling low in his throat, he brushes his mouth against mine—"it's a full-time job."

I don't kiss him back, but something softens inside me. "You didn't bite off more than you could chew when you got involved with me, did you, Tomasetti?"

"I can handle you just fine."

"You're pretty sure of yourself."

"I am."

Falling against him, I raise my face to his. "I need you to trust me," I tell him. "That's all I ask."

"I do." He dips his head and kisses my neck. "Will you do me a favor?"

I loop my arms around him. "Well, now that you're being nice . . ."

"Listen to your gut, Kate. Don't take any chances. Don't trust anyone."

"Okay."

"If you get into trouble, call me."

"Every chance I get."

He pulls back and looks down at me. "I mean it, Kate. Promise me you'll be careful."

"I promise."

Dinner forgotten, he pulls me tightly against him and lowers his mouth to mine.

CHAPTER 5

Sleep is invariably most elusive when you need it, and last night was no exception. Tomasetti slept restlessly, too, but he was snoring softly when I rose at three A.M., showered, and dressed. I grabbed my suitcase, loaded the cardboard box containing the quilts, potholders, and my sewing kit into the Explorer. It's nearly four when I kneel next to the bed and press a kiss to Tomasetti's cheek. Then I'm down the stairs and through the door. I run into the darkness, rain cold on my face, sliding behind the wheel of the Explorer.

My headlights slice through black, driving rain. I'm backing up to turn around when I see the bedroom light flick on. For an instant I consider going back inside to spend a few minutes with him. One more kiss before I leave. My foot hovers over the brake, but I don't stop. We said our good-byes last night, and I don't want to do it again. Instead, I hit the gas and barrel down the lane.

An excruciating loneliness chases me as I pull onto the road, but I don't look back. I don't want to see the light in our bedroom window or think of Tomasetti watching my taillights disappear into the night. The temptation to stay will be too great. I'm loath to admit it, but I don't want to leave. Already, I miss him. Already, I'm apprehensive about what lies ahead.

By the time I hit Ohio 83 north, I'm crying. I know it's stupid, and I'm unduly relieved there's no one around to bear witness. That's the thing about loving someone. You no longer own your heart, and that small, beating organ can turn on you without warning and shred you from the inside out.

As the lights of Wooster disappear in my rearview mirror and my headlights illuminate the road ahead, I regain control of my emotions. By the time I merge onto Interstate 71 north, my thoughts slide toward the assignment I've taken on. Roaring Springs, New York, is a nine-hour drive. Ample time to concentrate on details I undoubtedly overlooked and develop contingency plans in case things don't go as anticipated.

I'm half an hour out of Erie, Pennsylvania, when dawn breaks, revealing a sky the color of rusted iron. A few more miles and the rain turns to sleet. By the time I hit the outskirts of Buffalo, the sleet has transformed into snow. Driving conditions deteriorate with every mile, and by the time I reach the south side of Rochester, the interstate is down to one lane. I jam the Explorer into four-wheel drive and creep along at forty-five miles an hour. The remainder of the journey is a white-knuckle-two-hands-on-the-wheel event peppered with four spun-out cars and a jackknifed big rig.

Ten miles from Brushton, I call Tomasetti. He doesn't pick up. *Meeting*, I think. But that keen sense of loneliness presses into me again. I force it back into its hidey-hole and leave a message.

The blinking neon sign for Skelly's Diner welcomes me at just after three p.m. The "S" has burned out and the sign reads KELLY'S DINER. It's a dive, seemingly in the middle of nowhere. The building had once been a service station; there's a covered portico and an island where the gas pumps were. The windows are steamed up. There are two cars parked in front. In the gravel lot behind the building, a white SUV emblazoned with the New York State Police insignia is hitched to an unmarked travel trailer. I pull around and park next to it, out of sight from the street.

I've just shut down the engine when I see Frank Betancourt exit the trailer. He's wearing a black parka and gray slacks. A second man who I assume is Sheriff Dan Suggs exits the passenger door of the SUV as I'm getting out. He's tall, with a pear-shaped body stuffed into a Franklin County Sheriff's Department jacket. The three of us meet between our vehicles.

"Good to see you again, Chief Burkholder." Betancourt extends his hand. "I hope the snow didn't make the drive too difficult."

"Four-wheel drive helped." I turn my attention to the other man.

"Sheriff Dan Suggs." He reaches for my hand with both of his and shakes it with a good bit of vigor.

I guess him to be nearing fifty. Receding hairline. Red hair that's going gray at his temples. Mottled complexion. Eyes the color of faded denim. Tall with a generous pudge at his middle. He looks like someone's favorite uncle. The one who brought you candy when you were six and made you laugh about stuff you weren't supposed to laugh at.

His gaze is genial and direct. "I appreciate you coming all the way up here to do this, Chief."

"I'm glad to help."

"Coffee's on." Betancourt motions toward the trailer. "I brought our portable office."

I toss an admiring look at the RV. "Nice digs."

Betancourt moves ahead and ascends the steps. "Twenty-seven-foot Winnebago. Confiscated it during a drug bust a couple years back," he says, opening the door. "Comes in handy for long assignments or when we need a mobile base."

"Or to keep someone out of sight," I add.

He holds the door open for us. "That, too."

"Staties get all the good toys," Suggs grumbles good-naturedly.

The interior smells of coffee and the pressed-wood redolence inherent to all trailer homes. This one has been transformed into an office, replete with built-in shelves that accommodate a copier/fax machine, a flat-screen TV, police radio, and a plethora of complicated-looking electronics. Ahead and to my left, a sleek laptop and a short stack of manila folders sit atop a table that had originally been a dining booth.

The trailer rocks slightly when Suggs comes up the stairs behind me. "This thing's nicer than my own living room."

"You guys want coffee?" Betancourt asks.

"I'd kill for a cup." Suggs looks at me. "He's been fussing with that fancy coffee maker for fifteen minutes. You'd think he was some kind of connoisseur."

Betancourt grins as he goes to the stove and pours. "We can sit at the booth there. Facilities are in the rear if you need them, Chief."

I slide onto the bench seat. Through the mini blinds, I notice that the snow has dwindled to flurries, but the sky to the north threatens another round. Betancourt sets three cups on the table and then slides in next to me, careful not to get too close. Professional.

Suggs takes the seat across from us. "We thought it would be a good idea for all of us to sit down and talk before you go in."

I sip coffee that's hot and strong and very much appreciated. "I have questions and some ideas I want to toss out."

"We were hoping you would," Suggs tells me. "We're not exactly in our element here."

Betancourt opens the folder on top and slides a single sheet of paper toward me. "This is everything we have on Eli Schrock, the bishop."

"Kind of a skinny file." Suggs reaches for a folded newspaper beneath his coat and passes me the latest edition of *The Bridge*. "The Amish newspaper as per your request."

"Thanks." Setting the newspaper in front of me, I look down at the information sheet on Schrock. He's forty-eight years old. Born in Lancaster, Pennsylvania, to Swartzentruber parents. Six siblings. No education beyond the usual eighth-grade level. Married Anna Yoder at the age of twenty-six. She was killed in a buggy accident four years later. No children. Never remarried. His work history includes farming and a twelve-year stint as a furniture maker. He inherited his parents' farm when they passed, but sold it a few years later and used the money to buy eight hundred acres north of Roaring Springs.

Upon his arrival, he became active in the local Amish community and quickly earned the reputation as a rabble-rouser. A few years after arriving, he was elected ordained minister of the church district. During that time, he received two citations from the sheriff's department for failure to display a slow-moving vehicle sign on his buggy.

"Except for those citations, he's kept his nose clean," Suggs adds.

Betancourt slides a photo toward me. "That's the only picture we could find. I think it's a few years old."

The photograph is black and white with poor resolution, as if it had been taken from a distance and enlarged. Schrock has no idea his photo is being taken. He's not an attractive man, but his face is commanding. He's dressed in black. Long beard that's still dark. Angular face. Dark gray eyes with a piercing countenance. Heavy black brows.

"From what I've been able to piece together," Betancourt tells me, "he left Lancaster because of some problems with the other leaders of the district. The deacon. Even the bishop."

I look up from the photo. "What kind of problems?"

"I don't really have an ear into the Amish community, so most of this is hearsay, but from what the sheriff down there told me, Schrock thought the bishop was too soft when it came to enforcing the rules. There was some disagreement on the issue of excommunication. He pissed off some people and ended up on the wrong side of the bishop. A feud of sorts started. Evidently, Schrock isn't a very compromising individual and eventually left for New York. A few Amish families followed him. According to scuttlebutt, other Amish with similar beliefs came up from Ohio and as far away as Indiana. At some point he began calling himself bishop."

"Has he had any issues with neighbors since arriving?" I ask. "Any disputes? Things like that?"

"Neighbor to the north isn't Amish, so Schrock doesn't speak to him. To his east is an Amish family that's pretty much part of the community." Betancourt passes me a satellite image map of Roaring Springs and the surrounding area. "The eight hundred acres owned by Schrock are highlighted in yellow. Highways are marked in red. Lesser roads in blue."

"Schrock's place is off Highway 30 near Constable." Leaning closer, Suggs runs a stubby finger along the marked road. "You go north on Lucas Road and there's a two track that'll take you into the community."

"I looked at aerials last night and familiarized myself with the area." A sleepless night spent studying and memorizing maps.

Suggs nods. "That whole area to the north is a jigsaw puzzle of dirt roads and two tracks with a couple of good size creeks and ravines."

"There are some other players involved." Betancourt nods at Suggs.

The sheriff slides a second sheet of paper toward me. "This is everything I could find on the family Rachel Esh was living with when she died."

The information is sparse. Abe and Mary Gingerich. Forty-six and forty-three, respectively. They live in a house outside Roaring Springs, not far from Schrock's land. Four children are grown and out of the house. Special needs girl still at home. Fifteen-year-old Anna. Abe's occupation is listed as a farmer. Mary works part-time at a restaurant in town called The Dutch Kitchen.

I raise my gaze to Suggs. "Any idea why Rachel Esh was living with this couple instead of her parents?"

"The Gingeriches told me she was staying with them to help with Anna, the special needs girl. That's not the whole story. When I talked to her parents, Fannie and Samuel Esh, they let on that they were having some problems with her."

"What kind of problems?"

"They backtracked, but I got the impression she was acting out somehow. I tried, but couldn't get much more out of them."

"I'll try to make contact with them, but it might be tough with them grieving."

"They live on a farm six miles south of the settlement." Another sheet of paper comes my way. "Address is there, along with some info on her best friend."

The information on the best friend is sparse. Sixteen-year-old Marie Weaver. No photo. She works part-time at a mom-and-pop restaurant called Huston's outside Roaring Springs.

"Best friend might be a good source of information," I say. "Have you talked to her?"

"Girl's a piece of work." Suggs sighs tiredly. "I talked to all of them, Chief. No one knows shit about shit. Or else they're not talking."

"What's your gut tell you?"

"Frankly, I can't figure these people out. Here we are, trying to get to the bottom of a girl's death, and yet getting anything out of them has been like pulling teeth."

I nod, not surprised. "Does Schrock have a girlfriend?"

He shakes his head. "Not that I've been able to find."

"That seems odd," Betancourt says. "I mean, even for an Amish guy, right?"

"Most Amish men are married with grown children by that age," I tell them. "Most widowers remarry, so it's an interesting detail."

We fall silent, then I look from man to man. "I suppose I should ask about my accommodations."

Betancourt glances at Suggs, but there's something in his eyes, a look that tells me I'm not going to like what comes next.

"We considered putting you up in the Sleepy Time Motel, but it didn't seem quite right for an Amish woman," Suggs tells me. "Especially since you're supposedly going to be laying down roots." He clears his throat. "I looked at several rentals, and frankly, we're a little limited in Roaring Springs. I finally found a trailer home north of town." He grimaces. "It's fully furnished, including linens and dishes. The landlady, Brenda Bowman, keeps the place real clean. It's not the Ritz, Chief, but the location is damn near perfect."

The word "trailer" roils uneasily in my gut, but I quickly remind myself it's part of my cover and I'll only be here for a short time.

"Most important thing is that it's just half a mile down the road from Schrock's place," Betancourt adds, "and close to town."

"Close to the scene where Rachel Esh's body was found, too," Suggs adds. "Bowman rents almost exclusively to the Amish. She's no frills so you won't have to jump through any hoops. First and last month's rent." He jerks his head toward Betancourt. "We'll supply you with the cash."

"I'm sure you have a personal cell phone?" Betancourt asks.

"I do."

Reaching into his coat pocket, he pulls out a basic smartphone. "We got a backup for you. My cell number is programmed in. Same with

Dan's. And a direct line to the sheriff's department. All on speed dial."
He nods at Suggs. "We'll have our cells with us at all times while you're
here, day and night, and that includes when we're in the shower."

"I'll have to leave it on vibrate when I have it on my person," I tell
him.

"Let's check it now." Suggs pulls out his own phone.

I pick up the phone and set it to vibrate. The sheriff hits a button,
and the phone vibrates soundlessly in my hand. "Good enough," I tell
them.

"Can't have it ringing while you're at church." Betancourt's gaze
meets mine. "You have your sidearm with you?"

"Both of them."

"I'll take care of any paperwork so we're on the up and up with
that," Betancourt says. "Once we finish here and you're dressed and
ready to go, you'll walk into the diner with your suitcase and box, and
ask the waitress to use the phone."

"Dee Dee—the waitress—can be a little persnickety," the sheriff
tells me. "If she gives you any shit, I'll be at the counter. I go in all the
time for coffee. She knows me and I'll make sure she lets you use the
phone."

"Most phones have caller ID, and we thought it was better for
Skelly's Diner to come up," Betancourt clarifies, "rather than your
personal ID or anything to do with law enforcement."

"All this will get the rumor mill humming, by the way," Suggs tells
me. "We don't get many new residents around here."

The grapevine is a powerful mode of communication in most Amish
communities. Word of a new resident will travel fast.

Suggs passes me a sheet of paper with two names and phone num-
bers, and a Roaring Springs address at the bottom. "The driver's name
is Marcella Jennings, but everyone calls her Marc. Drives a beat-up

blue van and hauls the Amish around all the time. Everyone knows her, so she's legit."

"Good," I say.

"You'll also need to call the landlady and tell her you want to rent the trailer," Suggs continues. "Just tell her you saw the ad in *The Bridge*; it says something about the trailer being Amish friendly."

"Got it," I say.

"Once you set a time to meet Bowman out at the trailer, call Marc. Tell her you need a ride from Skelly's in Brushton to the trailer home." He nods to the paper. "Address is there. Marc'll pick you up and drive you out there for fifteen bucks."

The men fall silent. Now that we've touched on some of the details, I suspect the complexity of the assignment is hitting all of us.

After a moment, I say, "I have some thoughts on how to insert myself if you want to hear them."

Both men look slightly relieved, as if they're fresh out of ideas and unsure as to what else they can contribute from this point forward.

"I brought some Amish quilts with me," I tell them. "Baby quilts I picked up at a shop in Painters Mill. I can pass the work off as my own and sell them at one of the shops in town. It'll be a good way to meet some of the Amish women."

"That's good," Betancourt says.

"I think getting a job in town will be beneficial, too, especially in terms of meeting the Amish," I tell them. "I cruised around the Internet last night and found several Amish-owned businesses that might suffice." I glance down at my notes. "The Coffee Cup. The Calico Country Store. And The Dutch Kitchen restaurant."

Suggs nods vigorously. "The Coffee Cup closed last month. Used to be a dozen or more Amish-owned businesses, but most of them closed once Schrock got in there as bishop. Hated to see The Coffee

Cup go. I swear they made the best strawberry-rhubarb pie I've ever had." He grins. "Don't tell my wife I said that."

I smile back. "Attending worship will be one of the best ways for me to get to know people. Generally, the Amish will use someone's home or farm and rotate every other week so hosting such a large event doesn't become a hardship for any one person or family."

"I don't think this community rotates Sunday worship," Suggs replies. "I'm pretty sure Schrock preaches every Sunday out to his place."

"That's unusual," I say. "At his home?"

"I went out there one Sunday morning to talk to him about the lack of reflective signage on his buggy," the sheriff tells me. "There were fifty or sixty people in chairs out in his barn. He has a big potbellied stove in there."

I nod. "Do I have a form of transportation?"

He offers a hangdog frown. "We considered setting you up with a horse and buggy, but we didn't have the funds or the time or the right kind of place for you, frankly. There are no facilities for a horse at Bowman's trailer."

"In Ohio," I begin, "some of the Amish get around on bicycles or scooters. Would that be an option?"

"We can definitely purchase either for you," Suggs says. "Or you can pick up whatever you need and we'll reimburse the cost. But Chief, I can tell you that this time of year there's just too damn much snow for that to be practical."

My heart takes another dive. With several inches of snow on the ground and the temperature below freezing, I'm wondering about the physical logistics of getting around. The notion of trekking through miles of snow in a dress isn't pleasant.

"How far is Roaring Springs from the trailer home where I'll be staying?"

Suggs renders a pained look. "Half a mile south. Like I mentioned, Schrock's place is half a mile straight north. So you're pretty central, if that's any consolation."

"We're sorry, Chief Burkholder," Betancourt says. "We know the lack of transportation may present a hardship, especially with the weather this time of year, but it's the best we could do considering our budget and all those Amish rules."

I think about that a moment. "If there's an Amish family living nearby, I may be able to arrange it so I can pay them to take me places. And there's always the possibility of using a driver." Still, there's no doubt I'll be spending a good bit of time marching through snow.

"What can you tell me about the children in the settlement?" I ask.

"The kids live with their families, of course," Suggs replies. "Some of the families live on Schrock's land. Others live in the general area, on small farms mostly. I think we've got two or three families living in town."

"Is there a school?"

He nods. "It's on Schrock's property. Smallish white clapboard building a few hundred yards from the dirt road. One of the first buildings you come to when you drive in."

I pull out my notebook, scan my notes, then put it away. "I'll be going by the name Kate Miller. I'm a widow. My husband, John, died of cancer nine months ago. I'm Swartzentruber, so I'm looking for a community with like beliefs. I'm from near Millersburg, but I'll keep it vague, in case someone tries to check up on me. Since they have no reason to be suspicious, I don't think they'll go to the trouble. Back in Ohio, I found the Amish bishop too lenient. I heard about Eli Schrock from a cousin who'd heard about him from a friend. My parents are passed away." I shrug. "That's about it."

"Always best to keep things simple when you're undercover," Suggs says. "Good cover story."

Betancourt nods. "A few things to keep in mind, Chief Burkholder. In addition to information on the death of Rachel Esh, we're looking for any indication of child abuse or neglect. You know what to look for." He motions toward the phone. "It's set up for photos."

I nod.

"As we mentioned back in Painters Mill, local law enforcement also got wind of a rumor about people being held against their will. We got nothing concrete. Since these people are so damn secretive, you'll just have to keep your ear to the ground."

"I'm good at that."

Betancourt holds my gaze. "We're going to need you to report in at least once every twenty-four hours. More, if you can manage it. If you go past twenty-four hours, we'll have no choice but to assume you're in trouble."

Suggs interjects, "In which case, I'll check on you at your home. If you're not there, I'll get my deputies involved. We'll drive out to Schrock's place and find an excuse to look around."

I nod. "All right."

Suggs and Betancourt exchange looks. "Is there anything else we can do for you to help you get started with all this, Chief Burkholder?" Betancourt asks.

A uneasy silence echoes within the walls like curse words whispered by a child. I work to settle in my mind everything that's been said, but the mission ahead is unwieldy, with far too many variables.

"I think we've covered just about everything," I say after a moment.

Betancourt reaches into his coat pocket and pulls out a plain white envelope. "Eight hundred bucks cash. It'll get you into the trailer, buy your groceries, and keep you in petty cash for a while. Probably enough left to buy a bike over at the Walmart, if you need it."

I pocket the envelope without looking at the cash. "I think now would be a good time for me to get dressed."

Suggs rises. "I'll grab your suitcase."

CHAPTER 6

It's been eighteen years since I last wore an Amish dress. Even after so much time, the memories and old resentments rise inside me as I pull the clothes from my suitcase. This particular dress is slightly large for my frame, which isn't necessarily a bad thing when you're packing heat. The fabric is heavy for winter warmth, and dark gray, which is acceptable by almost all church districts. I'd forgotten what a pain the pins are, and my fingers fumble helplessly as I secure the *halsduch*, or cape, over the bodice. I poke myself twice before getting everything into its proper place.

I've chosen a thigh holster for the .22 mini Magnum. It's black neoprene. I adjust it so the weapon rests on the side and slightly in front of my right thigh. I drop the cell phone into my pocket. Both items are accessible yet undetectable. For now, I'll keep my .38 and extra ammo tucked into my suitcase.

It takes me another five minutes to secure my hair in a bun, roll the sides upward, and tuck all of it into the white organdy *kapp*. The black winter bonnet fits over the *kapp*. Fully dressed, I stand before the mirror in the bathroom at the rear of the travel trailer, a little shocked by my appearance.

"Hello, Kate Miller," I whisper.

Beyond the door, I hear Suggs and Betancourt talking. Waiting for me. Quickly, I fold my street clothes and cram everything into the canvas bag that will stay with my Explorer. A final glance in the mirror and I open the door.

Betancourt is standing near the dining table and does a double take upon spotting me. "That's quite a transformation."

A sense of self-consciousness steals over me. I feel vulnerable, and for the first time I realize how much of my identity is based on the uniform I wear and the badge that's now stowed in the canvas bag I'll be leaving behind.

Suggs is at the sink, drinking coffee. He swallows hard when he sees me. "You certainly look the part, Chief Burkholder." I give him points for trying not to stare, but he doesn't quite manage. "A deputy is on the way to pick up your vehicle."

Betancourt crosses to me and extends his hand for a shake. "If you need anything, call, day or night." He holds my gaze, doesn't let go of my hand. "You're going to do great."

"I'll do my best."

He jerks his head at Suggs and then leaves.

I blow out a breath, glance at the sheriff. "This feels weird as hell."

"I bet." He grins. "Ready?"

Plucking my coat from the back of the chair, I put it on. I've removed the buttons and replaced them with safety pins, which take another minute to secure. "Let's go."

My Amish clothes are squeezed into a single suitcase. I rolled the baby quilts to save space and fit them into the cardboard box. Tucking the box under my arm, I extend the suitcase handle and roll it to the door.

Outside, the engine of Betancourt's truck roars to life. Suggs opens the door for me. "Good luck, Chief Burkholder."

I look at him. My heart is pounding. I wonder if my face reveals the tension running like hot wires through my nerves. I force a smile. "Roger that," I tell him, and go through the door.

Snow falls from a sky the color of slate. I go down the steps with Suggs behind me. My Explorer is gone. The last link to my life. Behind me, I hear Suggs stowing the steps. I'm aware of the rumble of Betancourt's vehicle as I make my way toward the diner, but I don't look back. As I reach the front of the building, I see the travel trailer pull onto the road.

There are two cars and an old pickup truck parked in front of the diner. A few cars pass on the highway, but the sound of the tires is muted by snow. Propping the box on my hip, I open the door. A blast of heat and the smell of eggs fried in grease greet me. The Doors' "Riders on the Storm" crackles over a bad sound system. Two men in brown coveralls and Ray's Machine Shop caps sit at the counter. In an orange Naugahyde booth to my left, a woman and a little boy share a chocolate sundae. Behind the counter, a waitress in a blue uniform refills a ketchup bottle from a Sam's Club–size container. When the door closes behind me, she looks up and frowns.

I walk to the counter, my suitcase rolling beside me, and set the box on the nearest stool. "May I use your phone?" I ask, invoking the Pennsylvania Dutch inflection I'd fought so hard to eradicate.

The waitress doesn't acknowledge me. Taking her time, she sets down the condiment and screws on the lid. Behind me, I hear the door open. I glance over, see Suggs walk in and take a seat at the other end of the counter without looking at me. For a moment, I think the waitress is going to ignore my request, then she glances my way and rolls her eyes.

"There's a phone booth outside the convenience store in town," she tells me.

Before I can respond, Suggs's voice sounds from the end of the counter. "Aw, now, Dee Dee, let the girl use your phone."

The waitress sets her hand on her hip. "They're always coming in here to use the phone like this is their office or something and I'm their damn secretary. I ain't no one's secretary, and I sure don't have to take orders from you."

He chuckles. "Come on now. It's cold as a well digger's ass out there. This girl looks like she's been on the road awhile. Why don't you let her make her call so she can get to where she needs to go before the snow piles up?"

She glares at me and shakes her head. "No modern conveniences, my big toe. I wish you people would get your own damn phones. They're not free, you know." She reaches beneath the counter, produces an old cordless, and smacks it down on the counter. "I ought to charge you for it."

"I can pay," I tell her. "I just need to call a driver."

"Just use the damn thing," she snaps. "Make it quick, 'cause I got customers."

Pulling the number of the Yoder Toter from my coat pocket, I dial. I feel the waitress and the two men watching me as I wait for someone to pick up. Just when I think no one's going to answer, a gruff female voice answers. "'Lo?"

"This is Kate Miller. I'm Amish and I need a ride to Roaring Springs."

"Where you at?"

"Skelly's Diner."

"That far out gonna cost you, 'specially in all this snow."

"How much?"

"Fifteen bucks."

"I got it."

"All-righty. Give me ten minutes. Be out front, so I don't have to wait."

The line goes dead before I can reply. Keeping an eye on the cantankerous waitress, I disconnect and quickly dial the number for my soon-to-be landlady, Mrs. Bowman. She's a little less colorful than the driver and agrees to meet me in half an hour at the property I'll be renting.

I set the phone on the counter. Dee Dee the waitress is pouring coffee for Suggs. An oversized muffin sits on a saucer next to his mug. He says something and she giggles, slaps at his hand. She pauses at the two coverall-clad men, who've finished their meals, and refills their cups. Setting the pot on the burner, she heads my way and picks up the phone. "You done with this?" she asks.

I nod. I'm wondering if I have time for a cup of coffee when the coverall-clad man closest to me lays a five-dollar bill on the counter, rises, and saunters over to me. He's about thirty. A couple days' growth of beard. His coveralls are dirty, and he smells of ground steel.

"You need a ride somewhere?" He jabs a thumb at his friend. "My buddy and I just finished our shift and we can drop you somewhere if you want. No charge."

I look past him at his friend. I feel Suggs watching me, but I don't look at him. "I already have a ride."

"You sure? Save you some bucks?" He grins. "It's cold and snowy out there."

His friend leans forward and makes eye contact with me. "Warm in our truck."

"And we got four-wheel drive."

"Driver's on the way," I tell him.

He smiles, but it's not quite so friendly now. "Suit yourself. I reckon we can take a hint." He glances at his friend. "You ready?" He grins at the waitress. "See you tomorrow, Dee Dee."

"Be careful out there." She goes to where they were sitting, swipes the five off the counter, stuffs it into her pocket, and begins clearing the dishes.

Suggs does a good job of keeping the cranky waitress entertained while I wait for the driver. By the time I see the blue van pull up, she's laughing. Gathering my box and suitcase, I lug both to the door and walk into my new life.

I'm midway to the van when I hear the driver's-side door slam. A woman the size of a ten-year-old with curly gray hair, a red quilted coat, and a hunched back hustles around the front of the vehicle and meets me at the side. She gives me a quick once-over. "You Miller?"

"Yep."

She wrenches open the sliding side door. "You can put the suitcase on the seat. I got a bad back, can't lift nothing these days."

I load both and climb in.

"Where you headed?"

"Swamp Creek Road."

"I know it. You must be renting Bowman's old trailer."

"I'm supposed to meet her there."

"We'd best get moving then." She slams the door.

I'm no stranger to the dynamics of a small town. Still, it's disconcerting that the first person I meet knows where I'll be living before I do. She puts the van in gear and pulls onto the road. The interior smells of exhaust and cigarette smoke. She's got the radio on, but the reception is bad and there's more static than music. For the span of a full minute, the only sound comes from the rattle of something loose and the *thump* of wipers that need replacing.

On the outskirts of Roaring Springs, she glances at me in the rearview mirror. "I know most of the Amish in the area." She pronounces the word "Amish" with a long *A*. "Ain't seen you around before."

"I just arrived from Ohio."

"We don't get too many new ones." The brakes screech when she stops for a traffic light. "What brings you all the way up here?"

"Bishop Schrock."

"The bishop, huh?" Her eyes go back to the mirror, narrow on mine. "You heard about him all the way from Ohio?"

"I hear he's a good bishop. A strong leader."

"I guess that's one way to put it. You one of them Swartzenrubbers, or what?"

I don't bother correcting her mispronunciation. "My family was, but over the years we've drifted from the old ways. My church district in Ohio . . . the bishop had become mild."

"I reckon sometimes the old ways are the best," she says.

"Do you know Bishop Schrock?" I ask.

"He don't speak to us English folks. I seen him in town a time or two, though," she replies. "Kind of stands out in a crowd. Always wears black. Never seen him smile. Or heard him say hello, for that matter. I mean, if you ain't Amish, anyway. And he's got that stare. Sorta scares people off, if you ask me. I hear he runs a tight ship out there."

"My *datt* always told me that to be worldly is to be lost." It's the first truthful thing I've said so far.

When she looks at me in the mirror, her expression is perplexed. "If that's the case, you should be happy here because Schrock is strict with all them rules." She indicates my dress. "That gray dress you're wearing'll do fine, I suppose. A lot of the women wear black. That's about all in the way of color. From what I hear, he likes the women-folk to wear their skirts extra long. . . ."

I look out the window, but I feel her studying me in the mirror. "You all alone?" she asks.

"My husband passed away," I tell her. "Cancer."

"Hate to hear that." She clears her throat, motions to her left. "Grocery's right there, by the way. They're open till ten every day 'cept Sunday when they close at five."

Through the driving snow, I see the facade of a Big M grocery set close to the highway.

She makes another turn, heading north. We pass a cemetery with grass left uncut, some of the headstones leaning. A farm where a dozen or so cattle stand beneath the overhang of a tumbling-down barn.

The driver makes a sound low in her throat when we approach the sign for Swamp Creek Road. "County don't clear the gravel roads when it gets bad." She hauls the wheel right, hits the gas with enough force to send the van into a fishtail. "Should be okay as long as I don't stop."

I'm holding on to the armrest, wondering how she plans to drop me off without stopping.

She cackles as she barrels through the snow and I realize she's not kidding. "Mrs. Bowman meeting you out here?" she asks.

"Yes," I reply.

"Decent lady. Keeps a clean place and always fair to the Amish. Churchgoing, so she don't put up with no hanky-panky if you know what I mean. Frankly, I think that's why she likes to rent to the Amish. No teenage boys, though. 'Specially when they do that running around thing."

"*Rumspringa.*"

"They're as destructive as a herd of wild boars." She breaks into laughter and I hear phlegm rattle in her chest. "Course she won't have to worry about that with you being a woman, and a widow to boot." She slows the van. "Here we are. Home sweet home."

My heart drops into my belly at the sight of the mobile home. It's tiny, not much larger than a travel trailer, with pink siding striped with rust, and it doesn't look quite level. There's a bay window on the right end. From where I'm sitting I can see that one of the panes is cracked. The steel skirting is robin's-egg blue and there's at least one panel missing completely. I silently curse Betancourt and Suggs as the van rolls to a stop.

"I know what you're thinking. It looks kind of trashy, and I reckon it is, but I been inside and it's clean and warm. Trees are nice in the summer, keeps the place cool." She jams the van into park. "Looks like Mrs. Bowman beat you here. She's prompt, if anything."

I glance through the windshield to see a big red Suburban parked adjacent to a silver propane tank.

"That'll be fifteen bucks. Cash, if you got it." She holds out her hand.

Digging into my pocket, I pull out a couple of bills. "Thank you."

I reach for the handle and get out, relieved to be away from the stink of cigarette smoke and exhaust. Snow squeaks beneath my shoes as I pull out my suitcase and the box. I tuck the box under my arm and drag the suitcase through the snow toward the driver's-side door.

The van window rolls down. She's smoking. "You want me to wait for you?" she asks.

I look at the trailer and sigh. "No."

"Take care." With a wave, she backs up. The wheels spin as she pulls onto the road.

I direct my attention to the red Suburban. A forty-something woman, clad in a long, camel-colored coat and contrasting scarf, slides out and starts toward me. "You must be Kate Miller!"

"Hi." I wade through the snow. "Mrs. Bowman?"

"Nice to meet you, honey." She sticks out her hand without removing her leather driving glove, then motions toward the trailer. "Would you like to see the interior?"

"I would."

She shivers and looks upward at the lowering clouds. "Dreadful weather. Don't let the cold change your mind about moving here. This part of New York is gorgeous in the summertime."

"The trees are nice."

She tilts her head as if trying to decide if I'm being facetious, decides I'm not. "I keep a clean place here. Heat works good. Plumbing, too. I take care of it myself, and believe me, I'm careful about who I rent to."

"I understand."

"Let's get out of this blasted cold. Bring your suitcase and box." She's wearing boots with two-inch heels and wobbles slightly as she toddles through the snow. We go up metal steps, and standing on the metal deck, she jabs a key into a flimsy-looking knob lock. "I require first and last month's rent, and a one-hundred-dollar deposit. I pay all the utilities." She glances over at me, her eyes taking in my dress. "You won't be needing electricity, correct?"

"No." But I'm silently praying I'll have access to power to charge my phones.

The door swings open to a living room that smells of Pine-Sol and mothballs. Faux-wood paneling. Gold curtains. A mustard-brown sofa squats on newish beige carpeting. The air temperature hovers just above freezing.

"I had the carpet put in last year," she tells me, our footsteps muted as we walk inside. "Had it professionally shampooed last week after the last tenant moved out, so probably best if you take your shoes off when you come in." She sniffs, her brows lowering. "I swear the last tenant kept a cat in here. Never saw the litter box, but that smell . . ."

A bar-height counter separates the living room from a small kitchen to my right. An old-fashioned kerosene lamp sits atop the bar. The kitchen is comprised of cheap cabinets and circa 1970s wallpaper. Avocado-colored refrigerator and stove. A stainless-steel sink mottled with hard-water spots. A laminate table with two matching chairs is shoved against the bay window. A smaller kerosene lamp sits in the center and not for the first time I'm reminded that I'll be spending my evenings in the dark.

"It's a twelve-by-fifty-foot Liberty. I think it was built in the late 1970s. Built them solid back then." Mrs. Bowman motions toward a narrow hall. "Two bedrooms and a bath back there. Got lamps in every room, but you'll need to buy your own kerosene."

I'm trying to think of a way to ask her about electricity without letting on that I'm planning to use it. "What about heat?"

"I pay everything, so I'd appreciate it if you didn't crank it up too high. Hot water heater and stove run off propane. Fridge is electric." She raises her brows. "That's not a problem, is it? I know you people don't use electricity . . ."

"It's fine." I try to look pained, but I'm vastly relieved.

I follow her to the rear of the trailer. The floor creaks beneath my feet. The hall wears the same ugly paneling as the living room. We pass a closet-size bedroom, a twin-size bed taking up most of the space. Next is the bathroom. Someone has painted the paneling royal blue. There's a fiberglass tub with a shower curtain covered with seahorses. Blue vanity with a dinner-plate-size sink and pitted chrome faucet. A medicine cabinet with a cracked mirror is mounted above the sink.

I continue on, past a second exterior door on my right that leads to the backyard. The master bedroom takes up the entire rear of the trailer. It's small by any standard and contains a twin bed draped with a threadbare comforter, a closet with a sliding door, and a built-in dresser with four drawers. An alarm clock ticks from atop a plant stand that's being used as a night table. A fat candle on a plate sits on the floor next to the bed. A window unit air conditioner is jammed into the only window. I can feel the cold air pouring in from where I stand.

Mrs. Bowman comes down the hall to join me. "What do you think?" she asks.

"It's perfect," I tell her, trying not to be depressed. I lived in some dives in my early years, but nothing as dismal as this trailer.

"You'll be living here alone?"

I nod. "I'm a widow."

"My Harold has been gone nearly four years now and I still miss him every day." She clucks her mouth. "Alzheimer's. Do you have children?"

"No."

"Well, I don't allow pets." She pats the suitcase-size purse at her side. "I have the lease here, if you'd like to sign. Since you have your things with you, I'm assuming you want to move in today?"

"Right now, if that's all right," I tell her.

"Gotta love a no-nonsense Amish woman," she says. "Let's sit."

A few minutes later, we're seated at the kitchen table. The simple rental agreement is two pages long with a place at the bottom for us to sign and date.

"You're from Ohio?" she asks, looking down at the form.

"Holmes County." I sign and date the second page and slide it over to her. "I'm looking for a job, too. Do you know of anyone hiring here in Roaring Springs?"

"The pancake house off the highway is always looking for waitresses."

"What about Amish businesses?" I ask.

"Well, there aren't many left. The Amish around here keep to themselves." Slipping bejeweled bifocals onto her nose, she signs her name with a flourish. "There's a quilt shop in town called The Calico Country Store. And a restaurant called The Dutch Kitchen. I think they're still Amish owned. Last two left."

"I'll check them out."

She picks up the lease, folds it, and slides it into her purse. "I think we're all official now." She offers me a card. "If the temps dip below zero, keep the water dripping in the kitchen. Keeps the pipes from freezing." Another cluck of the tongue. "I need to get that skirting panel replaced."

I nod, pondering all the different ways I could kill Suggs and Betancourt.

"Toilet paper only flushed down the toilet. No sanitary supplies."

"Got it," I tell her.

"There's no garbage collection out here, so you'll need to take it to the dump. Don't leave it out for the critters. Coyotes will come right into the yard for scraps." She walks to the front door and opens it, shivering a little when the breeze lifts her hair. "Cats have been disappearing all over the place out here."

"No problem."

She steps onto the steel decking, pulling her coat tighter about her. "There's a snow shovel in the shed out back, if you want to make use of it. The closest phone is the Amish pay phone on the corner." She cocks her head at me. "Do you have some form of transportation?"

"Not yet," I tell her. "I may pick up a bicycle."

"Don't know how you people do it." Shaking her head, she descends the steps. "Especially in winter with all this snow. Give me a call if you need anything."

"Thank you."

Giving a final wave, she walks away without looking back.

CHAPTER 7

It's not until I'm alone and the events of the day settle that the enormity of the undertaking hits home. So far everything has gone as planned. But I'm fully aware that, while this first day was productive, the real work has yet to begin.

Nightfall is fast approaching and the trailer is dark, so I take a few minutes to light the lanterns. I check the heat and find that Bowman had it turned down to fifty, so I crank it up to sixty-five. I didn't bring much in the way of clothes—just the dresses and, for when I'm here alone, a heavy cardigan, sweatpants, and a couple of flannel shirts. It takes me ten minutes to unpack and stow everything either in the dresser or the closet. I've decided to keep my .22 and my personal phone with me at all times. I'll need to hide the other phone and the .38 in a safe place.

The trailer rocks slightly when I walk to the kitchen. The flames from the lanterns throw shadows against the ceiling. I look through the cupboards. There's a mismatched set of dishes, but not a scrap of food. I'll need to make a trip to the grocery, and once again I'm reminded that the lack of transportation is going to be a pain in the ass. I find a small pad of paper in one of the drawers and start a list.

I find an electrical outlet in the living room and plug in the phone given to me by Betancourt and Suggs. Relief sweeps through me when the charge symbol flicks on.

I call Suggs. "The eagle has landed."

"You getting settled in okay?"

"So far, so good. I have power to charge my phones. I'm probably going to end up buying that bicycle, even if I can't use it on snowy days."

"I can pick one up for you. . . ."

"As much as I'd like to take you up on the offer, probably best if I can find one for sale by an Amish person. Might be one more way for me to make contact with the community."

"I reckon that newspaper will come in handy after all."

"I plan to get out and make myself known tomorrow."

"Let me know if you need anything, and I'll get it done."

Next, I call Tomasetti and fill him in. "A fucking trailer?" he says. "I guess Suggs takes his budget constraints seriously."

"It's not quite as awful as it sounds." I laugh because we both know it is. "Not the best accommodations but it's close to all the places I need to be, including Schrock's farm."

He sighs. "You without electricity?"

"I've got access to electricity—there's a trusty little outlet here—so I'll be able to keep my phone charged."

"That's something. You're keeping your twenty-two with you?"

"My new best friend."

A lull ensues. I hear the TV in the background and I know Tomasetti is watching the news. I hear the wind tearing around the trailer outside and a pang of loneliness assails me. "I haven't even been gone twenty-four hours and I miss you."

"Kind of quiet around here without you," he tells me.

"You're not trying to tell me I talk too much, are you?"

"Well, now that you mention it . . ." Another silence falls, but it's thoughtful. "I miss you, too," he says quietly.

"It's cold as hell here. We might need to take that vacation when I get back. Someplace tropical."

"I'm going to hold you to it, so don't give me that I'm-the-chief-and-I-can't-get-away line."

"I won't."

"Will you call me if you need anything? Or if you get into trouble?"

"I will."

"I'm only eight hours away, Kate. Four, if I catch a flight out of Cleveland."

"I know. Thanks. I'll call tomorrow."

"Keep warm."

At first light, I'm fully dressed in my Amish garb and bundled in my barn coat, muck boots, and winter bonnet. I pack two of the crib quilts in a canvas bag, hoping to put them up for sale at the quilt shop in town. I'm craving hot coffee as I go through the front door and into a monochrome morning.

I didn't sleep much last night. The trailer is poorly insulated and drafty as a cave. Even with two blankets, I couldn't get warm. I could hear the coyotes yipping in the woods to the north, but they sounded like they were right outside my window. I spent most of the night huddled beneath the blankets, cursing Suggs and his bright idea of putting me up in a trailer. But as I make my way toward Roaring Springs, I have to admit it was a good choice with regard to logistics. The Walmart is about half a mile down the road. Roaring Springs proper is just a few blocks farther. Schrock's property is just as close, but in the opposite direction. My dumpy little trailer home is the heart of it all.

At least the weather has improved. The endless blue sky boosts my spirits, and though the temperature hovers somewhere around freezing, I feel the warmth of the sun on my back. I walk at a steady clip and it takes me just ten minutes to reach Roaring Springs.

The downtown area comprises a dozen or so two- and three-story brick buildings, some with interesting architecture. Most were built at the turn of the century; a few are marked with historical plaques. Despite both of those things, many are vacant, with the front windows boarded up and brick marred with graffiti. The main thoroughfare is cobblestone, but in desperate need of repair.

I'm midway down the first block when I spot the sign for The Dutch Kitchen. It might've been quaint in its heyday. Those glory days are long past, evidenced by a cracked front window, an antique door in need of restoration, and a crumbling sidewalk. I recall Suggs telling me this is where Mary Gingerich works. The woman Rachel Esh had been living with when she died.

I jaywalk and stop to read the whiteboard that has been set up on a tripod displaying the day's breakfast special, which is biscuits and gravy. The coffee of the day is Colombian dark roast. Hefting the bag onto my shoulder, I go inside.

I'm met with the pleasant aromas of sage sausage and freshly brewed coffee. The restaurant is a narrow space with a black-and-white-checked tile floor. A row of red booths lines the wall to my left. To my right, a long counter with old-fashioned stools separates the dining area from the kitchen. There's a smattering of tables at the rear and a battered door marked RESTROOM. The place is doing a decent business this morning. Locals, farmers, and merchants alike sit at the counter. A family of four shares a table at the rear. The waitress is a heavyset blond woman with pink cheeks and a harried expression. The second woman behind the bar is Amish. Wine-colored dress. Dark hair tucked into an organdy *kapp*. Hazel eyes. Her nametag tells me her name is Mary.

I climb onto the nearest stool and set the canvas bag at my feet. The Amish woman glances my way; her eyes brighten at the sight of me, telling me she's pleased to be in the company of another Amish woman.

She works her way over to me. Before she can speak, I greet her in Pennsylvania Dutch. "*Guder mariye.*" Good morning.

"*Wei geth's alleweil?*" she asks. How goes it now?

I offer a grin, continue the conversation in *Deitsch*. "Good, because I know if there's an Amish woman in the kitchen, the food will be good."

"And if she's behind the counter, the service will be even better."

Snagging a glass from beneath the bar, she scoops ice, fills it with water, and sets it in front of me. For the first time I notice the pass-through window and kitchen behind her. A young Amish man wearing a white cook's apron, with a bowl haircut and gaunt features, watches me through the opening.

"I haven't seen you around here before," the waitress says. "Are you visiting?"

My gaze slides away from the cook and I introduce myself. "I just moved here from Holmes County."

"Nice to meet you. I'm Mary Gingerich."

"You're the first Amish I've spoken to since I've been in Roaring Springs."

"We'll have to remedy that, now, won't we?" She scans the customers, looking for coffee cups that need filling. "What brings you to New York?"

"My husband passed a few months ago." I add a grave note to my voice. "We'd become discontent with our church district. The *Deiner* had become high," I tell her, meaning the district leadership had developed a loose interpretation of the *Ordnung*. "Especially the *Velli-cherdiener*." The bishop. "After John passed, I realized I wanted to go back to the older traditions. A lower church." I shrug. "We'd heard about Bishop Schrock and talked about moving, but then he got sick. . . . I decided to make the move on my own."

"All alone?"

I nod.

"That's a very brave thing to do."

"God was with me the whole way."

She nods, like-minded and understanding. "You know of Bishop Schrock, then?"

"A little. Things I've heard."

"Well, he believes in *das alt Gebrauch*." The old ways. "He believes in *Regel und Ordnung*, too." Rules and order. She lowers her voice. "Bishop Schrock still uses *Meidung*."

It's the Amish term for "shunning" or "social avoidance." Contrary to popular belief, the *bann* isn't a form of punishment. Most often, it's used to induce a person to confess their sins and apologize to the church, at which point they're usually reinstated.

"It's brought back a lot of backsliders who might've otherwise been lost," I say.

She shakes her head. "If Bishop Schrock puts you under the *bann*, it's for life."

A man wearing insulated coveralls and a John Deere cap enters. Mary glances toward the door and goes back into waitress mode, addressing me quickly. "*Witt du wennich eppes zu ess?*" Would you like something to eat?

"Coffee and the breakfast special," I tell her.

"Coming right up."

By the time I've finished eating, I know a lot more about the Amish community in and around Roaring Springs than when I walked in. I know that worship is on Sunday and it's always held in Eli Schrock's barn. I know that when Mary Gingerich speaks of Schrock, it's in a hushed tone and with reverence.

I strike up another conversation while she clears my dishes. "I'm looking for work," I tell her. "Is The Dutch Kitchen hiring?"

"Things are slow," she replies. "Work's hard to come by around here. Do you sew?"

"Yes."

"You might try The Calico Country Store down the street."

"Thanks, I will." Leaving a five-dollar bill on the counter, I slide from the stool and heft the bag onto my shoulder.

I start for the door, but she calls out my name. "Do you have a way to get to worship tomorrow?"

I stop and turn. "I was going to walk."

"Abe and I will pick you up in the buggy. We've plenty of room and your trailer's right on the way."

I smile. "See you then."

Situated in the first level of a historic building at the intersection of Main and Fourth Street, The Calico Country Store is the shining star of Roaring Springs's downtown. The windows are retail artistry, an Amish-style display of locally made furniture, hand-carved toys, and an iconic nine-patch quilt in burgundy and cream.

The cowbell mounted on the door jingles when I walk inside. The aromas of lavender and yeast bread invite me to venture deeper. The place is a far cry from the slightly chaotic atmosphere of The Dutch Kitchen down the street. This store is orderly, with a character that's uniquely Amish. The plank floors have been sanded and polished to a high sheen. The wall to my left is affixed with dozens of metal arms from which quilts hang. I see a red and blue double wedding ring quilt, a brown and white patchwork quilt, a stunning blue and red star pattern quilt. Beyond, a wall of crib quilts in pink and yellow, lavender and blue.

"They're beautiful, aren't they?"

I glance right to see a pretty Amish woman standing a few feet away, admiring the quilts, same as me. She's about fifty years old, with a freckled nose and eyes as deep and green as a country pond. She's generously built, but carries the weight well.

"Yes, they are," I tell her.

"Most of our customers are *Englischers* these days." She sighs. "And there aren't nearly enough of them, so it's nice to see the Amish come in."

I offer her a questioning look, but she waves it off. "Downtown Roaring Springs isn't exactly a bustling retail center," she tells me.

"It should be." Reaching out, I run my hand over one of the quilts. "I've never seen a prettier collection."

She stands back, studying me, while I pretend to peruse. "I know all the Amish faces around here and I don't believe we've met."

"I'm Kate Miller. I just arrived from Ohio."

"It's nice to meet you, Kate. I'm Laura Hershberger." Her eyes brighten. "What part of Ohio?"

"Holmes County."

"I was born in Dundee."

Uneasiness quivers through me. The last thing any undercover cop wants is for someone to be familiar with their hometown. "I've been through Dundee many times," I return easily.

"Is the Amish Door Village still in business?" she asks.

"And they still have the best meat loaf and mashed potatoes around."

Smiling, we share the moment. Two strangers longing for home and knowing they may never see it again.

"How long have you lived in Roaring Springs?" I ask.

"Going on twelve years now." She cocks her head. "What brings you all the way up here to New York?"

I give her the same explanation I gave Mary Gingerich. "Our church district had become too lenient." I shake my head. "John and I wanted to get back to the old ways. When we heard about Bishop Schrock . . ." I shrug. "But John got sick. The Lord took him before we had a chance to move. I knew it was something I needed to do on my own."

"I'm sorry you lost your husband. Do you have children?"

"No."

"Oh, I'm sorry."

I lower my gaze. When you're Amish and childless, you're somehow diminished. I work to shift the conversation away from me. The less people know, the less chance I have of getting caught in a lie. "I met Mary Gingerich at The Dutch Kitchen earlier."

"Good thing she's back at work." She tuts. "She and Abe were pretty broken up after that business with the Esh girl."

My cop's antenna pricks up. "The girl who died?"

She tosses me a surprised look.

"I read about it in *The Bridge*," I explain.

"News travels, especially when it's bad." She shakes her head. "It was an awful thing, made worse because she was so young. Mary and Abe were just beside themselves. Fannie and Samuel"—she shakes her head—"were inconsolable. Bishop Schrock spent that first terrible night with them."

"I can't imagine losing a child."

"At first everyone thought Rachel had run away. But there were all sorts of rumors flying around."

"Rumors?" I muster a puzzled look. "But it was an accident, right? She got lost in the woods and succumbed to the cold?"

"That's what everyone says." There are no customers in the shop, but she looks left and right just to make sure. "I think there was more to it."

I lower my voice. "What do you mean?"

"Not to speak ill of the dead, but Rachel Esh was a wild little thing. Pretty as a peach, but she didn't care much for the rules, and spent a good bit of time breaking them. Wearing *Englischer* clothes and whatnot. She didn't get along with her parents, so she moved in with Mary and Abe. Didn't work out so well there, either, from what I've heard."

"*Rumspringa* can be a confusing time for young people," I say, staying neutral, trying to keep her talking. "A lot of temptation these days."

"The sheriff's department has been sniffing around and asking all sorts of questions. Word around town is, Rachel wasn't out there by herself."

I stare at her, trying not to look too interested, not sure I'm succeeding. "Who?"

"No one knows. I heard she had a boyfriend. She went to see him. Got lost on her way home and died."

"How sad." I press my hand to my chest. "The boy is English?"

Another look around. "Word is, he was older. And married." She whispers the last word as if the walls themselves have ears. "No one knows for sure."

"The police must be anxious to speak with him."

"I wouldn't know." She shrugs. "Most of us don't deal with the

Englischers much. Bishop Schrock is strong on separation from the unbelieving world."

I want to keep the conversation focused on the death of Rachel Esh, but I'm not sure how to do so without garnering suspicion, and the moment slips away.

The Amish woman doesn't notice, and motions toward the window facing Main Street. "Before Eli Schrock became bishop, there were six or seven Amish shops. We have such an entrepreneurial spirit, you know. But the government came after us with all their taxes and regulations." She huffs a laugh. "Can't even put in a new front door without some kind of permit. The bishop defended us; he knows how to deal with them. But he lost. A week later, he held a meeting and told all the shopkeepers here in town that when their leases were up, they shouldn't renew."

"Such a shame," I say.

"A lot of Amish sell things from their homes or farmhouses now. Most of them make a pretty penny doing it. I have a three-year lease here. Time's up in ten months." She heaves a wistful sigh. "I love this place, but right is right, and of course the bishop has the final say. When the time comes I'll say good-bye to it and not look back." She laughs. "Listen to me, gossiping like some old woman."

"It's good to know these things," I tell her.

We fall silent, so I move to keep the conversation flowing. "Mary and her husband were nice enough to offer me a ride to worship."

"Well, that's kind. Daniel and I will be there, too."

"I hear Bishop Schrock is a good preacher."

"Barely has to read because he keeps all of it in his head."

"I'm planning to join the church," I tell her.

"He's taken in many, including a few who were lost." Offering a small smile, she reaches out and pats my shoulder. "He believes a strong

Ordnung bestows a free heart and a clear conscience. But if you came here because of Bishop Schrock, you already know that now, don't you?"

I offer my best smile. "I'm looking forward to meeting him."

"Well, a lot of the church districts have fallen to having worship every other Sunday. Bishop Schrock preaches every week. You'd be wise not to miss one."

"I don't plan to."

Sighing, she looks down at the bag in my hand. "What do you have there, Kate?"

"I was wondering if you take quilts on consignment."

"Ah! You're a quilter." Nodding her approval, she motions toward the rear of the shop. "Let's take a look and see what you have."

I follow her to an open area where a large rectangular table is set up with five chairs around it. There's no one else present at the moment, but I know by the sheer number of quilts for sale that most days the chairs are filled by Amish women. If the walls could speak . . .

I set my bag on the table and pull out the two crib quilts. Laura assumes a deadpan expression, but I see her eyes light at the sight of the craftsmanship. She looks at me as if seeing me for the first time. "That's some fine work."

"My *mamm* and *grossmuder* were quilters," I say, trying not to feel guilty for passing someone else's work off as my own. "I learned from an early age."

She takes the quilt from me and runs her fingertips over it, taking in the texture of the fabric, the intricate stitching. "The colors are pretty for a little one. You just have the two?"

"I'm working on two more. One is nearly finished," I tell her, pleased I left them back at the trailer, which gives me a reason to return to the shop. "A pink and blue tumbling block."

"I'm happy to take these on consignment." She tries not to look too excited, but I can tell she's more than a little impressed. "I might be able to get two fifty or so for them." Putting her hand on her hip, she gives me a that's-my-final-offer look. "It'll cost you twenty percent."

"Fifteen percent and you have yourself a deal."

She huffs, looks back down at the quilt in her hand, and sighs. "I can tell you're from Ohio."

"How's that?" I ask.

"Because we're a frugal bunch and we can drive a hard bargain when we need to." Her stern face breaks into a grin. "You have yourself a deal, Kate Miller. Fifteen percent it is." She hefts the quilt and looks at it admiringly. "You'd best get to work on those others. I suspect these will go fast."

CHAPTER 8

A quick stop at Walmart for groceries, an extra blanket, and a pair of wool socks, and I'm back at the trailer by noon. When I walk in the door, my hands and feet are numb and I'm shivering so hard I nearly drop the key. Filling the kettle with water, I set it on the stove for hot tea, using the flame to warm my fingers.

After stowing the groceries, I dig out my phone and call Suggs. "Did you know Rachel Esh was rumored to have had a boyfriend?"

"Some of the Amish hinted at it, but no one would say for sure so I could never confirm it or identify him," he replies. "Did you get a name?"

"The woman I talked to didn't know. It's just rumor at this point, but she mentioned he may be older and married."

"That's interesting as hell."

I tell him about my conversation with Laura Hershberger. "Sometimes there's a grain of truth in a rumor."

"Think you'll get the chance to work on her some more?"

"I'll probably see her at worship tomorrow. Everyone in the community will be there, so I'll have the opportunity to meet a lot of people."

"Nice job, Chief. This is exactly the kind of thing we were hoping you'd be able to do."

"Whether anything will pan out remains to be seen, but it's a start." I pause. "I also met the woman Rachel Esh was living with when she died."

"Mary Gingerich. You work fast."

"Roaring Springs is a small town. The Amish community is even smaller. I knew she worked at the diner. . . ."

"Anything new?"

"Not really, but I'm starting to get a better picture of Schrock." I tell him everything I've learned about the bishop so far. "He's very Old Order. Everyone I've met seems devoted. The only hint of discontent I heard was from the owner of the quilt shop. Apparently, Schrock told her not to renew her lease when it's up."

"Sounds like him."

"An unhappy follower is more likely to talk, especially if she's got something negative to say. I'll do my best to cultivate a relationship."

"You get a bike yet?"

"No, but I will," I tell him. "Mary took pity on me and offered to drive me to worship."

"She drives?"

I smile. "A buggy."

"Gotcha."

"So I'll have the chance to meet her husband and their daughter, too."

"Excellent." He pauses. "I don't have to remind you to be careful, do I?"

"The most dangerous thing I did today was go to Walmart," I tell him. "I'll check in tomorrow."

•   •   •

I've never been the domestic type. I sure as hell don't remember the last time I made date pudding. Probably as a teenager, when my *mamm* was still alive and doing her utmost to instill some semblance of domesticity in her unreceptive daughter. She would drag me into our big country kitchen and my sister, Sarah, and I would help her bake. It wasn't always the tranquil ritual you might imagine. I was difficult; Sarah outshone me, which only made things worse. Still, it's a good memory.

My current kitchen is a far cry from my *mamm*'s, my hands not nearly as capable as hers, but I get the job done with a good bit of sampling along the way, and the pudding turns out better than I anticipated. The entire trailer smells good—and it's blissfully warm. I bought some plastic cups, and tomorrow after worship I'll serve the pudding with caramel sauce and chopped walnuts on top. Hopefully, it will help get things off to a good start.

By late afternoon, the kitchen is cleared, the pudding is stowed in a sealable food storage bowl, and I'm poring through *The Bridge* for a bicycle that will make it easier to get around, at least when the roads are clear. There are no adult bicycles for sale, but there's an ad for a scooter bike, which is even better. It's an added bonus that there's a phone number, which tells me the owner is local and probably Mennonite.

After bundling up, I hike it down to the Amish phone booth at the intersection a couple hundred yards down the road. The phone is inside a frame building the size of an outhouse. There are dozens of buggy wheel marks in the snow, but there's no one here now. I slide the quarter into the slot and dial. A man picks up on the second ring with an enthusiastic, "*Ja!*"

"*Guder nochmiddawks,*" I say, greeting him with the Pennsylvania Dutch words for "good afternoon." "I'm calling about the scooter bike."

"It's a nice one. Aluminum, with twenty-inch wheels and a basket in front for the grocery or whatnot. Good to get around on if the snow isn't too deep."

I've seen the Amish around Painters Mill travel on kick scooters, even Amish women, and the contraptions are amazingly fast and easy to power. "How much?"

"It's used, so I'm asking two hundred."

"Where are you located?"

"East of Roaring Springs."

My heart sinks. I'm west of town, which tells me his place is too far for me to travel on foot. "I'm without transportation," I tell him. "Any way you can haul it over to my place so I can take a look? I'm pretty interested and I have cash."

"The cash part is talking. Where are you located?"

Twenty minutes later, a pickup truck pulls in to the driveway. Grabbing my coat, gloves, and bonnet, I go out to greet him.

He's lifting the scooter bike out of the truck bed when I meet him in the driveway. "I'm Kate Miller," I tell him.

"Christian Kempf." We shake and then he motions toward the scooter. "What do you think?"

I give the contraption a skeptical look. "I would have preferred black."

"Most of the Amish do around here. You could paint it."

"Why are you getting rid of it?"

"My wife and I are Mennonite now, so we don't need it."

"You used to be Amish?"

His gaze moves away from mine. "*Ja.*"

I return my gaze to the scooter, pretend to study it, but it's the seller I'm most interested in. "What made you decide to leave the church?"

He looks down at the ground, then he shrugs. "I'm a furniture maker and sell cabinets to the builder over at Ellenburg Center. Schrock didn't like it and asked me to stop."

"Must have been difficult."

"Hard for the wife. He put us under the *bann*. Her friends won't speak with her. Our daughter . . ." His voice trails off as if the words are too painful to utter.

I'm about to ask about Schrock's use of *Meidung*, but he shakes his head. "I have a car now, so we no longer need this." He turns his attention back to the scooter bike. "There are a few chips in the paint. Otherwise, it's in good condition. Would you like to try it?"

I glance toward the road, where most of the snow from yesterday has melted. "Sure."

He wheels the scooter to the asphalt and offers it to me. "Keep one foot on the platform and push off with the other."

I take the handlebars, and keeping my left foot on the platform, I shove off with the right. It's awkward at first, but I know immediately that it'll be easier—and faster than walking. I take it down the gravel road about fifty yards, make a U-turn, and come back.

"What's your bottom dollar?" I ask.

"Like I said. Two hundred."

"Basket's bent," I say, indicating the wire rack mounted on the handlebars.

"Well, I might take one seventy-five. That's as low as I can go without getting my wife riled up." But he grins.

I grin back. "I'll get my cash."

CHAPTER 9

Sunday morning dawns brilliant and cold—and with me rethinking the wisdom of bringing food to my first worship service. It's a small concern in the scope of things, but it kept me up last night. I don't know the congregation or its unwritten rules—and apparently there are a lot of them. I'm not even sure if my welcome will be warm.

I do, however, know the Amish, and I'm well aware that they appreciate good food. While I don't want to draw undue attention to myself, I do want to make a good impression. Most important, I want to meet and speak with as many people as possible. When you're Amish, food is usually a pretty decent icebreaker.

Mary and Abe Gingerich arrive ten minutes early, but I'm ready. I've stowed the date pudding and plastic containers in two paper bags. Grabbing both, I go through the front door and into a morning cold enough to steal my breath.

Abe has already turned the buggy around. Mary sits in the rear along with a teenage girl, their legs covered with a hand-knitted afghan.

"*Guder mariye!*" I call out as I make my way to the buggy.

A rotund Amish man of about fifty grins at me. "*Wei geth's alleweil?*" How goes it now?

"*Ich bin zimmlich gut.*" I'm pretty good. "You must be Abe Gingerich."

"And you must be Kate Miller."

I stop outside the buggy and offer my hand for a shake. "I appreciate the ride this morning."

"It's right on the way," he tells me.

I peer into the back. "Hi, Mary. You look nice and warm back there."

"We're plenty toasty." The Amish woman smiles back at me. "This is our daughter, Anna."

I recall Suggs mentioning that the girl is special needs and about the same age as Rachel Esh had been. She's got a round face and chubby cheeks mottled with acne. Though she's wearing a black cape, I can tell she's overweight. Her pale blue eyes are slightly strabismus, or cross-eyed, and possess the guilelessness of a much younger child.

"Hi, Anna." I reach out for a shake. "Cold enough for you this morning?"

The girl smiles, looking uncertainly at my hand. "Even my nose is cold."

"She's shy until she gets used to people." Mary elbows her. "Get on up front with your *datt* so Kate and I can sit back here and talk."

I raise my hands. "Thank you, but I don't mind riding up front."

The woman reaches into a slot behind her and pulls out another afghan. "Figured we might need an extra this morning."

Taking the cover, I climb into the buggy and settle onto the seat a respectable distance from Abe.

"What's in the bag?" comes Anna's voice from the rear.

"Anna!" Mary exclaims.

Smiling, I turn. "Date pudding," I tell her. "Do you like it?"

The girl's eyes light up. "It's my favorite. I helped Mamm and Rachel make it once and it was good."

I hold my smile, not even allowing myself to blink. "Is Rachel your sister?"

Anna falls silent, her eyes dropping to the afghan.

The woman picks up her daughter's hand and rubs it between both of hers as if to warm it. Sighing, Mary turns her attention to me. "Rachel is a girl who stayed with us for a while. She wasn't getting along with her family. We tried to help. . . ."

"She went to live with God," Anna adds.

"Oh." I feign shock. "I'm sorry."

"It was a bad thing," comes Abe's voice from beside me.

"Rachel was a troubled child," Mary adds.

"She went out in a snowstorm and died in the cold," Abe finishes.

"How incredibly sad," I murmur.

"It was truly awful and a terrible loss," Mary says.

Though I'm already privy to the details of Rachel Esh's untimely death, it doesn't take much effort to show that I'm aghast at the thought of a young girl freezing to death.

"It must have been devastating for her parents," I say with a shudder.

Abe clucks to the horse and jiggles the reins. "She's in a better place," he says as the horse breaks into a working trot.

No one mentions the possibility that Rachel may not have been alone. I don't press the issue; I've probably already asked too many questions. Instead, I make a mental note to get Anna alone at the first opportunity.

Mary makes small talk as Abe drives the rig onto the main road and heads north. Within minutes, we fall in behind another buggy. At the next turnoff, a third buggy pulls onto the road behind us. We pass a group of teenage boys decked out in their Sunday best—black overcoats, black flat-brimmed hats, and black trousers—walking alongside the road.

The frigid air chafes my face as the horse sets a fast clip. By the time we turn into the narrow dirt road that will take us to Schrock's place, there are six buggies in the caravan. My cheeks are numb, and though I've pulled the afghan up to my waist, I'm shivering. I attribute it to the cold, but my nerves are stretched taut beneath my skin as we draw closer to our destination.

The area is heavily treed with ancient hardwoods that soar sixty feet into the air. Abe makes a final turn. We pass a white clapboard school-house, and then a massive bank-style barn looms before us like some primordial beast. The two-story structure is painted white with a tin roof gone to rust. It's nestled in a clearing with horse pens to the right and a small pasture that slopes down to a creek on the left. The large sliding front doors stand open and I see a dozen or so men milling about inside. Vaguely, I wonder where the women have congregated.

Abe makes a U-turn and stops the buggy in front of the barn with a low "whoa." A boy not yet in his teens goes around to the horse and, watching Abe, waits for us to disembark. Picking up the bags of date pudding, I slide out of the buggy and wait. Mary climbs down, but I can tell immediately that Anna needs assistance, so I jump in to help. Once we're out, Abe nods to the boy, who will take the horse to the paddock where the animal will be unharnessed, stalled, and given water and hay.

Worship is a time of anticipation for the Amish, but it's also a time filled with quiet reflection and hope. Conversation is hushed and re-spectful. Smiles are subdued. Laughter is not appropriate, even among children.

"This way, Kate."

Carting the bags, I follow Mary and Anna to the barn door. Some of the men have gathered beneath the overhang at the end of the build-ing. Having grown up in Painters Mill, I'd attended hundreds of worship services before leaving the fold. Generally, the ordained men enter first, followed by the older men, the married men, the married women, the unmarried, and, finally, the teenagers. The order of things is atypical here; the women are nowhere in sight, and I remind myself that this is a different church district, a different state, and that Eli Schrock is originally from Lancaster County.

I keep my gaze cast down, but I feel the men's eyes on me as I go through the door. We enter a common area where I imagine the farm implements, wagons, and buggies are usually stored. All that has been cleared to make room for the congregation. The interior is dimly lit by several lanterns. It's warmer, but not by much. The smell of wood smoke fills the air, and I spot an old-fashioned potbellied stove in the corner. A boy of about ten years of age has been charged with keeping it stoked.

A scarred wooden table has been set up at one end of the main room. Dozens of backless benches have been arranged in rows separated by an aisle. At the rear, a dozen or so chairs have been neatly arranged. Several are occupied by elderly women.

"We'll put the pudding in the tack room." Mary motions to a door with a step up to a wood plank floor.

Nodding, I take the two bags into a room that smells of molasses and leather. A lantern flickers from atop an oak barrel. Two women stand next to a rectangular table already teeming with food: pies, rustic breads, and a ham dotted with cloves that looks home-cured. Steam rises from the spout of an old-fashioned enamel coffeepot.

"Hello," I say.

A stout older woman wearing a black bonnet and heavy black cape smiles at me. "You must be the widow from Ohio."

I introduce myself.

"Welcome to New York," the younger of the two says. "You settling in okay?"

I tell them I'm renting Bowman's trailer and the two women exchange looks. "It'll be a nice cold winter for you."

They get a good chuckle out of that.

The older woman jabs a thumb at the bags I brought. "What do you have there?"

"Date pudding," I tell them. "Where shall I put it?"

"Just set it up there with the rest." The older woman looks past me. "I believe Bishop Schrock is about to begin, so we'd best get in there."

By the time we enter the main part of the barn, the last of the unmarried men and teenage boys are coming through the door single file and making use of the benches in the back. As is usually the case, the women are seated on one side of the aisle, the men on the other.

The smell of kerosene from a large space heater mingles with the aromas of woodsmoke, the food in the back room and the lingering scents of hay and sweet feed and horses. I haven't attended a preaching service in years, but already I feel the anticipation of that first hymn building inside me.

It's a reverent moment and, though I don't know any of the people around me, a shared kinship. In unison, the men remove their hats, placing them beneath the bench upon which they're sitting. I don't feel like a cop as I take my place on the bench with the rest of the single women and visitors at the rear of the room. I'm young and Amish and the words to the first hymn venture from the recesses of my memory.

Mer misse glawe an sell was unser Harr un unser.

Heiland Jesu Christi uns g'sagty hot.

Ja, sell hot er g'sagt. Ja ich glab, sell is recht.

We must believe in that which our Lord and our

Savior Jesus Christ told us.

Yes, that's what He said. Yes, I believe that is right.

The hymn is followed by a period of silence. I should be observing those around me. Taking an inventory of the number and ages of the children present. Scrutinizing those children for signs of abuse. Instead, I close my eyes and the old prayer from *Die Ernsthafte Christenpflicht—The Prayer Book for Earnest Christians*—pries into a brain that doesn't necessarily welcome it.

O God and Father of all light and comfort . . .

The words come back to me with astounding clarity and ease. When you're Amish, some things are so entrenched, become such a sacred and immovable part of your life, that you can't escape them. Worship is one of those things, and not for the first time my roots threaten to overshadow who I am today and why I'm here: to infiltrate this group, ask questions, and, hopefully, glean new information that will either exonerate them from wrongdoing—or put me closer to unraveling the mystery of Rachel Esh's death.

I've moved on to a silent reciting of the Lord's Prayer when a male voice calls out the number of the next hymn. I open my eyes to see an older Amish man with a long salt-and-pepper beard standing at the bench where he'd been sitting. He begins to sing and within a few syllables, the rest of the congregation joins him until everyone is standing and singing.

When the second hymn is finished, the congregation falls to silence once again. The squeak of a hinge echoes within the room. The steady tread of boots thuds against the wood plank floor. I glance toward the front to see a tall, black-clad Amish man approach the preaching table. His beard is shot through with gray and reaches his waist. He moves with a masculine grace and a certain physical power that reveals he's comfortable with who and what he is. When he looks out at his audience, I can't help but notice piercing eyes the color of a nor'easter. A full mouth that would have been feminine on another man. His face seems to be cut from sculpted leather, the kind that's weathered sun and sleet in equal measure but never lost its sheen.

I know immediately that the man is Eli Schrock.

Looking at him, I'm reminded of a painted portrait, the kind in which the eyes follow you, judging and weighing, and never look away. I know that's not the case, but in the seconds before he speaks, I feel his eyes on me, as if he's sought me out. I actually experience a rise of alarm, as if he knows my weaknesses, my lies, the sins of my past.

He sets large hands against the preaching table, leans slightly and begins the *Anfang*, the introductory sermon, in a deep, singsong voice. For the next three and a half hours, Schrock takes his congregation through the main sermon, several prayers from *Die Ernsthafte Christenpflicht*, benediction, and, finally, the closing hymn.

Once Schrock makes his exit, the congregation rises. The men replace their hats. The crowd exits the same way they entered, according to age and status. I'm in one of the last groups, so I use the time to introduce myself to several women, taking a few minutes to get myself noticed as "the newcomer" before heading to the food area.

The aromas of cinnamon, yeast bread, and coffee titillate my olfactory nerves as I move closer to the tack room. I'm exchanging pleasantries with a cute twentysomething woman who is expecting her first child when I notice a line of sorts has formed and I'm somewhere in the middle of it. Through the crowd I catch a glimpse of the cause. A quiver of anxiety ripples through me at the sight of Eli Schrock standing in the doorway, greeting everyone as they enter the room.

He takes his time and seems to relish speaking with each and every member of his congregation. I watch him carefully as I move ever closer. He shakes the hands of both men and women. With an elderly woman, he takes her hand into both of his and bows his head slightly as he speaks to her. He holds the most elevated position in the church district, and yet he's respectful of his female elders. Even from a distance I discern his charisma. He's engaging and attentive, with a demeanor that oozes benevolence and beckons trust. But there's power there, too, and the strength to make the tough decisions when needed.

The woman behind me says something. I turn to her and we exchange a pleasantry. Then suddenly it's my turn. Eli Schrock stands just two feet away. So close I can smell him: a combination of hand soap, alfalfa hay, and coffee. Tilting his head, his eyes find mine, and in that instant the rest of the crowd melts away. Anxiety scratches at the back of my neck as he scrutinizes me. I know it the moment he realizes he's never met me, and he steps closer.

Bowing my head slightly, I extend my hand. "It was a good preaching service," I say in Pennsylvania Dutch.

"Humility is the way of the Lord." His hand closes over mine. I'm keenly aware of the heat of it. The scuff of calluses against my skin. His eyes are dark gray, nearly black, but a light seems to radiate from within.

"You're the widow from Ohio," he says.

The statement takes me aback; I know better than most how quickly word of a newcomer travels among the Amish. Still, I'm surprised he knows who I am. "I'm Kate Miller and I'm happy to be here, Bishop."

"We welcome you." He's still gripping my hand, looking at me with such intensity that I struggle to maintain my poise. "You'll be living permanently here in Roaring Springs?" he asks.

"Yes." I'm cognizant of the woman standing behind me, waiting her turn.

Schrock doesn't seem to notice her. He's still holding my hand, looking at me intently, unhurried. "You're planning to join the church?"

"As soon as possible."

"Good." He releases my hand. "We'll make it official next Sunday." He turns his attention to the woman behind me.

Giving myself a small mental shake, I continue on.

CHAPTER 10

The tack room bustles with activity. It's ten degrees warmer than the rest of the barn and filled with conversation in *Deitch*. Suggs had told me there are approximately a hundred and fifty people in the community. I don't know if that's an official number, but I'm guessing the number is closer to two hundred.

Many of the teenagers have already eaten and fled. Sunday is a big day for socializing for them. Chances are there will be a singing later, and I'm betting a few of the boys have gone off someplace private to smoke cigarettes. Because they're teenagers and not yet baptized, the adults won't give them too much static.

I make my way to the place where I left the date pudding, plastic-ware, and serving spoon, and I busy myself filling the dessert cups. I've filled a dozen or so when I see Mary's daughter, Anna, looking at me from across the room. She's standing a few feet from her *mamm*, looking bored—and hungry.

I motion her over. "Would you like to help me fill the cups?" I ask.

"*Ja!*" the girl says enthusiastically.

I catch her mother's eye and the woman gives me a nod. For a few minutes, Anna and I work in silence. All business now, she separates the cups and slides one to me. I dip the spoon into the pudding and ladle a dollop into the cup. As people converge, I introduce myself and make small talk, doing my utmost to engage them. I share the recipe for the date pudding with the women who ask. I discuss Schrock's sermon with a couple of the men. And there's always the weather, which seems to be a favorite topic.

After half an hour or so, the crowd at my table thins. Making sure Mary Gingerich is out of earshot, I turn my attention to the girl helping me. "I think everyone liked the pudding," I say.

"Brick Ivan had two cups!" the girl exclaims.

"Brick Ivan?"

"His real name is just Ivan but everyone calls him brick because he lays bricks."

"Ah." I smile, trying to come up with a way to get her talking about Rachel Esh. "You said your friend Rachel liked date pudding, too."

"She helped me and Mamm make it once."

"Were you good friends?" I'm not sure how close she was to Rachel Esh and I don't want to upset her, so I tread carefully.

Anna nods vigorously. "She was my best friend."

"You must miss her."

"*Ja.* Everyone thought she was too old to be my friend. You know, because I'm stunted. But my *mamm* said that's okay because God made me that way and whatever God does is okay."

"Your *mamm* is right." I shovel a spoonful of pudding into a cup and hand it to her. "What kinds of things did the two of you do together?"

The girl's eyes light up as she digs into the pudding. She's a good little eater and gives me only half her attention as she chews. "She played the clapping game with me. Me and my *mamm* and Rachel made soap once."

"I bet that was fun."

"She was so pretty and grown-up." A wistful sigh. "She smelled good and she used to let me brush her hair."

"I bet she had lots of friends."

"*Ja*, but I was her best."

I try again. "Who were her other friends?"

"Emma next door." She lowers her voice and whispers in Pennsylvania Dutch, "Don't tell, but Rachel told me Emma smells bad."

I can't help it—I laugh. "What about Marie Weaver?" I ask, recalling Suggs's notes.

"I almost forgot about her. Rachel loved Marie." The girl's face scrunches up. "I always thought Marie was kind of mean, though."

"Mean? How so?"

"I dunno." She shrugs. "My *mamm* says Marie has a sharp tongue. And she's always getting into trouble."

"What kind of trouble?"

"She wears English clothes." Again the girl lowers her voice to a whisper. "And she says bad words."

"I bet her parents don't like that."

"Neither does the bishop."

"The bishop? Really?"

She glances left and right and whispers, "Rachel told me he put Marie in the chicken coop."

I almost don't know what to say to that. "The chicken coop?"

For the first time, wariness enters her expression, as if she's realized she's talking about something she shouldn't be talking about. Trying not to feel guilty for plying a kid with dessert, I add a small dollop of pudding to her cup.

"You mean to *clean* it?" I ask.

"No, he locked her in."

"Why would he do that?"

Her eyes skate away from mine. "I'm not supposed to talk about that."

"You mean the chicken coop part? Or Rachel?"

She takes a big bite of pudding. "I dunno," she says around the food.

I help myself to some of the pudding, let the silence ride for a moment. "How do you like the pudding?"

"It's the best I ever had." She stops mid chew. "Don't tell my *mamm* I said that."

A wave of affection rolls through me and I reach out and squeeze her shoulder. She's so innocent and unsuspecting. The kind of girl a counterpart might confide in or speak freely before without the worry of repercussions. But does she know anything about Rachel Esh?

I glance over at Anna, who's finished her pudding and is eyeing another cup. "Is the chicken coop for teenagers who've misbehaved? Or do bad chickens get put in there, too?" I ask with a grin.

The girl flashes a smile, then looks down, her shoulders curling in. "I dunno."

Her reticence hints that there's something there she doesn't wish to discuss—or has been told not to. I don't want to frighten her with too many questions, so I go to another topic. "Is Marie here today?"

Twisting in her chair, she points at a girl sitting alone at another table, eating a wedge of rhubarb pie. The instant Anna points, the girl glances our way, as if knowing she's the topic of gossip. She gives Anna a withering glare and then her eyes slide to mine. She's got auburn hair. Brown eyes alight with intelligence. A sprinkling of freckles on an aquiline nose. A full mouth that's far too sensuous for a sixteen-year-old kid. She's unusual looking and extraordinarily pretty. A troublesome combination, even if you're Amish. Rolling her eyes in that universal annoyed-teenager way, she goes back to her pie.

"She's pretty." I place a spoonful of pudding into the next cup. "I bet the boys like to court her."

"She's mean to them, too."

"Did any of the boys like Rachel?"

She separates two cups, sets both in front of me. "Jacob Yoder."

I put the name to memory. "Did they go to singings together?"

She looks at me as if I'm naive, and I remind myself not to underestimate her or how much she may know simply because she's special needs. "My *mamm* says *Er harricht gut, awwer er foligt schlecht.*" He hears well, but obeys poorly, which basically means he's willfully disobedient.

Over the next twenty minutes or so, I try a few different angles with Anna, but she's grown bored with me, makes an excuse and wanders away.

The date pudding was a hit and the container is empty. I keep an eye on the crowd as I pack things away. A dozen or so elderly women are seated at a folding table, drinking coffee and speaking quietly. Most of the men have gone to another section of the barn; through a wide doorway I see them standing around an ancient-looking manure spreader. Several groups of girls are scattered about, sitting at tables or packing leftover food and utensils. A couple of boys are breaking down tables, folding and stowing them.

I glance toward the place where Marie Weaver had been sitting but she's left. I'd wanted to meet Rachel's parents, Fannie and Samuel Esh, but I have no idea what they look like or if they're even here. Normally, a briefing would have included photographs of all the players involved. But since most Amish do not have their photos taken, I can't rely on recognition.

I spot Mary Gingerich sitting at a table with some other women, one of whom is crocheting. Picking up my bags, I carry them over to the table.

"Hi, Kate." Mary addresses the other women. "This is Kate Miller. She just moved here from Holmes County."

All eyes turn to me. I smile demurely. "Hello."

"Kate's a widow," Mary informs them.

Eyes are averted, heads bowed slightly, and the women make a collective sound of sympathy. "How long ago did your husband pass?" a white-haired woman asks.

"Nine months," I reply. "John and I wanted to move here, but he got sick."

"You're here permanently?" the crocheting woman asks.

I nod. "I've rented Mrs. Bowman's trailer home."

"You have children?" another woman asks.

It's a question I've fielded several times now. Children and family are the heart of Amish society. I purposefully look away, glance down at the tabletop. "No, it's just me."

The white-haired woman shakes her head. She's probably too kind to say it aloud, but I know what she's thinking. If you're Amish, unmarried, and without children at my age, you're living an unfulfilled life.

"Welcome to Roaring Springs, Kate Miller." A red-haired woman whose face is mottled with freckles offers a kind, sympathetic look. "My cousin, Ruth, lives in Berlin."

The crocheting woman looks up at me. "I was in Holmes County last summer for my *grossmuder*'s funeral. It's beautiful, and the Amish are so friendly."

"Lots of *Englischer* tourists, though," the red-haired woman puts in. "They come right up to you and start taking pictures!"

"Gawking at the Amish as if they've never seen a plain person before," another asserts, and chuckles ensue.

It's harmless small talk, but the nerves at the back of my neck tingle with unease and I remind myself the Amish world can be a small one. While most adults don't use phones, they write letters. If one of them happens to mention me by name, I could have some explaining to do. . . .

"How did you like the preaching service?" a thirtysomething woman asks, looking at me from beneath impossibly long lashes.

The group falls silent and I realize this is the most important question I'll be asked today. I wait a beat, letting the anticipation build. "It was without blemish," I say. "Bishop Schrock observes the true ordinances of Christ."

Heads nod, but not all of them, and I'm intrigued. "My church district in Ohio was . . ." I pause as if seeking the perfect word. "—fallen. All the Amish were mixed in with the rest of the world. Some of our young people were confused. You know, drinking and smoking with their English friends."

"Here, we are separate," the red-haired woman tells me.

"Schrock protects us from the blind and perverted," says another.

Again, it doesn't elude me that not all the heads nod in concurrence, and I realize not everyone agrees with that assessment.

I spend twenty minutes with the women before excusing myself under the guise of needing a restroom break. I'm told there are two outhouses behind the barn, one for women and one for the men. "Just go through the barn door and to the left," Mary tells me. "You can't miss them."

After being inside for over three hours with so many people and having to be "on" the entire time, I feel as if I can breathe the instant I step outside. The wind has kicked up and smells of woodsmoke and snow. Clouds have gobbled up the sunshine from earlier. I shiver as I make my way around the side of the barn toward the rear.

To my right a dozen or so buggies are parked in a neat row. The two young hostlers stand nearby, watching me. I wave, but they turn away without returning the gesture.

I reach the back of the barn and take the stone steps to a path of trampled snow that wends through the trees. Ten yards away, two white clapboard buildings stand side by side. The one to my right is marked FRAW, so when the path splits, I go right. The outhouse is exactly that, but more closely resembles the kind you might find in a park. After making use of the facilities, I walk to the rear of the building to see what's there.

I find myself staring into an ocean of winter-dead trees tangled with vines and a few evergreens. To the west, the land dips down and over the tops of the trees, I see the smooth white surface of a plowed field. Remembering the aerial photos, I realize that beyond the field is a good-size creek.

A shriek breaks the silence. I look around, try to discern the direction from which it came and the nature of the sound. Spotting tracks, I leave the walkway and follow them down the hill. I've only gone a few yards when I hear male laughter. Youthful. More than one. I change direction slightly, my boots nearly silent against the snow.

The trees open to a clearing where four Amish teenagers have gathered. Three boys and one girl. At first I think they've slipped away to hang out and have some harmless fun. Then one of the boys lunges forward and shoves the girl using both hands. She reels backward, arms flailing, and lands on her behind in the snow. Instinct kicks in and before I can stop myself I move out of the trees. The three boys turn toward me, mouths open, arms loose. I see surprise on their faces. A topical uneasiness tells me they're not overly alarmed by my presence.

The boy who shoved the girl casts me an annoyed glare. He's disappointed I had the gall to interrupt.

I look at the girl, recognize her immediately: Marie Weaver. "Are you all right?"

Getting to her feet, she brushes snow from her coat. "I'm fine."

I turn my attention to the boy who shoved her. He's about nineteen years old. Sandy hair. Bad haircut. Vivid blue eyes. An attitude I'm no stranger to, especially when it comes to young males pumped up on testosterone. He might've been attractive if not for the angry patches of acne on his cheeks and the bad attitude in his eyes.

"What's your name?" The question is out—in my cop's voice no less—an instant before I remind myself who I am and why I'm here. Amish women aren't pushovers, but they're not as assertive as I am, especially when it comes to men.

In the periphery of my vision, I see the other boys exchange looks that relay the question: *Who the hell is she?* The one I'm addressing meets my gaze head on and holds it. "Jacob Yoder."

The boy who'd been courting Rachel Esh.

"What are you doing out here?" I ask.

"We could ask you the same thing."

I glance over to the other boy to my left. Dark brown hair. Too long with blunt-cut bangs. Pale skin. Brown eyes. A sharp retort dangles on my tongue, but I curb it. Instead, I stare hard at him until he looks away and I turn my attention back to the girl. "What's going on?"

She looks over her shoulder as if the answer lies somewhere within the trees. "We were just goofing off," she mumbles.

"Is that why he pushed you down?" I ask.

Yoder steps closer. "I didn't—"

"I saw you." I stand my ground, and he doesn't come any closer.

"We were just playing around," Yoder says. "Ain't that right, Marie?"

I make eye contact with the girl. She looks down at her shoes. "We were just playing."

A little voice inside my head warns: *Be careful.*

"Who are *you*?" The third boy, in his late teens with strawberry-blond hair, looks at his friends, emboldened by them. "I ain't seen your face around here before."

"Yeah." The dark-haired boy moves closer, stops a few feet away, looks me up and down. "You're not even from around here and you think you can tell us what to do."

Under any other circumstances, the last thing I'd do is give up ground, literally or figuratively. These young men are up to no good, and the cop inside me would like nothing better than to shove their bad attitudes down their throats. But I need to maintain the persona of a newly relocated, recently widowed Amish woman. Dropping my gaze, I take a step back. "I'm Kate Miller," I tell him. "I heard this girl call out, and I thought she needed help."

"Well, she don't need any help," Yoder tells me. "From you or anyone else." He grins at the girl. "She likes it rough. Ain't that so, Marie?"

I look at the girl. For the first time I notice the red welt on her cheek. The anger and humiliation simmering in her eyes. I wonder if she has other marks in places no one can see.

"I could use some help loading my things into the buggy," I tell her. "Would you give me a hand?"

For an instant, she looks torn. She doesn't want to be here, and yet she doesn't want to acquiesce in front of these boys. I turn my attention to Yoder. "You can help, too, if you'd like."

No one moves. No one replies. I look at Marie, sending a silent communication that she should come with me. She gives me nothing in return. Nodding at the boys, I turn and take a few steps toward the barn. When I glance back, I see the girl following.

Raucous laughter chases us as we wend through the trees and take the path toward the barn. Neither of us speaks until we reach the outhouses.

"What was that all about?" I ask as we step onto the stone walkway.

"We were just goofing off," she mumbles.

I motion toward her cheek. "Is that how you got that mark on your face?"

"I did that on a tree branch." She stops walking and gives me a who-the-fuck-are-you-anyway look. "Why do you care? I don't even know who you are."

"I just moved here." I jab a thumb in the general direction of the boys. "I didn't like what I saw back there."

She stares at me, her expression set and stubborn. "You don't know what you saw."

"Maybe I ought to tell the bishop."

Her mouth opens. Apprehension flashes in her eyes. "That'll only make things worse."

"You didn't do anything wrong."

"The bishop doesn't like me."

"Why not?"

"I don't know. He just doesn't. He thinks . . ." She lets the words trail. "Forget it."

Her body language tells me she doesn't want to go back to the barn. But she doesn't want to stand here talking to me, either, so I let her off the hook. "I don't have anything that needs loading."

"I wasn't going to help you with it, anyway." Making a teen's customary sound of annoyance, she turns and walks into the outhouse. I wait, trying to decide if I should ask her about Rachel Esh. According to Anna, the girls were best friends. If anyone has an insight into Rachel's life—or her death—it's Marie. I go to the edge of the porch area and look out over the woods. Marie emerges a minute later, shoots me a nasty glare, and starts toward the barn without speaking.

I fall into step beside her. "I just realized where I heard your name," I say slowly. "You were the Esh girl's best friend."

She stops and swings around to face me. "How do you know about her? I thought you weren't from around here?"

I keep my answer vague. "One of the women inside was talking about what happened." I pause. "That explains why you're so sad."

"I'm not sad," she snaps.

"You were friends."

"Yeah, well, she's gone so it doesn't matter, does it?"

We continue toward the barn, but stop when we reach the concrete walkway where the roof extends out. "Do you know what happened to her?" I ask.

"No one does," she mutters.

"Did those boys know her?"

"Everyone knows everyone around here. In case you haven't noticed, Roaring Springs is a small town."

"She was too young to die." Noticing dried grass on the sleeve of her coat, I brush it off. "And you're too young to be so sad."

"Yeah, well, no one cares what you think."

I nod toward the woods where the boys are. "Look, you don't know me, but . . . I have a niece your age. If you ever get into trouble or need help, you can come to me. I'm staying at the Bowman trailer. Do you know where that is?"

"I don't need help from you or anyone else." Casting me a disdainful look, she walks away.

"You're wrong about one thing," I say to her back.

She keeps walking.

"It matters," I call out.

She doesn't look back.

CHAPTER 11

One of the unwritten rules of Amish etiquette is that you don't leave directly after the post-service meal. Sunday is the only day set aside for rest, and most take full advantage of the opportunity to visit with their neighbors and friends. By the time the Gingeriches drop me off at the trailer, it's nearly four P.M.

I've put in some long days in the course of my career; I've pulled all-nighters and worked around the clock more times than I can recall. I don't ever remember being as mentally exhausted as I am today. I've been "on" since this morning, unable to let down my guard even for a moment. Pretending to be someone you're not and trying to keep all the lies straight is taxing, to say the least.

On the bright side, it was time well spent. Though I didn't learn anything earth-shattering, I met dozens of people and came one step closer to establishing my place in the community.

The incident with Marie Weaver and the three boys niggled at the back of my brain all afternoon. It's true that some Amish teens fall prey to the same bad behaviors as their "English" counterparts; they're human, and as fallible as anyone else. But generally speaking, the vast majority are well behaved and respectful, especially when their elders are around.

When I confronted Jacob Yoder, he was not only unrepentant but defiant. As if he'd known there would be no repercussions. I was left with the impression that the incident wasn't an anomaly. I can't help but wonder if Rachel Esh knew them, too. If she'd been treated with the same level of disrespect. Or worse.

On the surface, today's worship service had been typical; it would have been an enjoyable and fulfilling experience for any visitor. But I'm no ordinary visitor, and more than once I'd sensed there was something off-kilter. Nothing I can put my finger on, but I felt a nearly indiscernible thread of tension, of watchfulness—maybe even paranoia. It's as if everyone was following some carefully written script and being cautious not to veer from it. Especially when the topic of Eli Schrock arose.

Every individual I met spoke highly of the bishop. His belief system. His kindness and generosity. His strength and leadership. But the reverence with which those words were uttered didn't quite ring true. There was something left unspoken.

My own impressions of the bishop are mixed. He gave me no reason to harbor suspicion. He's a charismatic man, a natural leader, and outwardly friendly, while at the same time commanding respect. He's an enthralling speaker and delivered a rousing preaching service. He knows the Amish tenets and certainly wields the power to enforce them. All that said, when I looked into his eyes, I saw a flash of something unexpected. Tucked beneath the layers of benevolence and caring and a keen intelligence, I saw secrets. An innate darkness I've observed before—in the eyes of criminals.

I'm trying to put all my observations into order and pin down the specifics of what's bothering me as I unlock the door and let myself into the trailer. More than anything, I want a hot shower and a few hours of downtime. I want to curl up on the sofa with my phone and a blanket and call Tomasetti. But there's one more thing I need to do before dark: I want to see the place where Rachel Esh's body was found.

Toeing off my boots, I pull on an extra pair of socks and put the boots back on. I run my hand over the .22 strapped to my thigh, find it secure. My phone is still tucked away in my coat pocket. Though it's only a little past four, dusk is already settling in. As much as I don't want to get caught in unfamiliar woods after dark, I'm glad for the added cover. If someone catches me sniffing around the scene, I'll have some explaining to do.

Locking the door behind me, I descend the steps and round the trailer to the rear. The backyard is small and fenced with chain link that's tangled with winter-dead vines. A rusty metal shed is nestled in the farthest corner. The door is bent and ajar, as if someone forced it open and didn't bother repairing it. I take a moment to look inside, but there's not much there. An old rotary push mower. A leaf rake. Snow shovel. A few clay pots. I move on to the fence at the back, shove open the gate, and then I'm in the woods and heading north.

I start off at a jog. It's not easy in muck boots and a dress, especially with four inches of snow on the ground. I can't imagine how silly I'd look to some casual observer. Luckily, I'm in the boonies, and chances are I won't run into anyone.

My boots are nearly silent as I weave through the trees. Somewhere in the near distance a hawk whistles. It's a melancholy, lonely sound in the silence of the forest. A light snow has begun to fall, and though my nerves are on alert, I can't help but admire the stark beauty all around me.

I have only a general idea of my destination. Suggs told me the girl's body was found near the lake. The tree nearest her body was flagged with orange marking paint. He thought there might be some scraps of crime scene tape left as well. He wasn't sure.

It doesn't take me long to reach the lake. It's a good-size body of water—about two acres—and completely frozen over. A deer path runs alongside the water's edge. I cut over to the trail and continue on. The snowfall is just enough to dust my shoulders and head covering. It's cold, but the physical activity has warmed my core. Ever cognizant of the coming darkness, I maintain a brisk pace. It'll be fully dark in half an hour. If I don't find the scene quickly, I'll have to turn around and wait until tomorrow.

I reach the end of the lake and stop, looking for the marking paint or any scrap of crime scene tape left behind. I turn, take a good look at my surroundings. I pick out a few landmarks, and then I leave the path and go left. I walk fifty yards, keeping my eyes on the tree trunks. When I think I've gone far enough, I go right for a few yards and then walk back toward the lake.

I'm about to give up when, twenty yards from the north end of the water, I find the orange X on the trunk of a massive birch tree. Of course there's nothing to indicate Rachel Esh had ever been here, but there are signs that this was the scene of a police presence. A six-inch-long piece of yellow crime scene tape is tied around a sapling. Another piece is stapled to a larger trunk. The underbrush has been trampled, some of it cut away.

I'm no stranger to crime or the knowledge of the things human beings can do to each other. Even for an experienced cop, it's unsettling to stand in a place where you know someone died, especially when their death was at the hands of another. I wonder about the girl's final moments. Did she come out here alone and lose her way? Was the snow coming down too hard for her to find her way home? Was she lost, alone and afraid? Did she know she wasn't going to make it out of these woods alive? Or did someone make sure she didn't? Someone who, for reasons unknown, didn't want her to survive?

I don't expect to make some profound discovery simply by looking at the scene; nothing's ever that easy. But I've heard it said that some places have memories. I'm not sure I believe it, but it's almost always useful to visit a crime scene. I spend fifteen minutes walking the area, trying to get a feel for it, the logistics of the surroundings, gain some sense of what might've transpired. Why would a fifteen-year-old Amish girl wander into the deep woods during a snowstorm? Where was she coming from? Where was she going? Was she alone? Running away from someone? *To* someone? I think about her recent pregnancy, the possibility of a home abortion. Did she do it herself? Or did someone help her? And who supplied her with the OxyContin that showed up in the tox screen?

I know one thing for certain: Rachel Esh kept a lot of secrets.

I make a mental note to ask Suggs about the OxyContin trade in the area, have him cross the names with some of the Amish I met today, see if any of them intersect. I walk the area a final time, but there's nothing there. Just the remnants of a police presence, the knowledge of a life lost before its time, and an unsolved mystery that will be forgotten all too soon if someone doesn't uncover the truth.

"What happened to you?" I whisper, my voice sounding strange in the silence of the forest.

I've just started toward the trailer when the toe of my boot nudges something beneath the snow. Kneeling, I brush away snow and pull out a faceless Amish doll. It's about eight inches long. The fabric is tattered and dirty. Stitched into the material are the words LIFE BEYOND DEATH.

The odd inscription gives me pause. No one puts words like that on a child's doll. More than likely they were sewn into the fabric subsequent to Rachel's death and left here as some kind of tribute after the crime scene people left. Someone had cared about Rachel Esh.

Mourned her death. Her parents? Her best friend, Marie Weaver? Her boyfriend? Or is this something else? The response of a guilty conscience from someone unknown?

I don't have an evidence bag, so I drop the doll into my coat pocket. I'll pass it off to Suggs later. Chances are it won't tell us anything, but it's worth a closer look.

It's fully dark now and I'm thoroughly chilled. I've just started for the trailer when I hear the whine of an engine. According to the aerial photos, the nearest road is Swamp Creek Road, which is to the south. The sound of the engine is to the north. I'm pondering possible sources when headlights flicker through the trees. Not a car or truck, I realize, but a snowmobile, and it's coming this way.

There's nothing sinister about a nighttime snowmobile ride. More than likely it's someone out to have some fun in the snow. Still, I don't want to be seen here in the very spot where Rachel Esh's body was found. I glance around for cover. There are hundreds of trees, but not all of them are large enough to conceal me if the snowmobiler gets close. I spy a snarl of bramble at the base of an evergreen, dash over to it, and drop to my knees.

The whine of the engine grows louder. Not one machine, but two. Headlight beams slash through the trees. Shadows cartwheel against the trunks. I hunker down, the brush snagging my coat. The headlights flash over me and move on. The machines stop twenty yards away. Engines rumbling. There are two people on each snowmobile. The drivers are wearing snowsuits and helmets. The passengers are smaller. Women, I realize. No helmets. Regular coats.

The men are talking, loudly to be heard above the engines. I'm shocked to realize they're speaking Pennsylvania Dutch. They're too far away for me to catch all of the conversation. Something about a dirt road. I'm puzzling over these Amish men utilizing gasoline-engine powered vehicles when one of the passengers launches herself from the snowmobile and throws herself into a sprint. Adrenaline burns through my gut when I realize her hands are bound in front of her.

What the hell?

"*Shtobba!*" the man with whom she'd been riding yells. Stop. "Halt!"

"*Sie is am shpringa!*" shouts the second driver. She's running!

The man she'd been riding with unfastens his helmet, throws it to the ground, and vaults from the seat. "Stop!" He sprints after the woman. Even mired by the snow and his bulky clothes, it takes him only a few strides to catch her. He takes her down in a full-body tackle. The woman makes a muffled sound, her face crushed into the snow.

The man gets to his knees, flips her onto her back, and straddles her. "Stupid woman!" he shouts. "Get on the machine."

She spits snow in his face and shouts something in a language I don't recognize. He draws back and slaps her in the face.

A hundred scenarios snap through my brain. Is this some kind of domestic dispute? Are these people intoxicated? Or is something more sinister going on? For a split second I debate whether to intervene. Of course, if I do, I risk blowing my cover. But there's no way I can stand by and let that son of a bitch assault her. The man takes the decision away from me when he punches her a second time.

I jump to my feet. Leaving the cover of the trees, I whistle. "Here, boy! Come on, boy!"

Then I'm walking toward them, using my hand to shield my eyes from the glare of the headlights. "Hello?" I call out, making an effort to lose my cop persona. It's not easy; nothing pisses me off more than seeing a bully punch the shit out of a woman.

"Who's there?" I call out in Pennsylvania Dutch.

Four heads swivel in my direction. The man on top of the woman jumps to his feet. The other man, still sitting on the snowmobile, swings his leg over the saddle and gets off. I hear him tell the woman behind him to stay put.

I don't see any weapons, but that doesn't mean they're not armed. The Amish generally don't own handguns, but these men are a far cry from typical.

"Who are you?" The man who'd punched the woman starts toward me. He's wearing a ski mask so I can't see his face, but his body language tells me he's pissed off that I've interrupted.

I'm aware of the .22 against my thigh as he closes the distance between us. Stopping, I watch him approach. He's young. No beard that I can see, which means he's not married. I don't like the look of him. Angry and high on adrenaline.

"I'm Kate Miller." I motion behind me. "I live down the road. I saw a stray dog. He looked cold and lost." I cock my head, the way a suspicious Amish woman might. "What are you doing on those machines?" I ask in Pennsylvania Dutch.

The two men exchange glances.

"We ain't seen no dog." The man who'd punched the woman stops ten feet away from me, looks me up and down. "You probably saw a coyote."

I look past him at the fallen woman and switch to English. "Was there an accident here? Are you injured?" I motion toward the snowmobile, then turn my attention to the man. "Isn't it against the *Ordnung* for you to be riding them?"

The woman stares at me, mouth open, breaths puffing out in a vaporous white cloud. A small dribble of blood on her chin. I can tell by the way she's looking at me that she's frightened. That she doesn't understand English *or* Pennsylvania Dutch.

The man sets his hand on her shoulder and pulls her against him, so that her bound hands are out of sight. I pretend not to notice and address the woman directly. "Did you fall off the machine?"

When she doesn't respond, I turn my attention to the man. "Look at her," I scold. "She's cold and hurt."

I start to go to her, a mother hen whose chick has been pecked by an aggressive rooster.

"She's fine." The man steps toward me, blocking my way. "We don't need your help."

I stop.

"Go home, lady," the second man calls out. "You're trespassing on Schrock land."

"I'm sure Bishop Schrock will be interested to know about these machines," I shoot back.

The man who'd hit her moves closer. For an instant, I think he's going to lay into me. Behind the ski mask, his eyes blaze with fury. I brace, remind myself the .22 is in easy reach.

But he stops, gives me another once-over. "She's fine. Now get out of here. There ain't no dog out here."

The woman says something in a language I don't recognize. Eastern European, maybe. She's young. Barely twenty. This is not a domestic situation. I'd lay odds she doesn't know the man she's riding with. But there's little I can do. . . .

I look away, pretend I didn't hear her. But my heart is pounding, my brain churning: *What the hell is going on?*

I can tell by the way the men are acting that my presence is making them nervous. Not because they've broken Amish rules, but because they're up to no good and don't want a witness. The man nearest me looks like he's considering doing something about it.

I step back, putting some space between us. "You sure she's okay?"

"She's fine," the man tells me. "She drinks too much. I'm taking her home. That's all."

I give the woman a judgmental look. *"Der Siffer hot zu viel geleppert."* The drunkard has sipped too much. "That's what happens, I guess."

The man points in the general direction of the road. "Go on. Get out of here."

I put their physical descriptions to memory as best I can. Turning away, I start toward the trailer.

Behind me, I hear the man order the woman back onto the snowmobile. The twin engines rev. Once I'm in the trees, I stop and turn. Through the trunks, I catch a glimpse of the woman's face. The cop inside me winces at the thought of letting them go. But I do, watching them fade into the darkness. When they're gone, I turn toward home and break into a run.

I'm still out of breath when I call Suggs. Quickly, I take him through everything I saw and give him the physical descriptions of all four individuals. "The men were wearing ski masks beneath their helmets, so I don't know what they looked like."

"Of course they were," he mutters darkly. "You're certain the women weren't Amish?"

"They weren't wearing Amish clothes. They didn't know Pennsylvania Dutch. I don't even think they knew English."

"Well, that's puzzling as hell." He goes silent a moment. "A couple of young Amish guys with foreign women? Is it possible they're on *Rumspringa* and picked up . . . er . . . dates? Some of those kids, especially the boys, can get pretty wild."

"I thought of that. But I don't think that was the case. Dan, I saw one of the men strike the woman he was with. Her hands were bound."

"Shit." We fall silent; I can practically hear our thoughts zinging over the line. "Were the men armed?"

"Not that I could see. No rifles. But they were wearing snowsuits, so hard to tell. And those snowmobiles were nice ones. New. Polaris."

"Not cheap."

"Why would young Amish men have snowmobiles?" I ponder.

"I suppose they could have borrowed them." But he doesn't sound convinced. "Were they part of Schrock's group?"

"Maybe. They told me I was on Schrock's land and that I was trespassing."

"Did you get a tag number?" he asks. "In New York state, snowmobile owners are supposed to display their registration number with a plate or decal."

"I looked, but it was dark and the headlights were blinding me. One of the machines was silver and blue. Couldn't see the other one well enough to tell."

"A lot of snow machines up here this time of year."

I'm still thinking about the women. "Are there any pockets of non-English speaking immigrants in the area? Eastern European, maybe?"

"We have a few immigrants here and there, but no concentrated pockets."

"Is there a snowmobile dealer in town?"

"There's one in Malone."

"Could you check with them and see if any Amish have purchased machines?"

"Good idea. I'll do it."

"I'll call you tomorrow."

I disconnect and look around the darkened trailer. It's cold and smells of mildew and kerosene. I light the lantern on the bar, but it does little to penetrate the shadows. I take a few minutes to settle down, then carry the phone to the sofa and dial Tomasetti's number.

He picks up on the first ring. "Hey, Chief," he says. "How's it going up there on the tundra?"

"I'm sitting here in the dark and cold, missing you."

"Hmm. Sounds tough. Are you wearing a dress?"

I smile. "Yes."

"Head covering?"

I can't help it; I laugh. "Tomasetti, are we having phone sex?"

"I'm pretty sure we are."

"This dress is a bit of a stretch."

"This is about the woman, not the dress," he tells me. "Besides, I have a good imagination."

"Good thing."

But I can hear the smile in his voice. He misses me, too, I realize. The thought warms me from the inside out.

"You all settled in?" he asks.

"As settled in as I can be in a twelve-by-fifty circa-1980 trailer."

"Sounds homey."

"If you like caves."

"How's the assignment going?"

I tell him about attending worship earlier in the day. The women I met in town. Mary Gingerich and Laura Hershberger.

"Quilting? Worship? You like living the edge, don't you?"

I laugh again. "Tomasetti, it's really good to hear your voice."

"That's what all the female chiefs of police tell me."

"Just for the record, you're full of shit."

"They usually tell me that, too."

I debate whether to get into the incident in the woods. I don't want darken the conversation. More important, I don't want to worry him when I'm so far away. But I need his opinion, so I lay it out. "There's no doubt something unsavory was going on. At the very least an assault. I feel like I should have done something about it."

"You are. You're there, trying to figure out what's going on."

I hadn't thought about it that way, but he's right. Still, it isn't an immediate fix and that part of it doesn't sit well with me.

"So what's your take on the Amish community there?" he asks.

"Friendly. Welcoming." I try to find the right words, can't. "But I'm getting some odd vibes."

"How so?"

"Still trying to pin it down. Outwardly, people are fiercely supportive of Schrock. Almost *too* supportive. I'm not sure everyone is being honest about their feelings. I guess I'm sensing some undertones of discontent."

"What's your take on Schrock?"

"He's charismatic. Intelligent. Personable. Commanding. Hell of a preacher."

"Joel Osteen meets Amish Mafia."

Leave it to Tomasetti to make me laugh about something that really isn't funny. That's one of the things I love about him. "He's very Old Order. One of the women told me there's no plumbing in any of the houses on his land. Their dresses have to be a certain length and only a few colors are approved. No slow-moving vehicle signs on the buggies. Steel wheels. No windshields. No gas- or kerosene-powered engines, even on the dairy farms."

"Makes the appearance of those snowmobiles even more baffling."

"Exactly." I'm still thinking about Schrock. "Interestingly, he practices *Meidung*."

"Shunning?"

"Right. Only he takes it to the extreme. Usually social avoidance is used to bring the wayward souls back into the fold. Schrock doles it out as punishment. He bans for life and for relatively minor offenses."

"Sounds like you don't want to find yourself on his shit list."

"If he only knew, right?"

Tomasetti pauses. "If you want to make points with Schrock, maybe you ought to tell him about the two guys on snowmobiles."

"You're right. It'll give me an excuse to visit his farm and talk to him."

"Might make you an enemy or two," he says. "Something to keep in mind."

"I'm not here to make friends."

"Will you do me a favor before you start beating the beehive?"

"If I can."

"Watch your damn back."

CHAPTER 12

When I was a kid, my brother, Jacob, would help our neighbors bale hay for extra cash. The summer he turned thirteen, he used that money to buy his first bicycle. My sister, Sarah, and I—being females—were handed down his skateboard. I wasn't very good at sharing and spent a good bit of time haggling with Sarah, trying to convince her I should be the one to ride it. I was a persuasive child, and most of the time, I got my way. I loved that skateboard; it gave me the freedom I craved—but got me into a lot more trouble than my parents bargained for.

Of course my short-lived love affair with that skateboard was twenty-five years ago. Now, looking down at the kick scooter propped against the deck rail, I'm pretty sure I'm going to kill myself with it. The Schrock farm is only half a mile away and the roads are clear, so I decide to try it. The day is overcast with temperatures hovering in the mid-twenties, so I'm bundled up. Knowing Schrock is strict with regard to dress, I don my longest black dress and black winter head covering and strike out at nine A.M. with the hope that I don't bust my ass on the way.

I take the same route the Gingeriches took yesterday and it takes me just ten minutes to reach the mouth of the lane. The gravel is too rough for the scooter, so I park it on the shoulder and strike out on foot. There are several inches of old snow striped with buggy wheel marks. Around me, the woods echo with birdsong and I hear the whistle of a hawk in the distance. I pass by the clapboard schoolhouse and the barn where worship services were held the day before. An Amish woman in a gray dress and black coat is sweeping the concrete beneath the covered porch.

"*Guder mariye.*" I wish her a good morning as I approach.

She responds in kind and I'm relieved to be greeted with a smile. "*Wie geth's alleweil?*" How goes it now?

"I'm Kate Miller. We met yesterday at worship."

"You're the young widow from Ohio." She bows her head slightly. "What brings you here this morning?"

"I'm looking for the bishop."

She blinks and I detect surprise in her eyes. "Is he expecting you?"

I smile. "Do I need an appointment?"

"Of course not, but if he's in counsel . . ." Letting the words trail, she looks at me with a little more scrutiny. "Is everything all right?"

"Yes, I just need to speak with him about something that happened last night."

Curiosity flashes in her eyes. I smile inwardly. The Amish may be pious, but they share all the same human weaknesses as the rest of us, including a propensity for nosiness.

"Something that will concern him?" she asks.

I lean a little closer. "I saw two young Amish men on snowmobiles." Looking in both directions, I lower my voice conspiratorially. "They were with women. *Englischers*, I think."

"Bishop Schrock has been known to be a little more lenient with the young men," she tells me, "especially if they're on *Rumspringa*."

"These men are older. I think one of them wore a beard." I don't know that for fact; I couldn't see his face because of the ski mask. But

132

a married Amish man gallivanting with strange women makes for a more interesting story and will hopefully expedite access to Schrock— and get the tongues wagging in the process.

She presses her lips together. I can't tell if she's displeased by the news or with me for relaying it. "What makes you think that's something he'll be interested in?"

I laugh outright. "They were riding motorized vehicles. I'm sure that's against the *Ordnung*."

Stepping away from me, she goes back to her sweeping. "I don't see why that's any of your concern. You're not a member of the congregation yet, are you?"

"I will be." I pause, but she says nothing. "I saw one of the men strike the woman he was with." I add a bit of attitude to my voice. "Do you think the bishop will be interested in that?"

She stops sweeping and looks at me as if she'd like nothing more than to hit me with the broom. Instead, she shakes her head. "The house is that-a-way." She motions to a point farther down the lane. "Big farmhouse on the left. Can't miss it."

The trees thicken as I make my way down the lane and a sense of isolation surrounds me. Two hundred yards in, the branches curl overhead like black, arthritic fingers. I'm starting to wonder if the not-so-helpful woman gave me the wrong directions when I spot the old farmhouse nestled in the trees to my right. It's a two-story brick structure that's been painted white with a tin roof. No shutters. No winterized flowerbeds. No landscaping to speak of. Just hundreds of trees and, farther back, a massive bank barn and what looks like a good-size coop where a dozen or so hens scratch and peck at the yellow grass poking up through snow mottled with chicken shit.

A big dog of indistinguishable pedigree lumbers over to me, ears flopping, tongue lolling, emitting the occasional *woof.* He doesn't look like a biter, or much of a watchdog, for that matter, but I give him a wide berth and head toward the front door.

I step onto a wood-plank porch that's been painted gray. My boots thud softly as I make my way to the door and knock. A young Amish woman opens the door. I guess her to be in her late teens. Pretty face. Big brown eyes. She's dressed modestly in a dark gray dress, black apron, and *kapp.* Plain clothes only go so far when it comes to obscuring the feminine silhouette, and this girl is hugely pregnant. Interesting.

"*Guder mariye*," I begin. Good morning.

She opens the door wider. The smell of vinegar wafts out and I realize she's cleaning. "*Guder mariye.*" Her voice is soft, like a child's.

"I'm Kate Miller. I live down the road."

I wait, but she doesn't respond.

"Are you Bishop Schrock's daughter?" I ask.

She looks down at the broom. I notice her red chapped hands. Nails chewed to the quick. "I just clean for him," she tells me.

I want to ask her age, but fearing too many questions will set off red flags, I don't. "What's your name?"

"Esther."

"What's your last name?"

The girl looks away, doesn't respond.

"Okay." I clear my throat. "Is the bishop here? I need to speak to him."

"In the barn." She motions toward the bank barn, looking relieved to be rid of me.

"*Danki.*"

She closes the door without responding.

I leave the porch, cross the wide gravel area and start toward the barn. One of the big sliding doors stands open. Inside, I see the silhouette of a horse in crossties standing in the aisle. A young Amish man is next to the horse, bent at the waist. As I draw closer, I hear the *clang* of a hammer against steel and I realize he's shoeing the horse. A second animal is tethered to the stall door, awaiting its turn.

"Hello," I say to him as I step into the shadows of the barn.

The farrier lowers the horse's hoof to the ground and straightens. He's thickly built, with bright blue eyes and a clean-shaven face, which tells me he's unmarried. Though it's cold this morning, he's removed his overcoat and wears a black jacket over work trousers, a blue work shirt, and suspenders. "Hello," he says.

"Is Bishop Schrock around?" I ask.

He nods toward the back part of the barn. "He's unloading hay."

"*Danki.*" I run my hand over the horse's rump as I pass, its coat warm and soft beneath my palm.

I find Schrock standing in a hay wagon that's been backed up to the rear door. His back is to me; he's using a pitchfork to drop loose hay from the bed of the wagon to several horses in the paddock below. "Hello? Bishop Schrock?"

Slowly, he turns to me. His dark eyes zero in on mine with startling directness. He's clad in black. Overcoat. Jacket over a white shirt. Work pants. Black felt hat.

He doesn't offer a smile, but I discern recognition in his expression. "Kate Miller," he says. "Good morning."

"You remembered my name."

"You have a memorable face." He jams the pitchfork into the hay and climbs down from the wagon, moving with the surety of a man in good physical condition. "What can I do for you?"

"I wanted to talk to you about something that happened last night."

Concern enters his expression. I can't tell if it's practiced or genuine or somewhere in between. "Of course."

"I heard the sound of engines outside my trailer, so I put on my coat and walked outside and I saw two Amish men on snowmobiles."

"*Amisch?*" His brows snap together. "On *snowmobiles*? Who were they?"

"They wouldn't give their names. They were wearing ski masks beneath their helmets."

"You're certain they're Amish?"

"They spoke *Pennsilfaanisch Deitsch*." I grimace, take a half step closer. "Bishop, there were women with them. *English* women. I saw one of the men strike the woman riding with him. Hard enough so that she fell to the ground."

He stares at me, dismay spreading over his features. "Was she hurt?"

"Her lip was bleeding." I drop my gaze, pretend to struggle with the weight of the message with which I've burdened him. "I didn't know what to do. I thought you should know."

He nods. "Tell me, Kate, are the men of the age where they might be on *Rumspringa*?"

I shake my head. "Had that been the case, I wouldn't have come to you. I understand sometimes the young men who've not yet been baptized . . . do things." I let my expression become pained. "Bishop," I say in a low voice. "I can't be sure, but I think one of the men wore a beard."

Sighing, he reaches out and sets his hand on my shoulder. I suppress the urge to cringe when he squeezes gently. "Thank you for bringing this to me. I'll see if I can figure out who they are and what I can do to help them."

If I hadn't been watching him closely, I might've missed the flash of condescension, of *amusement*, in his eyes. He didn't ask a single question that might help him identify the men. *You already know who they are*, a little voice whispers in my ear.

Giving me a nod, he climbs back onto the wagon.

I'd wanted to speak to him longer to see where the conversation might take us, but I've been dismissed. I start toward the door. I'm midway there when he calls out to me, "Do you need a buggy ride back to your trailer?"

"No, thank you, Bishop. I have my scooter bike."

As I turn and start toward the door, it occurs to me that even though I hadn't mentioned it, he knows where I live.

CHAPTER 13

My exchange with Schrock niggles at me all the way back to the trailer. When I told him about the men in the woods, he made all the right noises. He said all the right things. But he wasn't convincing. I didn't see genuine concern. There were no questions. Granted, he's a reticent man; he's difficult to read. I'm not sure if my perspective is tainted because of the suspicion that has been laid at my feet. But I know if I'd brought the same information to my former bishop in Painters Mill, he would have been all over it—and enormously displeased.

I drop the kick scooter at the trailer and continue into town on foot. My first stop is The Dutch Kitchen for a mug of dark roast and some conversation with Mary Gingerich. There are only three other customers in the restaurant. Two men sit in the nearest booth. A silver-haired man wearing a John Deere cap and insulated coveralls sips coffee at the end of the counter. I take my usual place, where Mary is pouring pancake syrup into a glass container.

"Morning," I say as I upend the coffee cup in front of me.

She looks up from her work and grins. "Can't stay away from my coffee, eh?"

"Or the biscuits." I slide the cup toward her and tell her about the men on snowmobiles. "I think they were Amish."

Mary pauses mid pour. "None of the Amish around here use snow machines." Topping off my cup, she replaces the carafe, grabs a towel from the edge of the sink, and begins to wipe the counter. "It's against the rules."

"They were speaking *Deitsch*," I tell her.

"Probably not from around here. Or maybe young men on *Rumspringa*, then. You know how they are when they're that age."

"One of them wore a beard." I lean closer and lower my voice. "One of the men hit the woman in the face."

Something akin to caution flickers in her eyes. "An *Englischer*, more than likely. A loose woman. Drinking alcohol or whatnot."

"Maybe." I sip the coffee, wondering why everyone is so ready to dismiss such blatant rule breaking. "It was a disturbing thing to see."

"And what exactly were you doing out in the woods at night?"

"I thought I saw a stray dog." I shrug. "He looked cold and I didn't want him to be eaten by coyotes."

She sends a scowl my way. "You'd best be careful out there all by yourself."

I watch her work for a moment, sipping my coffee. "I went to see the bishop this morning."

"The *bishop*?" She stops wiping and straightens, her gaze meeting mine. "You told him about the boys?"

"I thought he should know."

"What did he say?" she asks in a low voice.

"Just that he'd look into it and take appropriate action."

Taking the towel to the sink, she runs it under the tap, twists out the excess water, and takes it back to the counter. I don't miss the way her eyes flick to the window behind her.

I glance past her and notice the Amish man in the kitchen area. The same one I saw before. Bent slightly, he's watching us through the pass-through window. I stare back and he looks away, slinking deeper into the kitchen. *Eavesdropping.*

"I didn't know the bishop has a daughter," I say conversationally.

"He doesn't have any family here that I know of."

"I just assumed . . . The girl that answered the door. Her name's Esther." I shrug.

She wipes the counter harder, her mouth tightening. "I don't see how that's any business of yours. Or mine."

"She's in the married way," I say, using the preferred Amish term for pregnancy.

She stops wiping. Giving me a cross look, she sets her hand on her hip. "I'm no fan of gossip, Kate Miller. Or tall tales, for that matter."

"I just thought—"

"You misunderstood what you saw, is all."

I set my cup on the counter, look down at it. "I'm sure you're right."

She continues wiping the counter with a little too much vigor. "Such things aren't spoken of here."

I add a trace of hurt to my voice. "I hope I didn't offend you. I was curious—"

"Not here," she hisses.

My cop's antennae cranks up. "What do you mean?"

"I've got to get back to work now, Kate."

"But . . ."

"You'll have to get your biscuits another time." Sliding the condiment tray aside, she wipes beneath it. "Probably best if you just left."

I stand outside the door of The Dutch Kitchen for a minute, trying to figure out what just happened inside. Only two options make sense. Either Mary knows the men on snowmobiles and didn't appreciate my going to the bishop, or she knew the man in the kitchen was listening to our conversation and didn't want to speak openly in front of him. But in either case, why?

I puzzle over the odd exchange as I start toward The Calico Country Store. Hopefully, I haven't alienated her and decide I'll try to make good with her tomorrow.

I'm surprised and pleased to see the quilt shop bustling with activity. Like yesterday, I'm greeted by the homey aromas of lavender and yeast bread. I spy a platter of sliced bread on the counter. I snag a piece and nibble the crust as I make my way to rear of the store to check on the status of the quilts I left. I find Laura Hershberger using a telescoping retriever pole to snag a crib quilt from its place on the wall. Next to her a woman in a red leather jacket and matching boots watches.

"That's a pretty one," I say to no one in particular.

The woman in the jacket glances at me and offers a toothy smile. "I'm buying it for my grandbaby."

The portly man standing next to her bends slightly and makes eye contact with me. "She's our first," he tells me. "Just a week old, so our daughter will get a lot of use out of this one."

I offer a smile. "The quilts are made to swaddle as many babies as a mother and father wishes to have."

The woman looks delighted by the notion.

Laura Hershberger retrieves the quilt and steps down from the short ladder upon which she'd been standing. "The double wedding ring pattern has always been my favorite."

"And the pink and blue is perfect for a little boy *or* a girl," I add.

Laura hands the quilt to the woman in the red jacket. The woman holds it up, beaming, and actually rubs the thing against her cheek. "Oh, I love it. And Christine will, too. I don't care how much it costs."

Not looking quite so sure, the man finds the tag, turns it over for a look, and winces. "Do you take credit cards?" he asks.

Ten minutes later, Laura and I are sitting at the table at the rear of the store, drinking coffee. We've both helped ourselves to another piece of bread.

"Did you enjoy worship yesterday?" she asks.

"Very much," I reply. "Everyone in the congregation is friendly and welcoming. Bishop Schrock is a good preacher."

She smirks. "A little long-winded if you ask me, but then that's the bishop for you."

I let that settle, thinking about my exchange with Mary, and decide to give the beehive another poke. "I went to see him this morning."

She looks at me over the rim of her cup and raises her brows. "About what?"

I tell her about the men on snowmobiles.

"What on earth would Amish men be doing on snow machines?"

"I was wondering the same thing." Lowering my voice, I tell her about the two women. "Laura, I don't think they were Amish."

Her frown conveys disgust. "Boys that age have the brains of a chicken. I suspect Bishop Schrock will show them the error of their ways."

I stare at the chunk of bread in my hand, unmoving, playing the role in which I've been cast. "I saw one of the men hit the woman he was with. Right in the face."

She stiffens and for the first time looks uncomfortable. "Maybe they were just roughhousing. You know how the young people are these days, especially the boys."

That was one of the attitudes I despised most growing up. People were always making excuses for the boys when they misbehaved. Not so for the girls, who have much less in the way of freedom and are held to a higher standard. "These were not boys," I say firmly. "They were grown men. One of them had a beard."

Her mouth opens, forming a perfect oval. "You told the bishop as much?"

I break the piece of bread in my hand in half. "I thought he should know."

"What did he say?"

"He said he'd find out who they are and deal with them."

"The bishop is a man of his word." When she raises her mug to her lips, I can't help but notice that her hand isn't quite steady. "You're not afraid to make waves, are you, Kate Miller?"

"I'm not afraid to do the right thing."

"Let's hope it was."

I shoot her a puzzled look, but evidently she's had enough talk of wayward Amish men. Brushing crumbs from her apron, she rises. "Some of the women come in to sew a few days a week. If you're working on something, you're welcome to join us."

My nerves tighten at the thought of exposing my sewing skills—or lack thereof—to any of the women, most of whom know their way around a sewing kit. But since the Amish grapevine begins with the heart of the family—the women—it's an opportunity I can't pass up.

"I'd love to."

Misconceptions about undercover work run rampant—even within law enforcement circles. While there's no doubt it can be high octane, the lion's share consists of building your cover, making yourself visible, and, of course, waiting—the bane of most cops. There's not much you can do to rush the process. Push too hard, and you risk the suspicion of those you're investigating. Sit back on your heels, and you get nothing.

I like to think I've found the middle road. I've made myself known, asking questions without ruffling too many feathers, and I've garnered a good bit of information. It's premature to determine if any of it will result in anything useful, but it's a solid start.

I spent the afternoon at the shop—time that passed with particular slowness. There were few customers, and although I tried multiple times to strike up a conversation with Laura, she wasn't in the mood for chitchat. I used the time to purchase a few additional sewing supplies: several yards of fabric, four spools of thread, and a new pair of shears. I left town a little after two o'clock, and back at the trailer, I set to work on the simplest sewing project I could think of: potholders—an activity I haven't partaken in for twenty years.

It doesn't take long for me to realize I've lost what little skill I had acquired as a teenager. As I use the seam ripper to remove my less-than-stellar stitching, I find myself wishing I'd purchased a few more items from the sewing shop in Painters Mill so I could pass them off as my own work and avoid sewing altogether.

By four P.M., restless and frustrated and freezing cold, I pull my personal cell phone from beneath the mattress and dial the one person who can make me feel better.

"I thought the Amish went to bed early," he begins without preamble.

At the sound of his voice, the tension clamped around the back of my neck relaxes. "Not this early."

"Everything okay?" he asks.

"You mean aside from me freezing my ass off, dying of boredom, and basically getting nowhere?"

"You knew going in that impersonating an Amish woman wasn't exactly going to be life on the edge."

"No TV. No radio. No electricity. And very little damn heat." I sigh. "It makes me realize just how far I've moved away from my roots."

"Or maybe being Amish isn't just about going without the things the rest of us take for granted," he says. "Maybe it's something you carry inside. You know, faith. A kind heart."

I smile. "Tomasetti, you're full of surprises this afternoon."

"I like to keep you on your toes."

"You do." Snuggling more deeply into the blanket I've thrown over me, I tell him about my visit to see Schrock earlier. "He didn't ask any questions."

"He already knew."

"Exactly." I tell him about the young woman who answered the door. "She's pretty and young. She could have been there to clean or to cook for him, but I got a bit of an odd vibe."

"You think she's there for another reason?"

"The Amish are generally aware of appearances. They care what people think. With Schrock being unmarried, relatively young, and in a position of power, I thought it was odd that he'd have a pretty young woman cleaning his house." I think about that a moment. "Most Amish would go to great lengths to avoid any hint of impropriety."

"Was this girl a minor?"

"Late teens. Maybe early twenties. And pregnant."

"Interesting."

"I thought so, too." I think about bishop. "I'm no schmuck when it comes to reading people, but I can't get a handle on this guy."

"Sometimes that happens when people put forth a false front," he says.

"I've only met him twice. Both times, he was relaxed, said all the right things. Body language matched his words."

"But?"

"I know it sounds melodramatic, but there's something about him that seems . . . off." I think about my visit with Mary Gingerich earlier in the day, about Laura Hershberger's reticence. "Nobody wanted to talk about those men. I don't know if they're protective of their bishop or . . . scared of him."

"Maybe he's abusing his position. Intimidating people."

I think about my conversation with Anna Gingerich. "Remember what Suggs said about people being locked in a chicken coop?"

"Unfortunately, I do."

"I was chatting with a girl on Sunday and she told me she knows of another girl who'd been locked in a chicken coop."

"That kind of extreme punishment would explain why people don't talk about him."

"They want to stay off his radar."

"They sure as hell don't want to piss him off." He sighs unhappily. "I know I don't have to remind you, but somehow a fifteen-year-old kid ended up dead. Don't let down your guard. Don't trust anyone. And keep your fucking eyes on Schrock."

Despite my best intentions, the conversation has gone in a direction I didn't want it to go. "I'm being careful."

We go silent and I'm suddenly aware of the hiss of the miles stretching between us. "I could drive up there," he says quietly. "We could shack up for a couple days."

"That would get the tongues wagging."

"Probably get us locked in the chicken coop."

I can't help but laugh, but I don't miss the serious note in his voice.

At just before five P.M. I'm saved by a knock on the door. Setting my ruinous sewing project on the sofa, I go to the window and part the

AMONG THE WICKED

curtains, surprised to see Jacob Yoder standing on the deck, his hands in his pockets, snow gathering on the shoulders of his black overcoat. Beyond, I see a bony-looking Standardbred gelding hitched to a buggy. He's alone.

I open the door and give him a look that's not quite friendly. "What do you want?"

Amusement flickers in his eyes. "Bishop Schrock wants to see you."

It's the last thing I expected him to say. For an instant, I'm not sure how to respond. "Why?"

"He didn't say."

"Right now?"

"That's what he said."

I stare hard at him, looking for a lie or some deception, but there's nothing there. "All right." I start to close the door, but he stops me.

"I'm supposed to take you." He motions toward the buggy.

"I have my scooter bike." If things go south with Schrock, I don't want to rely on Yoder for transportation.

He gives me an incredulous look. "He doesn't like to be kept waiting."

"Tell him I'll be there in twenty minutes."

"If I were you, I'd make it ten."

I close the door without responding.

147

CHAPTER 14

I watch Yoder pull away. When he's gone, I rush to the bedroom, kneel next to the bed, pluck the .22 from its hiding place, and holster it. I double check the charge on my phone, make sure it's on vibrate, and stow it in my pocket. Grabbing a black scarf, I cover my head, pull on gloves and my coat, and then I'm out the door and into the cold.

I push the scooter bike hard, and it takes me ten minutes to reach Schrock's place. The snow is coming down in earnest now and starting to accumulate. Stopping at the mouth of the lane, I hop off the bike, lean it against a tree, and set off on foot.

The hem of my dress is damp and cold even through my tights, but my feet are dry in my boots as I tromp through snow. There are buggy tracks, telling me someone has driven by recently. I pass the barn where worship was held yesterday. The main door is closed and there's no one in sight.

The house looms into view like something out of a gothic movie. It's a grim place in the semidarkness. It's isolated and, with the falling snow and trees, somehow menacing. I see the flicker of lantern light in the living room window. Taking the steps to the porch, I cross to the door and knock.

While I wait, my mind scrolls through possible reasons Schrock might want to see me and how I might use the visit to my advantage. I look out over the woods, and even with my nerves zinging, I have to admire the beauty of the place. The black trunks of the winter-bare trees. The softly falling snow. The blanket of leaves slowly being covered with white.

The creak of hinges sounds. I turn to see Eli Schrock standing in the doorway, looking at me as if I'm lost and wandered to his door-stop for directions.

"*Guder nochmiddawks*," I say. Good afternoon.

He doesn't offer a smile. His eyes are direct and probing. Clad in all black—hat, trousers, and jacket—he makes an imposing figure. I'm not easily intimidated, but the knowledge that we're wholly alone and I'm miles from help hovers in the forefront of my mind.

"Kate Miller." He bows his head slightly. "I thought you'd ride with Jacob."

"I didn't want to put him to any trouble, so I rode the scooter bike."

"You must be cold. Come in."

Stepping aside, he ushers me through the door. I'm keenly aware of his size as I walk past him. He's well over six feet tall and probably two hundred pounds. He stands so close I discern the smell of fresh-cut wood on his jacket and coffee on his breath. The first thing I notice is the fire blazing in the hearth. A braided rug covers a rough-hewn plank floor. On a table next to the sofa, a kerosene lantern flickers, casting shadows on the ceiling. I notice a copy of *Martyrs Mirror* lying facedown on a sofa cushion.

"I've interrupted your reading," I say.

He closes the door. "You've read *Martyer Schipiggel?*"

"When I was a teenager."

"The Anabaptists have suffered many torments because of their faith." He motions to a straight-backed chair across from the sofa. "And yet they forgave, even loved their persecutors."

"Dirk Willems," I reply, referring to the story of the martyred Anabaptist who fled from his captors, risked his life crossing thin ice, and made it to the other side. When his pursuer gave chase and fell through the ice and into the frigid water, Willems went back onto the ice and rendered aid. Because of his kindness, Willems was recaptured, tortured, and burned at the stake.

Schrock smiles, pleased that I'm familiar with the story. "It's the Amish way."

My boots are nearly silent against the floor as I cross to the chair.

"Would you like *kaffi*?" he asks.

"Thank you."

He walks into the kitchen. I watch as he removes a plain mug from the cupboard, lifts an old-fashioned percolator from the stove, and pours. I lower myself into the chair, lean back with my hands in my lap, and try to settle my nerves.

"Sometimes I make it too strong." He returns with a mug in each hand and passes one to me. "When you're a widower, you learn to do all the things your wife would normally do." He smiles. "And usually not as well."

"How long have you been a widower?" I drink some of the coffee. He's right; it's strong, but good.

"A long time."

"I'm sorry."

He offers a kindly look. "God had another plan. Perhaps it was His way of bringing me here to Roaring Springs where I could dedicate myself to serving as *Vellicherdiener*."

I expected him to go to his chair and sit, but he sets the coffee on

150

the mantel above the hearth and remains standing. "You'll be joining the church on Sunday?"

"Yes."

He studies me for a moment. "What about you? How long have you been a widow?"

"John has been gone for nine months now." I say the name with reverence. "He was a good husband. A good man."

"You never had children?"

"We weren't blessed with children."

"Children are important." His eyes bore into mine. I look for disappointment, but he gives me nothing. "But we are blessed with only what God gives us."

I look away, take another drink of coffee. "Yes."

"There's still time if it's the Lord's wish."

It's an overly personal statement, so I don't respond. I try to get a handle on the source of my discomfort, identify it, stave it off, but I can't. I don't know why I'm here or where he's going with this line of conversation. I'm not sure what to say next, so I pick up the cup and drink.

"It must be difficult," he says.

"What's that?"

He walks to the hearth, lifts a log from the rack, and places it on the fire. "Being alone at such a young age. No children. No husband."

"I have my faith," I tell him. "It fills up my life. It's enough for now."

He straightens and crosses to me, looks down at me, studying me intently. I'm no stranger to odd individuals or awkward situations, but my unease is making itself known. My palms are damp. My heart beats a little too fast. I'm sweating beneath my coat, but I don't want to take it off.

"A young woman has needs," he says softly. "Without a husband . . ." He shrugs. "Even an *Amisch* woman."

Incredulity rises inside me, but I bank it. I look up at him. He's standing too close, his head cocked. His gaze searches mine, as if he's waiting for a reaction. Or something I've not yet revealed to him. For the first time it strikes me that I feel strange. My heart rate is too high. My hands and feet are still cold from the ride over, but the back of my neck is damp with sweat. The heat from the fire is making me sleepy, which is unusual because I'm "on."

I startle when he reaches out, takes my left hand, and pulls me to my feet. For an instant I feel light-headed, but it quickly levels off. In the back of my mind I wonder if I'm coming down with something. Or if the stress is getting to me . . .

We're standing face to face, about two feet apart. Around us, the house is so quiet I can hear the crackle of the fire, the wind driving snow against the window, the steady thrum of my heart. I know better than to let the moment unnerve me, but it does.

"Did your husband forgive you?" he asks.

"Forgive me for what?"

"You never gave him children."

I glance down where my hand is enclosed within his. I try to tug it away, but he doesn't release it. Despite my best efforts, I'm flustered. I feel unsettled and spaced out. I raise my gaze to his and find his eyes probing mine. I'm aware of my heart tapping hard against my ribs. The .22 against my thigh. The weight of my phone in my pocket.

"That's private." I say the words slowly, enunciating each syllable because suddenly I'm having difficulty speaking. "I prefer not to talk of such things, even to you, Bishop."

"Artificial birth control is against the rules here. It's against our conscience and is considered taking a life."

Kate Burkholder would have told him to piss off. Kate Miller, bound by her faith and the *Ordnung*, is obligated to submit.

"I've never used it," I murmur.

"Then why no children?"

"I don't know."

"Were you a good wife?"

"Of course I was."

"You submitted to your husband?"

"Yes."

"Always?"

I say nothing.

Gently, he turns my hand over so that it's palm up. Again, I try to withdraw it from his, but he maintains his grip. I'm keenly aware of his proximity. The warmth of his skin against mine. Raising his other hand, he runs his index finger across my palm. A feather-soft touch, but I feel it with the power of an electrical shock.

"Did you have thoughts of other men?" he asks.

I stare at Schrock, taken aback. "Bishop, that's an . . . inappropriate question."

"So you did, then? While you were with your husband, you were thinking of another man?"

"Never."

"Do you plan to remarry?" he asks.

"One day. God willing."

"Sadly, many widows never do. Some, of course, are too old. They have difficulty finding a suitable husband. Not you, of course." He shrugs. "Some of the young widows have too much guilt."

"Guilt? I have no guilt."

"Some Amish women find it difficult to open their bodies to another man. After taking their vows."

Had the circumstances been different—had I not been required to maintain my cover—I would've laughed in his face and left him with a resounding *fuck off.* Of course I can't do either of those things. As distasteful and outrageous as this exchange has become, I'm bound to participate.

"I have no such guilt." I'm alarmed when I slur the final word. It's then that I know the light-headedness isn't my imagination. Something's wrong. My vision is off. I stare at him, aware that my face is hot. I can feel sweat beading on my forehead and upper lip. Not embarrassment or discomfort. More like a fever. . . .

Only then does the possibility that I've been drugged strike me. A warning bell clangs in my head. Did he put something in the coffee? I didn't drink much, but I'm definitely feeling the effects of . . . something.

"I can help you," he whispers. "As your bishop, I will counsel you. Prepare you for your husband. Teach you to be a better wife in the eyes of God."

I yank my hand away and stumble back. His fingers scrape my skin as he lets go. "I don't need any of those things."

A smile plays at the corners of his mouth. A sort of dark amusement peeks at me from behind his eyes. He's enjoying this, I realize. He enjoys intimidating people. Toying with their emotions. Manipulating them to get what he wants. Bending them to his will. Finding a weakness and taking advantage of it.

Hurting them.

I have to hand it to him: he's good at it, at least when it comes to grieving widows and vulnerable teenagers. But I'm a cop, and at the moment it's taking every bit of restraint I possess not to blow this whole thing for the sheer satisfaction of taking him down a few notches.

"God came to me last night, Kate Miller. In a dream. He told me your husband died because you were not a good wife to him. You had impure thoughts."

I step back. "That's not true."

"I know these things. I look at you and I see a woman who is lost and alone. A frightened woman who wants to belong but she doesn't know how to reach out. A woman who longs for the return of the faith she's lost. I know everything about you."

"No, you don't," I whisper.

"I know John never forgave you. Because of that he cannot get into heaven. Come with me tonight, and I'll show you the way to forgiveness."

"I have to go." Turning abruptly, I run to the door, throw the lock.

He reaches the door at the same time I do and sets his palm against it, blocking me. He bows his head slightly, his face coming within inches of mine. Too close. "Wait."

"No."

"I didn't mean to upset you."

"I have to go."

He straightens, his expression disapproving, disappointed. "All right." His eyes go to the window. "It's dark and snowing. At least let me hitch the buggy and drive you home."

"I've got the scooter bike."

He looks at me for what seems like an eternity. As if he's trying to decide whether to let me go. For an instant, I'm afraid he won't. I'm not incapacitated; I'm armed and able to defend myself. But I'm impaired. And for the first time, he's frightened me.

After an interminable moment, he opens the door. "As you wish."

I rush through. My head spins as I cross the porch to the steps and stumble down them. What did he put in that coffee? The tox screen done on Rachel Esh showed she had OxyContin in her blood. Was it from Schrock? Is that what he gave me? Something worse?

At the foot of the steps, I glance over my shoulder, find him at the door leaning against the jam.

Goddamn predator.

"Be careful out there, Kate Miller," he calls out. "It's very, very cold."

I feel eyes tracking me as I walk swiftly through the falling snow. I wonder if he's laughing because my coordination is off. The son of a bitch. A chill that has nothing to do with the falling temperature hovers at the base of my spine. I resist the urge to look over my shoulder until I reach the trees, where I break into a run.

I'm out of breath when I reach the scooter bike near the end of the lane. As I push it toward the road, I notice there's at least two inches of new snow, and I hope I can get the damn thing home.

It's not easy. After a few hundred yards, I get off and push it the way a kid would push a bike with a flat tire. All the while I fret over what I might have ingested, my mind replaying every moment. The way he looked at me. The way he touched me. The things he said and the manner in which he said them.

I'm not easily shocked; in the years I've been in law enforcement, I've seen things I wouldn't have believed if I hadn't witnessed them with my own eyes. I've seen things I later wished I could erase from my brain. I've met more than my share of people who were violent or foaming-at-the-mouth crazy or both. Individuals whose minds are as putrid and dark as a rotting carcass.

Eli Schrock is none of those things. He's charismatic, with a gentle demeanor and kind eyes. He's well spoken, outwardly religious, and caring to the point of discomfort. All of which makes him the most dangerous kind of criminal.

This community into which I've been thrust isn't merely an Amish settlement. Eli Schrock is no more an Amish bishop than I am. He's taken something sacrosanct and twisted it to meet his own self-fulfilling and perverse needs.

By the time I reach the trailer, my head is beginning to clear. I'm immensely relieved; as far as I know, he could have slipped me a dose of something nasty. Something fatal.

I check for footprints around the trailer before going inside, but the snow is coming down too hard for the precaution to do much good. Shivering, I open the door and go directly to the sink, yank a glass from the cupboard and down a full glass of water. Working the phone from my pocket, I dial Suggs.

"I just got back from Schrock's place," I tell him. "I think the son of a bitch drugged me."

"Drugged you? Kate, Jesus Christ." His voice takes on an urgency I hadn't heard before. "I'll get an ambulance out there now. Get you to ER."

"That'll draw too much attention. Dan, I'm not finished with this bastard."

"But—"

"Can you pick me up?" Even as I say the words it occurs to me that someone could be watching. Frustrated, I smack my hand down on the counter. "Meet me at the Amish phone booth."

"Damn it, Chief. Are you sure you're okay to do that?"

"Make sure there's no one around to see us." I hear stress in my voice, make an effort to edge it down. "Don't drive your official car."

He curses again. "I'll be in my wife's SUV. Be there as soon as I can. If you get into trouble, call."

Three hours later I'm sitting on a gurney in the emergency department of Alice Hyde Hospital in Malone, my legs sticking out of a worn hospital gown that refuses to remain closed in the back. Upon my arrival—and thanks to Suggs's position as sheriff—I was immediately wheeled into an exam cubicle and assessed by the on-call physician. Once my vitals were taken and deemed normal, three vials of blood were drawn. As a precautionary measure, I was given an intramuscular injection of Naloxone, which, I was informed, is a routine treatment for an opiate overdose. It's a safe medication and has no side effects if, in fact, I did not ingest an opiate narcotic. The blood tox screen will tell all in a few days.

"Knock, knock," comes Suggs's voice from the other side of the privacy curtain.

I reach for the sheet lying across the head of the gurney, snap it open, and cover my legs. "I'm here."

The curtain is shoved aside and the sheriff peeks in. "How you feeling?" he asks.

"I think they're about to spring me."

"You gave me a hell of a scare," he growls. "I guess it's safe to say you don't have any qualms about putting yourself in the line of fire."

"If you want the honey, you've got to poke the hive," I return.

"What did the doc say?"

"Schrock may have dropped some type of opiate into the coffee he gave me. Doc says I probably didn't ingest much. They sent my blood to the lab for a tox."

"Anything turns up and we'll nail him to the wall with it."

"Felony assault might earn him a few years." I look at Suggs. "I think he's guilty of worse."

He cocks his head, curiosity sharp in his eyes. "So what happened?"

I tell him about Yoder coming to my trailer with a summons from the bishop. "Initially, Schrock was on his best behavior. Once he gave me that coffee, the situation got strange. He began saying things an

Amish bishop would never say. Had I been a civilian, there's no doubt it would have culminated into something else."

He makes a sound low in his throat. "Fucking charlatan."

"Dan, this guy's a predator. He's preying on these people. He's in a position of power and he's using it to manipulate the people who believe in him." I recall the sensation of his finger as he traced it over my palm and suppress a shiver. "He's no bishop, and we're not dealing with a typical Amish community."

"Look, Kate, I think this gig just got a hell of a lot more dicey. Maybe we ought to end it now. We'll wait for the tox. Get a warrant. And we'll settle for what we can get as far as charges—"

"I want to finish this."

He releases a long sigh. "You're sure?"

"Yup."

"All right." He pauses. "So what's next?"

"The same. I'll keep talking to people. Keep digging. Sooner or later I'll find someone who knows something and get them to talk to me."

"Do you need anything?"

"A car. Cable TV. A decent furnace."

His laugh is halfhearted, as if he knows I'm only partially kidding. We fall silent. Suggs is trying hard not to look at my gown, my bare feet sticking out from beneath the sheet. He isn't quite succeeding.

"Kate, you need to be careful," he says. "I mean it. Especially with Schrock."

"You bet I will." I tell him about the man who works in the kitchen at The Dutch Kitchen. "He was watching us. Eavesdropping. I think that's why Mary Gingerich wouldn't talk to me."

"That's so far out there, I don't even know what to say," he snaps. "Fucking spies." Shaking his head, he shoves his hands into his pockets. "You think someone's watching your trailer?"

"It's possible, but I don't think they're suspicious of me."

Yet.

The word hangs in the air, but neither of us acknowledges it.

"You can't walk home tonight," he says. "Too far. Too cold."

"Since it's late and you're in a civilian vehicle, I think it would be okay for you to drop me at the Amish pay phone."

"I guess it's a chance we'll have to take." But he looks worried as he scrubs a hand over his jaw. "I'll be in the waiting area. Come get me when you're ready."

CHAPTER 15

My encounter with Schrock haunts me through the night. When I'm not tossing and turning, I'm dreaming of being trapped inside that house with him, unable to escape, and when I reach for my sidearm it's not there . . .

I had every intention of calling Tomasetti to let him know what happened, but I couldn't make myself pick up the phone. I know that's not fair. Nor is it honest. He's a strong man and I'm not giving him the credit he deserves. But telling him about a dangerous incident when I'm so far away didn't feel like the right thing to do. I'm ever cognizant of the anguish he endured after the deaths of his wife and children. He doesn't speak of it, but there are still nights when his demons come calling. Nights when he wakes in a cold sweat, shaking and choking back panic. I don't want to add to that.

I rise at dawn, take a hot shower, careful to leave my cell and .38 sitting on the edge of the tub. At nine, I pack my sewing supplies in a canvas bag and head into town.

Though it's a workday, downtown Roaring Springs is deserted. A leaden sky presses down with the weight of some massive boulder. As I make my way along Main Street, with its vacant storefronts and cracked sidewalks, a plastic bag catches in a whirlwind at the entrance to an alley. The scene is postapocalyptic and leaves me feeling isolated and alone.

There are two cars and a pickup truck parked outside The Dutch Kitchen. I lean the scooter bike against a parking meter at the curb and head inside for coffee and hopefully some conversation with Mary Gingerich.

A skinny man with shoulder-length hair and a scruffy beard nurses a cup of coffee at the counter. Two women dressed in jeans and sweatshirts are having breakfast in one of the booths. I feel their eyes on me as I start toward the counter. I don't miss their not-so-covert comments about my clothes as I pass, and I try not to shake my head. I've just taken a seat on a stool when Mary comes through the swinging double doors leading to the kitchen.

"Looks like we might be in for some snow later," I say in Pennsylvania Dutch.

Instead of responding, she turns her back, plunges her hands into soapy water and begins to wash coffee cups. "We get that a lot this time of year."

The sense that something is off—that something has changed since we last spoke—strikes me immediately. When Mary and I initially met, she was welcoming and friendly and open. Yesterday, and now this morning, she won't so much as look me in the eye.

"*And Wei bischt du heit?*" I ask. How are you today?

"Busy." She turns to me, her expression cool and unsmiling. "*Witt du wennich eppes zu ess?*" Would you like something to eat?

"Just coffee," I tell her.

She sets a steaming cup in front of me, but she doesn't linger. Something cold scrapes up my back when I notice the bruise below her left eye. Amish women do not wear makeup. Evidently, she made an exception and stopped by the drugstore for concealer; I can see where she tried to cover the bruise. I suspect her eye will be fully black by the end of the day. When she turns to refill the man's cup, I notice an abrasion the size of a quarter glowing angry and red on the side of her neck.

My first thought is that Abe hit her. But I'm a decent judge of character; I don't think her husband is a wife beater. But if not Abe, then who? And why?

When she passes by me again, I reach out and touch her arm. "Mary, are you okay?"

She slants me a look. "I'm a klutz, is what I am. Ran into a cabinet door last night."

Watching her closely, I sip the coffee without tasting it, hoping I'm wrong, knowing I'm not. "Cabinet door must have been pretty angry."

She laughs self-consciously, her hand fluttering to the abrasion on her neck. "Well, that's just crazy talk."

I lower my voice. "Who did that to you?"

Her eyes dart left. I glance over her shoulder to see the Amish man staring at us through the serving window between the counter area and the kitchen in the rear.

I let my gaze slide away from his and address Mary loudly enough for him to hear. "I'm willing to bus tables. Or wash dishes if that's what you need."

She blinks, then I see her shoulders relax. "You'll have to come back when the owner's here."

"Can I fill out an application?" I ask.

Gathering herself, she turns to the man watching us. "Do you know when Mr. Pelletier will be here?"

He shrugs. "Tomorrow, I guess."

Nodding, she turns her attention back to me. "You'll have to come back then."

I bring the cup to my mouth. "Come to my trailer when you get off," I whisper.

"Can't." Using the damp towel clutched in her hand, she wipes the counter. "They'll know."

"Who?"

Wiping vigorously, she shakes her head. "Can't talk about it," she says. "Please, just leave."

"I can help you."

"No one can help," she whispers. "No one."

On the short ride to The Calico Country Store, Mary Gingerich's words replay uneasily in my head. *They'll know.* Who the hell was she talking about? Schrock? His followers? The man in the kitchen? I think about the marks on her face and neck. Who would do such a thing, and why? Is physical violence somehow part of this community? If so, to what end? Does it have something to do with Rachel Esh? She had been living with the Gingeriches at the time of her death.

It's nearly ten A.M. when I reach The Calico Country Store. The cowbell on the door jingles merrily when I enter. I'm greeted by the aromas of cinnamon bread and cardamom. It's a pleasant, homey space that beckons one to leave her problems at the door and come in for a decadent snack, a bit of shopping, and some harmless gossip.

There are no customers in the store this morning. A Mennonite girl stands behind the cash register, reading an inspirational romance novel. She glances up at the sound of the bell and smiles.

"Hi," I greet her. "Is Laura around?"

The girl points toward the rear of the store. "She's at the sewing table with the other women."

"*Danki.*"

Midway there, the sound of laughter reaches me. I round the corner to find Laura and three other Amish women sitting at the table in a "sewing circle," drinking coffee. Spread out before them is a gorgeous tulip basket pattern quilt. Hefting my sewing bag higher on my shoulder, I approach.

"*Wie geth's alleweil?*" I call out to them. How goes it now?

"Ah, Kate!" Laura tosses a grin at me, her eyes flicking to the bag at my side. "Glad you could make it. I see you brought your work with you."

"I'm just finishing up a couple of potholders. For my niece's hope chest."

"We've plenty of room if you'd like to join us." Laura introduces me to the three women as she clears a place at the end of the table. Wearing a dark gray dress and black winter bonnet, Ada is in her mid-fifties with a round face and a figure to match. Naomi is the elder of the group. She's tall and lean with black hair gone to salt and pepper, dark eyes, and nineteen grandchildren. Lena is forty-two with dishwater-blond hair, a pretty girl-next-door face, and a surprise baby on the way. She and her husband live in a house not far from Eli Schrock's land.

"Rebecca isn't here yet," Laura says to no one in particular.

"Missed last week, too," Ada says as she pushes her needle through fabric.

Naomi glances toward the door as if expecting her to come through it at any moment. "Odd for her to miss two weeks in a row."

Laura addresses me. "The five of us meet every few days to catch up on our sewing."

"Catch up on our gossip, more like," Ada puts in.

Using her front teeth, Naomi severs a thread. "There's plenty to be had."

"*Es waarken maulvoll gat,*" Lena comments. There's nothing good about that.

"I suppose that depends on who's the topic of the day." Laura motions toward the quilt spread out on the table. "Been working on this one for a couple of weeks now."

"The thing would be finished if you girls spent more time sewing and less talking," Ada huffs.

I like Ada immediately; she's opinionated, with a spicy personality, and reminds me of my grandmother, who baked the best dry molasses cookies in the world—and was well known for taking you down a notch when you needed it. Ada may be a scant inch short of five feet tall, but she commands respect, and if you're smart, you'll give it to her.

Setting my bag on the floor next to a vacant chair, I pull out my supplies. Spool of thread. Pincushion. Thimble. One of the potholders I'd started. I spy scissors on the table, so I leave mine in the bag. I feel awkward and inept as I run the thread through the eye of the needle, but my hands are steady and I remind myself that even though it's been a while since I stitched, I've been practicing. I spent many an evening as a girl, needle and thread in hand, under the watchful eye of my *mamm*. I hope the memory comes back with enough steam for me to pull this off.

"We're having *siess kaffi* if you'd like some, Kate," Laura says without looking up from her work.

"I love sweet coffee." I'm about to get up to pour myself a cup when the Mennonite girl who'd been manning the counter brings one to me. "*Danki.*"

The coffee is strong and sweet, with just the right amount of milk. One sip and a hundred memories rush through me. I was sixteen years old the last time I had sweet coffee. My *mamm* took my sister, Sarah, and me to a neighbor's farm to see a new baby who had come into the world three weeks ahead of schedule. All the local Amish women had gathered, helping the new mother with her chores—cleaning and laundry—even putting up the tomatoes she'd been canning. Most brought a dish. I wasn't into socializing with my elders back then, but I recall there was such cooperation among the women, a lot of laughter—some of it at the expense of the men, most of whom were in the barn smoking cigarettes. And there was such love for that new baby. As angry and unhappy as I'd been back then, I remember laughing because they passed him around for so long that he fell asleep, and even then they didn't put him down.

"Has anyone heard from Fannie?" Lena asks of no one in particular.

"Not since I took them over that strawberry-rhubarb pie last week," Ada says. "Poor thing is trying to be brave, but she just sits at the kitchen table crying all day."

"They weren't at worship on Sunday," Naomi comments.

"Seems like that would have brought them some comfort," Lena puts in.

Laura gives me a somber look. "Fannie and Samuel are the ones who lost their daughter, Rachel."

"There was a story in *The Bridge*." I feign a shudder. "Such a terrible thing.

"And they're such nice people," Ada says.

I keep my eyes on my stitching. "I've not met them yet."

"I was thinking about taking them a chicken casserole," Laura says. "Maybe we can go together."

"I'd like that," I tell her.

No one speaks for several minutes, as if in reverence to the grieving couple and their recently deceased daughter. Meeting Fannie and

Samuel Esh is high on my list of goals, but I know that with them still grieving—and me being an outsider—it will require delicacy and tact.

I've just sunk the needle into my index finger when Laura breaks the silence with a more upbeat topic. "I heard Viola Beachy had her baby," she announces with some flourish.

The women continue with their work, but sit up a little bit straighter. A new baby is momentous news among the Amish, especially the women. "Boy or girl?" Lena asks, pressing her hand protectively against her own protruding belly.

"Boy. Big, too. Nearly nine pounds," Naomi puts in.

Ada snips a thread with the scissors. "I'll take her and David a couple of my potpies tomorrow."

"They'll appreciate that," Naomi says with a nod.

I look at Lena. "When is your little one due?"

"Another month or so," she tells me. "Our fourth."

"Only four." Ada tuts. "You and Reuben had best get busy."

"One at a time," Lena snaps good-naturedly.

Chuckles break out around the table. I join in, hoping the women don't notice that my stitches aren't quite straight and not as evenly spaced as they should be. But the fabric I'm working with is pretty and the thread is a similar color, and hopefully won't be too closely inspected.

A few minutes later, Ada sighs. "The quilt is going to be a pretty one."

"Warm, too," Laura puts in.

"Are you going to sell it?" I ask.

She grins. "Haven't decided."

I don't know if it's the part of me that's still Amish—that will always be Amish—or nostalgia, but for the first time since arriving in Roaring Springs, I'm relaxed. I like these women; I'm comfortable with them. And it occurs to me how good it feels to belong. How easy it would be to slip back into the rhythm of the old ways. At this moment, Chief of Police Kate Burkholder is a distant memory, like someone I knew a long time ago. This afternoon, I am Kate Miller. An Amish widow trying a little too hard to fit in, make new friends, and start fresh.

The cowbell mounted on the door jingles. All eyes sweep toward the front of the store. The lights have been dimmed in the front section, but I see the silhouette of an Amish woman as she brushes snow from her shoulders and starts toward us.

"Hi, Rebecca," Lena calls out.

Naomi looks up and smiles. "*Nau is awwer bsll zert.*" Now it's about time.

"Sorry I'm late." The woman—Rebecca—approaches the table.

Laura starts to rise. "We've got *siess kaffi.*"

"Sit. I'll get it." She reaches us, looking harried and stressed out. I guess her to be around fifty years of age, with a pleasant face, rosy cheeks, and eyes as green as a springtime hayfield. She's generously built, tall, and solid looking. Her maroon dress falls nearly to her ankles. Red hair peeks out from beneath a black winter bonnet. A quilted sewing bag is slung over her shoulder. Her eyes take in the group, lingering on me.

"You're the widow from Ohio," she says. "Welcome."

I offer a smile and introduce myself.

Setting her bag on the floor, Rebecca pulls out a chair and sinks into it. I'm trying not to stare, but her body language seems odd. Her movements are tentative and jerky. She digs into her sewing bag, but doesn't remove anything. Ada has stopped sewing, her attention fastened on the newcomer. The other women have fallen silent.

Rising, Laura goes to the front of the store. Out of the corner of my eye I see her grab a mug and pour coffee. Back at the table, she sets it in front of Rebecca and reclaims her chair. "There you go."

Rebecca mutters a thank-you.

"I heard that Esther girl had her baby this morning." The words are spoken by Ada and in a tone reserved for unpleasant topics.

"Esther?" Naomi's hands still.

Ada clucks her mouth in disapproval. "The *maulgrischt* out at the farm." *Maulgrischt* means "pretend Christian" in Pennsylvania Dutch.

"Girl or boy?" Lena asks.

"Boy," Laura tells her.

Naomi sets down the section of fabric she's working on. "How old is she, anyway?"

"Sixteen," Laura says. "Or so she claims."

"I heard she's not married. Never been married." Lena looks from woman to woman. "Is that true?"

"It's wrong, is what it is," Ada grumbles.

Laura nods. "You mean her not having a husband?"

Ada gives her a canny look. "I mean all of it. Living out there with the bishop like she is, and him allowing it."

I listen with interest as the women discuss the mysterious young woman living with Schrock. But some of my attention remains focused on Rebecca. I can't pin it down, but there's something going on with her. Tension seems to radiate from her. Is it stress? Anxiety? Fear?

"Bishop Schrock wouldn't . . ." Lena struggles to finish the sentence. "You know. He wouldn't. He's the *bishop*."

Ada frowns. "He's a man, is what he is."

"He saved her life," Lena says emphatically. "He saved her soul from the devil."

"Saved something for himself, more likely." Rebecca spits the words as if they burn the inside of her mouth.

170

Lena gapes at her, offended. "He took her in when she had nowhere to go. He gave her proper clothing. Taught her the Amish ways and the word of God."

Rebecca doesn't back down. "Or maybe she's the one teaching him a thing or two."

"I don't believe it," Lena hisses.

Naomi reaches across the table and pats Lena's hand. "No one knows any such thing for sure."

Laura concentrates on her stitching. "And who are we to judge?"

"Rebecca, how's the—" Across from me, Ada gasps, dropping the section of quilt she'd been working on. "Oh no. *Oh no.*"

All eyes fly to Rebecca. For the first time I notice the bandage covering the outside portion of her left hand. Oddly, she'd been trying to hide it. Upon closer inspection I discern the shape of her hand and realize her pinky finger is missing.

No group of people knows better than the Amish that farming can be a dangerous profession. Accidents are commonplace, even for the women who often help their husbands in the barn and fields. I'm not surprised by the sight of the missing digit. What I *am* surprised by is the reaction of the women. Surely this isn't the first time they've seen the result of a mishap that claimed a finger. Yes, those kinds of accidents are traumatic, but why the shock? And why would Rebecca try to conceal it? That's when it strikes me that no one has asked her what happened.

They already know, a little voice whispers in my ear.

The hair on the back of my neck prickles. I look down at the potholder in my hands, slide the needle into the fabric, and tug it through. "What happened?" I ask matter-of-factly.

Naomi stares at the bandage, her mouth open and trembling. Lena leans back in her chair, blinking. Laura looks down at her sewing, but her hands seem to be frozen in place. The room falls silent.

171

Shifting uncomfortably, Rebecca lowers her hand so it's out of sight. "It was such a fool thing." Her eyes flick to the door, then back to me. In the instant our eyes meet, I see fear in their depths. "I caught it in the meat grinder when I was making sausage."

The rise of tension is palpable. Eyes are averted. The women turn their attention back to their sewing, stitching faster, but not all hands are steady.

"How awful," I hear myself say. "Did you go to the doctor?"

"Levi took me to the hospital." She forces a laugh, but it's a loud, unnatural sound. "I don't think I'm going to be much help with this quilt."

Late afternoon ushers in a lowering sky with fog and another round of snow. By the time five o'clock rolls around, only Laura and I remain and the shop is empty of customers. Earlier, she taught me how to use the old-fashioned cash register. In the last hour, I've rung up only two sales.

"Might as well close up." Laura joins me at the register, lays a ten-dollar bill on the counter, and slides it over to me. "That's all I can afford to pay you."

"I can't take your money." I slide it back to her. "I didn't earn it."

"You've manned the register most of the afternoon."

"I spent most of the afternoon drinking sweet coffee and eating your cookies."

"Kate—"

"No."

She softens. "I wish the customers would come back. I love this shop. The people who used to come in." She lowers her voice. "Just between us, I even like the tourists."

I chuckle. "I won't tell."

"I'm going to miss this place when I walk out for the last time." She drops a short stack of bills into a cash bag and zips it.

I wipe the counter, trying to decide how best to broach the subject of Rebecca. "I like your friends."

"They're like sisters to me," she replies. "Some days I don't know what I'd do without them."

"Terrible about Rebecca's finger," I say easily. "My *grossdaddi* lost two in the corn thrasher when I was a kid. Never slowed him down, though."

Laura slides cookies from the plate into a container, concentrating a little too hard on the task. "It happens."

We work in silence for several minutes. "Ada and Rebecca were pretty tough on Bishop Schrock," I say, trying to land on a subject that will keep her talking.

"They've got their reasons."

I glance at her, trying to decipher the meaning, but her face gives me nothing. "Did something happen between them and the bishop?"

"Not Ada," she tells me. "Rebecca."

In my mind's eye I see her bandaged hand; I recall the reactions of the other women, and I know there's something there. Something important. I hope Laura trusts me enough to tell me what it is.

"What happened?" I ask.

Without replying, she walks to the front door and throws the dead-bolt. Glancing through the plate glass window at the darkened street beyond, she lowers the blinds. Once they're closed tightly, she lifts a slat with her finger and peers out at the street. Finally, she leaves the window and ushers me to a table at the rear of the shop.

"What I'm about to tell you . . ." she says in a low voice. "Probably best if you don't repeat it."

I offer a concerned, sympathetic look. "Of course."

"I'm a firm believer that there are some things best left unsaid. Some things most people are better off not knowing. I don't want to burden you, but I think you're a strong woman and I'd like your perspective." She lets out a long breath. "Honestly, I've been wanting to get this off my chest for some time."

Reaching across the table, I squeeze her hand. "What is it, Laura?"

"Rebecca and I have been friends for a lot of years. We've had babies at the same time, husband troubles, and we've eaten more than our share of fattening cookies." Smiling wistfully, she looks down at the cookie in her hand. "Last summer, she came to me, crying. Kate, the story she told me . . . I didn't know what to make of it." Shaking her head, she lets the words trail. "I didn't want to *believe* it, but let me tell you: It sent a knife through my heart."

"What happened?"

A gust of wind rattles the windows. Laura startles, her eyes jerking to the door. She covers her reaction with a laugh, but for the first time she looks frightened.

"Rebecca told me that two of her granddaughters, just thirteen and fourteen years old, and her sixteen-year-old grandson were taken in and 'counseled' by Bishop Schrock. The children spent four nights at the bishop's farmhouse." She looks down at the tabletop. "She said the two girls weren't the same when they came out. They wouldn't talk about it; wouldn't tell anyone what went on. Rebecca claims the bishop turned them against her."

"Turned them against her how?" I ask.

"Evidently, the girls wanted nothing to do with her. Wouldn't speak to her or visit with her and Levi, her husband. Rebecca blames the bishop. Says he took them from her. She's bitter, and that's not the Amish way." She shudders. "Some of the things she says about the bishop . . . Terrible things."

"Like what?"

She shakes her head, letting me know she won't repeat them.

"What do you think happened to the girls?" I ask.

She shrugs. "I know how it must look to an outsider. Like the bishop overstepped. But in his defense, those girls had become prideful. I could see a . . . wildness in them. And Little Andy, with the drinking and smoking. There's no doubt those kids were heading down the wrong road." She shakes her head. "There's so much temptation in the world for the young people these days."

"That much is true," I say.

"Kate, I've seen the bishop with the youngsters. He's *good* with them." But it doesn't elude me that she says the words as if she's not only trying to convince me, but herself. "Some might say he's too firm. But I think he's seen the devil at work and he knows the power of evil. I think he saw the direction they were going and somehow talked all that temptation right out of their heads."

I stare at her, my mind reeling with the knowledge that Schrock is a predatory son of a bitch. After what he did to me, the thought of what might have happened to two innocent Amish girls twists my gut into knots.

"Rebecca wants to leave Roaring Springs," she tells me. "She wants to go back to her old church district in Ohio. The bishop asked her and Levi to stay, but I don't think they will. Honestly, I don't blame her. With her grandchildren and children gone."

"They left?"

"Rebecca's son and daughter-in-law, Big Andy and Irene, packed up and left in the middle of the night shortly after it happened. Took the girls with them. Left without a word. Didn't even tell Rebecca. Poor woman didn't even get a chance to say good-bye."

I put the names to memory so Suggs can run them through the

various law enforcement databases. In the back of my mind, I'm wondering how Rebecca's missing digit fits into all this.

"Where did they go?" I ask.

"Shipshewana, Indiana, I think."

"What about the grandson?" I ask.

Though the shop is locked down tight, the blinds pulled, her eyes flick toward the front of the store, as if she's expecting someone to come through the door. I find my own gaze following hers, the hairs at my nape standing on end.

"Little Andy never came back," she whispers.

"What? But . . . where did he go?"

"Evidently, the bishop sent the boy to another church district in Missouri to help an elderly couple whose family was killed in a buggy accident."

Suspicion creeps over me, as cold and hard as January ice spreading over the surface of a pond. "Without speaking to his parents? I mean, did the boy *want* to go? Did he volunteer?"

"No one knows. And no one's talking."

"Did Rebecca confront the bishop?" I ask.

"She's not one to take things sitting down." The smile that follows is humorless and tight. "She's a strong-willed woman and isn't afraid to speak her mind. I don't know everything that was said, but there's bad blood between them now."

Around us the shop is eerily silent. The only sound is the occasional hiss of tires on Main Street. The rattle of heat coming from the vent overhead.

"Laura," I whisper, "did the bishop do something bad to the children?"

The words hover, like the smell of something long dead that neither of us wants to acknowledge. She stares at me, anguish and fear etched into her features. "I can't imagine, Kate. I mean, he's the *bishop*."

"He's a mortal man," I tell her. "A human being with weaknesses just like the rest of us. Maybe more, from what I've heard."

"I think I've said enough."

She starts to rise, but I reach out and set my hand on her arm. "Laura, did the bishop have something to do with what happened to Rebecca's hand?"

Pulling her arm away, she rises so abruptly that the chair legs screech across the floor. Without looking at me, she shoves it against the table. The shop no longer feels homey or cozy or even comfortable. It feels like a dangerous place that's exposed and watched.

"I can't." Turning away, she walks to the counter.

I rise and follow. "Did someone hurt Rebecca?"

"I shouldn't have told you any of this. I shouldn't be burdening you with my worries."

"I'm glad you did." When she says nothing, I add, "That's what friends are for."

When she turns to face me, she's pulled herself together. Her eyes are cool when they meet mine. "I think it's time you went home, Kate."

"But what about—"

She cuts me off. "If you're smart, you'll forget we ever had this conversation."

CHAPTER 16

Everything I learned from Laura Hershberger and the other women at the quilt shop churns in my brain as I take the scooter bike back to the trailer. Bishops don't take teenage girls into their home to "counsel." They don't send teenaged boys away without the blessing of the children's parents. Families don't flee their homes in the middle of the night.

Unless they're frightened of something. Or someone.

What really happened to Rebecca and her family? All I can do at this point is continue to ask questions. Keep digging. In the interim, I'll pass along the information to Suggs so he can run the names. Hopefully, he'll be able to locate them and find out what happened.

It's nearly dark by the time I arrive at the trailer. While soup heats on the stove, I call Suggs and recap my conversation with Laura Hershberger. "The grandson never came back. Allegedly, he was sent to Missouri to help an elderly couple after their family was killed in a buggy accident."

"That's checkable. I'll get with the highway patrol down there and see if they can get me stats on fatality accidents involving buggies. And of course I'll run their names."

"While you're at it run the parents and the two girls, too, will you?

Last name Beiler." I spell it for him. "I don't know the girls' first names, but I'll work on it."

"All right." He sighs. "Damn, this whole thing stinks. Kids disappearing. Entire families running in the middle of the night." He goes silent and then asks, "You been able to get a look at any of the kids around there?"

"I saw a few at worship on Sunday. No visible signs of physical abuse. Most were bundled up, but no odd behavior or marked up faces."

"Doesn't mean it's not there."

Neither of us mentions the fact that some of the worst kind of abuse doesn't leave physical marks.

"All these rumors," the sheriff says with distaste. "God only knows what the hell is going on out there. Remember what I said, Kate. If things get too dicey, we can pull you out any time."

"I got it under control," I tell him.

As I end the call, I wonder how many cops have said those very words only to realize they weren't true.

I spend a couple of hours struggling with my sewing project. By the time ten P.M. rolls around I'm frustrated and cold and ready to call it a night. It's not until midnight that I fall into a fitful slumber. Dreams of Rachel Esh invade my sleep. We're sitting at the sewing table at The Calico Country Store. I'm stitching a crib quilt that's nearly finished, but no matter how hard I try, I can't manage the final stitches. Rachel and Laura stare at the mess I've made of it, and I can tell by their expressions that they've realized the work isn't mine. That I'm no seamstress and my secret has been found out.

Laura looks at me with knowing eyes. "She's not one of us," she tells Rachel. "*Sie hot en falsh Amisch.*" She's a phony Amish.

The girl replies, but I don't hear the words. Her lips are blue and

I can tell by the gray hue of her face that she's dead. Her front teeth are broken to the gum. Blood between her teeth. Ice on her lips. Her smile is macabre.

"We're going to have to tell the bishop," she whispers.

"I'm trying to save you," I tell the girl.

Rachel throws her head back and a terrible laugh spills from her bloody mouth. "No one can save me."

I wake in a cold sweat and sit bolt upright. Around me, the trailer is quiet and freezing cold. I'm breathing hard and in the thin light slanting in through the window I can see the vapor of my breath.

Tossing the blankets aside, I throw my legs over the side of the bed and rise to turn up the heat. I'm midway down the hall when I see a shadow shift in the living room. I go still, squint into the darkness. Another wave of cold air wraps around my ankles and slinks up my legs. The front door is open, I realize, and a different kind of cold stabs me in the back.

Something scrapes across the carpet ten feet away, and in that instant I know I'm not alone. Adrenaline burns like fire in my gut. My .22 and phone are beneath the mattress.

I spin, dash toward the bedroom. Heavy footfalls right behind me. I reach the bed, drop to my knees, jam my hands beneath the mattress. My fingertips brush steel. Heavy hands slam down on my shoulders and yank me backward. The fabric of my flannel shirt tears. I lose my balance, fall onto my back, my head bouncing off the floor. Stars fly in front of my eyes.

"Drag her out here," a male voice says.

"Get your hands off me!" I draw back and punch at his face. My fist grazes his temple. "Get off!"

A second hand grasps my right arm, yanks hard, dragging me down the hall and into the living room. I twist, get my knees under me, try to scramble to my feet. I see the silhouettes of two men. Snowsuits and ski masks. Then I'm yanked forward. My knees go out from under me and I'm being dragged on my stomach.

Again, I twist, get one knee beneath me. I try to jerk my arm from the man's grip, but his hand is a vise, crushing bone and bruising flesh. Using my free arm, I drive my fist into his crotch. His gasp ends in a roar. His grip loosens. I jerk my hand away. In an instant I'm on my feet.

"Get out!" I scream. "Get out!"

Spinning, I sprint toward the bedroom for my weapon.

He tackles me midway down the hall. I fall hard on my stomach. My chin scrapes the carpet. My attacker comes down on top of me. I hear his laugh. Hear his partner running toward us. I twist, bring up both feet and mule kick him in the gut. He reels backward, crashes to the floor on his ass.

"Grab that bitch," he pants.

I flip over, scrabble toward the bedroom. My brain chanting. *Get the gun. Get the gun.* I dive toward the bed. A hand comes down on the back of my head, shoves me down hard, slamming my face against the floor. My nose crunches. Pain zings up my sinuses. My arms collapse beneath me. I feel the warmth of blood coursing from my nose, taste copper at the back of my throat.

"Son of a bitch!" I try to turn over to kick him again, but both men are on me now, pressing me down.

"Got a mouth on her, don't she?" one of the men hisses.

"Guess someone needs to teach her some manners."

My head reels. I lie still, taking physical stock, trying to regain my senses. Roughly, they flip me onto my back. I look up at them, keenly aware that my gown has ridden up, exposing my bare legs and underwear. My heart sinks when one of the men removes a roll of duct tape from beneath his coat.

"Don't do it," I say.

The other man's hand snakes out and clamps around my throat, cutting off the blood flow to my head. "Gimme your hands or I'll fuckin' knock you out."

I extend my hands. In front of me.

The other man tapes my wrists together. Fear crashes over me when I realize I'm done. I can't get to my .22. Can't get to my cell. I'm at their mercy and there's not a damn thing I can do to help myself.

"Who are you?" I try to maintain a level of authority in my voice. I'm appalled when it quavers. "Why are you doing this?"

The men ignore me.

"Get up," one of them says, and without waiting for me to comply, they haul me to my feet.

I look from man to man. Both are wearing ski masks and snowsuits. "I haven't seen your faces," I tell them. "I don't know who you are."

The men exchange looks, but say nothing.

"Let me go and we'll forget this happened," I say quickly. "I won't tell anyone. You have my word."

"Yeah, right," one of them mutters.

"Tell me what you want," I say. "I'll do it."

"You and that big mouth of yours will find out soon enough," one of the men tells me.

"Let's go," says the other.

He takes my arm, drags me into the living room. I know they're going to take me outside. God only knows what will happen once they do. Last time I checked my phone, the temperature was eighteen degrees. I try another tactic. "I need to get dressed," I tell them.

"You're dressed just fine," the man behind me replies.

"I'll freeze," I say.

"We better put a coat on her," the other puts in.

The man grasping my arm stops, gives me a rough shake. "Where's it at?"

My barn coat is draped over the back of the bar stool facing the kitchen. I cock my head toward it. "You're going to have to untie me. So I can put it on."

The other man brushes past us and snatches up the coat. Facing me, he drapes it over my shoulders, yanks it tight, and fastens it with the big safety pin—without putting my arms through the sleeves. "There you go. Nice and warm."

The other man kicks my sneakers over to me, then kneels and shoves them onto my feet, cinching the laces tightly. Together, they force me through the living room, out the door and onto the deck. As they drag me down the steps, I realize these are the same men I saw last night with the two women. They're Amish; I can tell by their accents. And I'm pretty sure they're going to kill me.

When you're working undercover and your gig goes south, it usually happens so fast that any hope of initiating some brilliantly conceived contingency plan flies out the window—usually at about the same time you realize Plan B wasn't quite as brilliant as you'd initially thought anyway. My emergency plan had been pretty simple: Grab the cell and the .22 mini Mag and hope five shots are enough. The best I can hope for now is the opportunity to run.

Don't let down your guard.

Tomasetti's words ring hard in my ears as we trudge through the snow to two snowmobiles parked a hundred yards into the woods. Before mounting, one of the men—the one I kicked in the groin— reaches out, grasps my throat with his right hand, and squeezes hard enough to cut off the blood to my head. Even in the darkness, I see the threat in his eyes as he peers at me through the slits of the ski mask.

"You do anything stupid and I'll put a rope around your neck and drag you," he snarls. "You got that?"

I nod and he releases me.

"Where are you taking me?" I ask.

The other man removes a stocking cap from beneath his coat, pulls it over my head, yanking it down over my eyes and most of my face. Then I'm lifted and put on the back part of the seat. I feel him climb on in front of me.

"Shut up and hold on to my coat," he tells me.

The engine revs and the snow machine lurches forward.

For the first few minutes of the ride, I entertain fantasies of jumping off and running into the woods under cover of the night. I'd take refuge in the trees, somehow loosen the binds at my wrists, and make my way back to the trailer. Once there, I'd arm myself with my .22, contact Suggs—and kill anyone who came through the door before the sheriff's department arrived.

All the while my mind races through a myriad of unpleasant reasons why I'm here. Are they taking me to Schrock so he can finish what he started? Worse, does he somehow know who I am? Are they planning to kill me?

The most pressing issue is the cold. I'm not dressed for temperatures in the teens. I'm certainly not dressed for a middle-of-the-night snow-mobile ride, when wind chills are undoubtedly below zero. As we zip through the darkness, weaving between trees and over deadfall, the cold is like a blade, cutting into my flesh and sinking deeper with every mile. It penetrates my clothes—a nightgown, flannel shirt, and barn coat—and sucks the breath from my lungs. Within minutes my entire body is quaking uncontrollably. My teeth chatter. My face and hands have long since gone numb. As much as I don't want to get close to the driver, I lean against him, using his body to block the wind.

I try to work at the tape binding my wrists, but it takes all my strength just to hold on. I use the driver's back to scrape at the hat covering my face; eventually, I'm able to inch it up enough so that I can see. Even then, all I can see are snow and trees flying by, none of which look familiar.

We're on the snowmobile for less than ten minutes. By the time the engine slows, the cold has rendered me utterly useless. My hands and knees and feet are numb. I'm shivering so violently, I can barely stay astride the seat.

Tilting my head back for a better view, I try to get a look at my surroundings. We've arrived at a farm surrounded by hundreds of sixty-foot-tall trees. A large bank barn and paddock ahead. Two-story frame house to my left. We've stopped a few yards from a small outbuilding. Nothing looks familiar.

The gravity of the situation drops into my gut like stone. I have no idea where I am or why these men have brought me here. I have no mode of communication, no weapon, and not nearly enough protective clothing. In cop speak, I'm in serious shit.

I can't help but think of Rachel Esh. She froze to death not far away from here. Is this the way it went down? Did these men come for her in the middle of the night? Did she get away from them and run into the woods? Did they look for her? Or did they know she wouldn't make it and simply let her die in the snowstorm?

In the back of my mind, I consider telling the two men that I'm a cop. That if I die, they'll be caught—and more than likely face the death penalty. As much as I don't want to blow my cover and waste the time and effort invested in this operation thus far, it might be the only way to save my life.

But despite the risks and the fact that I'm not in control of the situation, some inner voice urges me to wait. I'll keep my options open. For now, I want to see where this goes. I want to know who's behind it.

The driver of the machine I'm on dismounts. I'm aware of his partner behind us, headlight illuminating us. The next thing I know, the driver turns, sets his hand against my chest and shoves me hard. I slide from the seat and plop into the snow on my backside.

Laughter erupts.

Using my hands, I scrape the hat up over my eyes so I can see and look around. One of the men is standing next to the outbuilding. Only then do I realize it's a chicken coop. Shit. *Shit.*

"Get up."

I bend my knees, try to get my legs under me, but wobble and fall sideways. He doesn't give me a second chance. Bending to me, he wraps both hands around my biceps and hauls me to my feet.

"Cut the tape," he says to the other man.

A different kind of fear goes through me at the sight of the four-inch folding knife. I raise my bound wrists, watching as he severs the tape.

"Get in the coop."

I turn to face him. "I n-need t-to get warm," I sputter through chattering teeth. "Gloves."

"How 'bout if I knit you a pair? Now get in there."

His partner fumbles with a padlock on a hasp and with some effort shoves open the door. The other man clamps his hand around the back of my neck and forces me toward the door. Beyond, the interior is dark and smells of frozen chicken shit and dirt.

"I don't want to go in there." I say the words in Pennsylvania Dutch.

"This is what we do to nosy Amish women."

Raising his foot, he places it on my butt and shoves me through the door. I stumble into the darkened interior, smack my forehead against something, and fall to my hands and knees. Something scampers across the dirt floor to my right. *Rat*, I think, but I'm too cold to care. The door slams shut.

I struggle to my feet, strike my head against a low beam, and duck back down. A roost. Rushing to the door, I slam both fists against it. "Let me out!" I scream. "Let me out!"

A round of laughter ensues, followed by conversation I can't quite discern. The snowmobile engines rev.

"Don't leave!" I slam my fist against the door. "Bastards!"

The men drive away. I stand at the door. Through a gap between the wood planks, I watch the taillights fade into the darkness. The sound of the engines fade. Dismay spreads through me. And then the men are gone.

"Pricks."

I stand there, shaking with cold and rage and disbelief. I'm somehow incredulous the situation has deteriorated to this. If I don't play my cards right, it'll soon become a life-or-death scenario.

Turning, I face the interior of the coop. Weak gray light creeps in through the gaps between the weathered wood siding. There's a small door that's about two feet square and at ground level on the far end for the chickens, but it's closed. There are no chickens in sight. I can tell by the smell they haven't been gone long. The place is dirty and, though I'm protected from the wind, cold as hell.

I make my way to the chicken door and kick it. It's solidly closed; there's probably a cross board nailed across it on the outside. There are no windows. I go back to the large door, shove at it with both hands, but it's secure. Using my shoulder, I get a running start and bang against it. The door shudders beneath the force of my weight. I ram it again and again; I bring my foot up and kick it as hard as I can, but it refuses to give way. The sons of bitches put the padlock back on; I can hear it rattling on the outside.

I'm breathing hard from the physical effort. My shoulder hurts from the impact. My hands ache with cold. I can't feel my fingers at all. I'm wearing sneakers with the socks I went to bed in, but they're not enough to keep my feet warm, or even ward off frostbite. But the physical activity has alleviated the worst of the shaking. For now.

Half a dozen outcomes float uneasily through my brain. As far as I know, the men have left me here to freeze to death. I wonder if that's the way it went down for Rachel Esh. Did they leave her here to die and then dump her body in the woods so the police would believe she'd perished in the storm? But why? Did she spurn Schrock's advances? Did she see something she shouldn't have?

This is what we do to nosy Amish women.

Have I been asking too many questions? Is that what this is about? Or does this have something to do with the two women I saw with the men on snowmobiles? Were those women somehow harmed? Are the men afraid I'll identify them? The problem with that scenario is I didn't see their faces; I couldn't identify them. If not that, then what?

The bottom line is I've been careless. I spurned Schrock's advances. I've asked too many questions. I fooled myself into believing I was being careful. In reality, I'd committed the mortal sin of undercover work: I underestimated the perspicacity of my enemy.

Pacing the confines of the coop, swinging my arms to keep the blood circulating, I mentally catalog the people I talked to. Mary and Abe Gingerich. Their daughter, Anna. Laura Hershberger. The women at the quilt shop. Marie Weaver. The one event that supersedes the rest is my visit with Schrock. Of all the possible culprits, he's the one who wields the power and has the authority to direct someone to do this, all without getting his hands dirty.

If I freeze to death tonight, no one will ever know what happened. As with Rachel Esh's death, the coroner will be able to determine the cause of death—which would probably be hypothermia—but not the *manner* of death, which would be homicide. I made it easy for them.

Instead of letting the thought shake me, I use it to spur my temper. Starting in the nearest corner, I feel my way around the perimeter of the coop, testing each piece of siding as I go. The structure is about twenty by twelve feet. There are two roosts at about head level. The floor is hard-packed dirt. One wall is a maze of nesting boxes where the hens lay eggs. The large door is solidly secure, so I go back to the chicken door. I lower myself to the ground a couple of feet away from it, bring my feet up and plant a double barrel kick in the center. Once. Twice. Three times.

"Come on," I pant.

The fourth blow cracks wood. Encouraged, I kick it again as hard as I can. One of the planks splits. Half of it pulls away from the frame. Another kick and my foot blasts through the hole. A wood sliver slices my calf as I pull it back through. I don't care. A final kick and the plank flies off and lands in the snow outside. Then I'm on my knees, shoving at the loosened wood with my hands.

It's not a quiet process. If there's anyone nearby, there's no doubt they've heard my assault on the chicken door. Someone could be waiting for me on the other side. I pick up a split piece of siding to keep with me in case I need to defend myself.

When the opening is large enough to accommodate me, I go to my hands and knees and slither through. I find myself in an aviary constructed of chicken wire, steel T-posts and a few four-by-four wood braces. It's just high enough for me to stand upright. I wish for wire cutters as I walk the perimeter. Relief leaps through me when I realize the wire is attached to the structure with only a few fencing staples.

I try yanking it with my hands but the effort is unsuccessful, so I throw my shoulder against it. The chicken wire stretches and bends and then snaps away from the building. I work my way down to the bottom, peel back the wire and slide through.

Free of the coop, I dart around to the other side of the building. Though the moon is obscured by clouds and the shadows of the trees, there's enough light for me to make out the track marks of the snowmobiles. They went in the opposite direction from where we came in. Taking off at a run, I retrace the tracks back toward the trailer.

CHAPTER 17

By the time I arrive back at the trailer, I'm in bad shape. I'm no longer shivering. The cold burns my lungs. My heart is pounding so hard my chest hurts. I can't hear anything over the roar of blood in my ears. At some point, I dropped the piece of wood. Someone could sneak up on me and I wouldn't hear them approach. I sure as hell wouldn't be able to do anything about it.

I stagger like a drunk as I round the end of the trailer, and for a crazy instant, I can't remember where the door is. Then I see the stairs and lurch toward the deck. At the foot of the steps, I stumble and go to my knees. All I can think about is getting inside. I'm not sure I can stand, so I climb the steps on my hands and knees. Gripping the doorknob, I pull myself to my feet and open the door.

I totter to the bedroom, fall to my knees and pull my .22 from beneath the mattress. I know my phone is there, too, but in my confused state I can't find it. Gripping the .22 with both hands, I leave the bedroom, keeping my eyes on the windows as I walk back to the living room. I stand there a moment, my head swimming, trying to decide what to do next. I'm aware that I'm experiencing the initial stage of hypothermia, but the knowledge doesn't help.

I can't remember if I locked the door, so I go to it, twist the lock. I head to the kitchen, drag a chair to the door and wedge it beneath the knob. Dizziness presses down on me when I straighten and I have to lean against the bar. The shivers are starting to return. I make my way back to the kitchen, fill the kettle with water and light all four burners. I don't set down my revolver, instead warming one hand at a time over the flame, knowing it's going to be painful when the feeling returns.

I find a mug and a teabag and pour hot water. I sip the tea without tasting, trying to get the hydration and warmth into my body. My hand is shaking so violently some of it sloshes over the side of the cup. I go to the table and sit. I'm nauseous and hungry at once. My hands and feet ache. The skin on my face and my ears burn and for the first time I worry about frostbite. As bad as it is, though, my mind is beginning to clear. By the time I pour a second cup of tea, I feel steady enough to call Suggs.

"Yeah?" he answers in a sleep-rough voice.

I have no idea what time it is. "It's Burkholder."

"Chief, what the—Is everything okay?"

"No."

I hear rustling on the other end. "What's going on?" he says, urgency and concern sharp in his voice.

"A couple of guys on snowmobiles broke into the trailer. Caught me sleeping. I couldn't get to my phone or weapon and they hauled me away, locked me in a fucking chicken coop."

"*What?* Kate, what the hell? Who?"

"I'm pretty sure it was the same men I saw with those women night before last."

"You get names? Description?"

"No. Dan, they wore ski masks. All I know is that they're young. Early twenties maybe. And Amish."

192

"Shit. Are you okay?"

"I barely made it back to the trailer. Those sons of bitches left me in that coop to freeze to death."

"How long ago?"

I look at the clock on the stove. "Two hours."

"Look, Kate, you're slurring words. Unless you've been hitting the booze, you're probably hypothermic. I'm going to get an ambulance—"

"No," I cut in. "I'm fine now. I just need to get warm."

"You sure you don't need to get yourself checked out? I can be there in ten minutes and take you to the ER myself. No one will be the wiser."

"Sheriff, I'm okay. I made hot tea. I'm on my second cup. Going to bundle up in a minute, get my core temp back up. I thought you should know what happened."

"Hell yes I should know!" He snaps the words and I sense him reeling in his temper, trying to be patient with me. "I'm glad you're okay. How did they gain entry?"

"I don't know. The door was locked."

A beat of silence as he mulls that bit of information. "Is it possible they have a key?"

"If the landlady rents to the Amish and doesn't change the locks between tenants . . . it's possible."

"I use a locksmith here in Roaring Springs. I can get him out there first light."

"I know this sounds paranoid, but if someone's watching the trailer . . . might be better if I change it myself."

"What about tonight? What if they come back?"

"It'll be the last time they walk into someone's home uninvited."

He makes a sound of discomfort. "You sure you're okay?"

"I'm warming up. Hands and feet hurt."

"I meant what I said before, Kate. If you want to end this, just say the word. We'll get you out pronto. No problem. Do you understand?"

The prospect of going home tantalizes me. My mind flashes to my big farmhouse kitchen. The ever-present smells of coffee and potpourri. Tomasetti singing off-key in the shower. The police station with my cramped little office and beat-up desk. At this moment, they're the most comforting images in the world.

The cop inside me rejects any notion of comfort. I need to finish this assignment, especially now that someone has made it personal. Maybe it's my ego talking; a reflection of my anger at being bested and hurt, but there's no way I can walk away. I need to know who tried to kill me tonight and why. I have a feeling once I do, I'll know what happened to Rachel Esh.

"I'm going to finish this," I tell him.

"I appreciate that, Kate. I really do. But the last thing anyone wants is for you to put yourself at risk. You've gone above and beyond already." He pauses. "I don't have to tell you that what happened to you tonight could have turned out a hell of a lot worse."

"I know exactly what could've happened. I won't let my guard down again."

"All right." He shifts gears. "Any idea why these two men would risk getting into trouble with the law to lock you in a chicken coop? What could they hope to gain?"

"Since they believe I'm Amish, they're betting I won't go to the police. Most Amish—particularly the Old Order and Swartzentruber—would rather handle things on their own than involve outsiders."

"Okay, I'll buy that. I've seen it. But why do it at all?"

"To send me a message. Intimidate me." I repeat what one of the men told me. *This is what we do to nosy Amish women.* "It's interesting that he used the word 'we.'"

"That confirms it's a concerted effort. That there are others involved."

"I've been asking a lot of questions. Too many, probably."

"Someone noticed."

I consider that a moment. "Dan, had I died in that coop—and I was, indeed, an Amish widow from another state—my death probably would have gone unnoticed and unreported."

"That'll put a chill in your damn spine." He heaves another sigh. "I guess it's safe to say you've officially pissed off Schrock."

"I turned down his advances. Maybe that ruffled his ego."

"Do you think he made you as a cop?"

"No. He thinks I don't know my place."

"Or whoever you've been talking to went to Schrock or mentioned it to someone who did. Any ideas? The woman at the quilt shop?"

"I can't see her going to Schrock." I take a long swig of tea. "Dan, I've talked to a lot of people since I arrived. It could have been any of them." I sigh. "Guess I wasn't being as subtle as I thought."

"That son of a bitch is using some pretty heavy-handed intimidation tactics. If he's responsible for half the shit that's going on, he's dangerous as hell."

"There's no doubt in my mind."

"It goes against my better judgment to leave you in there."

"Dan, I'm just now getting to the meat of this. Just a few more days. I'll be careful."

Suggs groans. "Something like this happens again and you're out. You got that?"

"I got it." I choose my next words carefully. "Would you do me a favor and not mention this to Tomasetti?"

"Oh boy," he mutters. "Are you two . . ."

"Um . . . well . . ."

"I have no reason to mention any of this to Tomasetti. But I have to keep Betancourt up to speed."

"I'd appreciate it if the two you kept it between you."

"I'll do my best," he says.

"Thanks, Dan."

"If I were you, I'd start sleeping with that thirty-eight under my pillow," the sheriff tells me.

"I plan to," I reply. "Talk to you tomorrow."

"Night, Chief."

Fear and sleep make incompatible bedfellows. Throw post-hypothermic exhaustion into the mix and you have a long and excruciating night. To make matters worse, I bedded down on the sofa. I couldn't bear the thought of someone breaking in and not hearing them from the back bedroom. When I finally dozed off at five A.M., I had my .38 in my hand, the hammer back and my cell in the other.

Lucky for everyone involved, the men never showed.

I woke a couple hours later, clearheaded and fully recovered from my ordeal in the chicken coop. At some point during the night, it occurred to me that if the men had wanted to kill me, they could have done so. I don't believe that was their intent, though if I had succumbed to the cold they wouldn't have been too broken up about it.

Interestingly, I didn't see a firearm on either man. Often when a criminal is armed and wants control of his victim, he will brandish a weapon. I'm not convinced they were armed, which is telling.

I'm working on my second cup of coffee when I notice the chafing and bruising on my wrists from the tape. A small blister is beginning to rise on the pad of my left ring finger, probably from frostbite. I'll need to keep an eye on it in the coming days and watch for any sign of tissue loss or infection. I dress for the day, adding an extra layer for warmth, and at seven-thirty I leave the trailer and take the scooter bike to the farm store for a new lock.

The Roaring Springs Feed Store is about twenty minutes away. I arrive just as the cashiers are opening their registers. Grabbing a shopping cart, I head for hardware. I grab two commercial-duty bolt locks and the tools I'll need to install them. On impulse, I add a couple of heavy-duty, zinc-plated barrel bolt locks. Then I'm off to sporting goods. There, I'm quickly reminded that stun guns are illegal in the state of New York. It takes me less than a minute to locate the pepper spray. I choose a compact canister filled with the highest percentage of oleoresin capsicum. The label boasts twenty-five bursts with minimal blowback and it's made in the U.S.A. If my attackers return, I'll be ready.

Back at the trailer, I set to work. Installing a bolt lock isn't rocket science and I'm relatively handy—or so I'd imagined. The job isn't as easy as I anticipated. The lack of power tools doesn't help and a chore that would have taken a locksmith an hour ends up taking me close to three. The locks aren't quite straight and the jamb is nicked. But the trailer is secure.

I fix hot soup from a can for lunch. As I eat, I pull out my phone, call up Google and retrieve an address for Abe and Mary Gingerich. It's not far. I'll stop by under the guise of thanking them for driving me to worship on Sunday and see if I can get Mary to open up about the bruise on her face.

The afternoon has turned colder with a brisk wind whipping down from the north. Dark clouds roil above the tree line to my left, prompting me to push the scooter bike faster as I head west. It takes me just ten minutes reach their small farm.

It's a single-story stone house with asphalt shingles and a big chimney that's puffing smoke. A swaybacked outbuilding that had once been a detached garage is being used to house goats. A greenhouse in the side yard is missing half its panes and falling to ruin. Beyond, I see the raised landscape timbers of a garden. No shutters on the house. No clay pots left over from summer. No adornment of any kind. The place is plain.

I stop the bike in the gravel driveway, dismount and lean it against a bare-branched maple a few feet away. The wind cuts through my coat, its icy hands rushing up my skirt and down my collar. By the time I reach the front door, I'm shivering despite the physical exertion of the ride.

The door opens and Mary Gingerich appears. "Kate?" Craning her neck, she looks past me as if to see if I'm alone. She doesn't look pleased to see me. She has a full-fledged black eye now and I wonder: *What kind of person assaults a middle-age Amish woman?*

The same kind that leaves fifteen-year-old girl out in the cold to die . . .

"I thought I'd swing by to thank you and Abe for driving me to worship on Sunday," I say.

"No need to thank us."

"May I come in?" I add a shiver for effect.

She offers a pained expression. She doesn't want to invite me inside, but her good manners prevent her from refusing. "Come on."

The living room smells of woodsmoke and some kind of frying meat. It's a small space with a worn oak floor covered with a braided rug. The furniture is minimal: plain brown sofa covered with a half dozen homemade throw pillows. Rocking chair draped with a blue-and-white afghan. An overstuffed chair and ottoman face a potbellied stove in the corner. The curtains are black.

"I hope I'm not interrupting your afternoon," I tell her.

"I was just frying up some *schpeck* for sandwiches." Bacon. "Would you like to stay?"

"I can't, but thank you."

An awkward silence falls. The room is so quiet I can hear the bacon sizzling in the kitchen. Mary looks everywhere except at me.

"Mary, I need to talk to you about something that happened."

Her gaze jerks to mine. In the depths of her eyes I see apprehension, maybe even fear.

"Two men on snowmobiles came to my trailer last night," I tell her. "They broke in while I was sleeping, tied me up and took me to a farm where I was locked in a chicken coop."

She makes all the appropriate noises, even manages to widen her eyes. But it's a practiced response. She's not surprised, and she's not a very good liar. "But . . . why would they do such a thing?"

"To harm me. Intimidate me." I shrug. "I don't know."

Her gaze slinks away from mine. I wait, but she says nothing. It doesn't escape me that she fails to ask if the men were Amish or what they looked like.

I gesture to her black eye. "I thought you might be able to shed some light."

"I don't see how—"

"The men were Amish. Early twenties." I pause, push harder. "I'm betting they're the same men who gave you that shiner and put that mark on your neck."

Pressing her hand to her chest, she takes a step back. "Oh, Kate . . ."

It's the first honest reaction I've seen. It's obvious she's hiding something—maybe even protecting someone. But who? And why?

"Who put those marks on your face?" I ask.

A laugh squeezes from her throat. "I've no idea who you're talking about."

"I think those men came to you, too. I think they hurt you. And I think you're afraid to talk about it because you're afraid they'll come back and do it again."

"*Sell is nix as baeffzes.*" That's nothing but trifling talk. But her gaze drops to the floor as if she can't lie and look me in the eye at the same time.

"Who are they, Mary?" Tilting my head slightly, I make eye contact with her, refuse to release her gaze. "Why are they hurting people?"

Her laugh is the high-pitched trill of a nervous bird. "I don't know what you're talking about."

"Nothing you say will leave this room," I tell her. "You have my word."

A quiver moves through her, so minute I almost miss it. But I'm good at reading people, their thoughts, their emotions. She wants to open up. She wants to release the ugly truth trapped inside her. But this woman isn't merely frightened. She's terrified.

"I nearly froze to death last night," I tell her. "Those men are dangerous. They need to be stopped."

"There's nothing you can do," she whispers. "No one can stop them. Just . . . live quietly and they'll leave you alone."

"You live quietly and look what they did to you."

"You know nothing," she hisses.

I try a different tactic. "Maybe I should talk to the bishop."

"Do not speak of this to the bishop," she says quickly.

"Why? He won't stand for that kind of behavior."

She starts to turn away, but I reach out and gently grasp her arm. "Mary, talk to me. Please."

"Leave this house. *Now.*"

We both startle at the sound of Abe's voice. I turn to find him standing in the kitchen doorway. He stares at me without expression, his eyes as lifeless as a mannequin's.

"You think you know so much," he says quietly. "You know nothing of the way things work here. *Nothing.*"

"Then help me understand," I say back. "Talk to me."

"Leave us alone." He motions toward the door. "Go."

Uneasiness pricks the back of my neck when I notice the large bandage encompassing his right hand. The dime-size spot of blood.

"What happened to your hand?" I ask.

Mary turns away. A sob escapes her. Abe leaves his place at the doorway and moves closer.

No one answers for the span of a full minute. I'm aware of the fire crackling. Sleet striking the window on the west side of the house. The steady thrum of my heart. That little voice in the back of my head warning me to tread carefully.

"An accident," the Amish man tells me. "In the workshop."

I look from Abe to Mary and back to Abe. "You're lying."

Anger flashes in his eyes, but it's laced with something else I can't quite read. Fear? Panic? His face is such a jumble of emotions I can't discern which.

"You did this. *You!*" He looks down at his hand. "All the questions and sticking your nose in places it doesn't belong. Look at what you've stirred up. Look what you've done to us."

"Is this the way you want to live your lives? In fear?" I motion toward Mary. "Men coming into your home and hurting you?"

"No!"

"The people who did this need to be stopped."

"By you?" His smile verges on nasty. "What can you do?"

"Not me," I tell him. "The police."

"The English police." He spits the words with disdain. "Stupid woman." Abe stalks to the door, opens it using his uninjured hand. "Leave us. Now. Stay away from my wife. Stay away from me. And if you know what's good for you, you'll keep your mouth shut."

Never taking my eyes from his, I cross to the door. Instead of going through it, I loosen his grip, close it, and turn to face him. "That isn't the Amish way."

Abe narrows his eyes, cocks his head. "You don't act like an Amish woman."

"I'm as Amish as you are," I shoot back. "But I don't tolerate violence. Evidently, you do."

He looks down at the floor.

I wait.

"They came here," Mary says after a moment, "two nights ago."

"Who?"

The couple exchanges a look. Mary turns away and crosses to the door, twists the knob lock. There's no bolt lock.

Abe sighs tiredly and looks away. "Can't say."

"Were they on snowmobiles?" I ask.

When he doesn't answer, Mary turns to face me. "*Ja.*"

"Why did they come here?"

"To tell us to stay away from you," she tells me. "You're not one of us. You're an outsider and not to be trusted."

For an instant, I wonder if my cover has been compromised. Uneasiness quivers in my gut. Then I realize she's referring to the Amish edict of separation. "Because I'm from Ohio?" I ask. "Because I'm not a member of the church district? Or is it something else?"

"You don't know the rules here," Abe says. "You don't know how things are done."

"Exactly how *are* things done?" I send a pointed look toward his hand. The huge bandage. The blood soaking through. "What did they do to you?"

The Amish man looks away. I'm about to try again when Mary speaks. When she does, her voice is so low I have to lean close to hear. "They cut off his finger."

A shudder rises in my chest, but I tamp it down. "Who?"

"We think it was Jacob Yoder and Jonas Smucker," she replies. "They were wearing ski masks, but I knew. We've known them since they were boys."

Abe jerks his head. "Yoder held me down. Smucker cut it off."

"With bolt cutters," Mary adds. "There was nothing we could do."

A chill hovers at the base of my spine. "Why?"

Mary turns from the door and gives me a hard look. "We're to stay away from you."

"They didn't do this on their own," I say. "Someone told them to do it."

I give them time to respond, but neither speaks.

"Was it Eli Schrock?" I ask.

The couple stares at me as if I've said something blasphemous. "We can't say," Abe tells me.

"Can't or won't?" I drill Mary with a hard look.

Again, no response. Neither Abe nor Mary makes eye contact with me.

"An Amish bishop would never hurt anyone," I tell them. "Never."

Neither of them has anything to say about that.

I lower my voice. "Do you know what happened to Rachel Esh?"

Gasping, Mary puts her hand over her mouth, covers a sound of distress, of pain. I can't help but notice her fingers are trembling.

Her husband reaches for her, moving between us as if to shield her from my words, from me. "Do not speak ill of the bishop." He's so upset his voice quavers. "Leave us," he orders. "I think it would be best if you didn't come back."

"Cut off his fucking *finger*? Are you *shitting* me?"

Suggs's voice is so loud I have to hold my cell away from my ear. "Just like the woman at the shop."

"Jesus. That's . . . brutal." He takes a moment as if to let the image I described to him earlier settle in his mind. "It's enough for me to pick up Yoder and Smucker."

"They wore ski masks, Dan. A positive ID is iffy. And if the Gingeriches refuse to testify or if they make up some story about a workshop accident, you'll get nothing and Schrock gets off scot-free."

Suggs utters a curse. "I know where this is going and I don't fucking like it."

"If we want Schrock, we're going to have to wait this out. Leave me in place until I can get something better."

"So let me get this straight, Chief. If our friendly neighborhood bishop decides a member of the church district has broken the rules or crossed him, he sics his goons Yoder and Smucker on them and cuts off their goddamn fingers?"

"Unfortunately, I think that's the gist of it."

"And now you're on his radar."

I'm not sure how to respond to that, so I move on. "No one suspects me of anything. I'm an outsider. I've asked a few too many questions."

"You pissed off Schrock when you turned him down."

I scramble for a rebuff, but there's nothing there. He's right. "The situation here is a lot worse than we imagined. We're talking physical assault on a regular basis. Probably sexual assault. Maybe even murder."

He makes a sound of disgust. "Kate, I want you out."

"If we walk away now, we end up with nothing," I snap.

"Shit." Suggs sighs heavily. "Proof of *something* would be nice."

"I can get it. I just need more time."

"Kate, I know you can handle yourself. You proven it and then some. But I don't like the idea of you being out there all alone with these crazy shits running around chopping off people's fingers and doing God only knows what else."

"I'm being careful," I tell him. "Especially after what's happened. I know what I'm up against. I've secured the trailer. I'm armed."

"How much longer?"

"A couple more days. Give me some time to poke around the rat hole. Sooner or later, something's going to run out."

"Hopefully, it won't be your luck."

"This isn't about me. It's about the death of a fifteen-year-old girl and a religious sect run amok. If we don't stop them, more people will be hurt. Maybe even killed."

He's thoughtful for a moment and then asks, "Knowing what you do now, what do you think happened to the Esh girl?"

"She saw or heard something or maybe she simply knew too much. Or maybe it's worse than that. Maybe Schrock was supplying her with drugs. Maybe he was having sex with her. She got pregnant. She wanted out. He was afraid she'd go to the police so he murdered her."

"Powerful motive," he says.

I run with it. "Maybe the bishop told Smucker and Yoder to stop her. They accost her in the middle of the night, the same way they did me. Drag her out of bed. Take her into the woods. Maybe they didn't intentionally kill her, but something happened and the situation spiraled out of control. Maybe she got away, ran into the woods and ended up dying of hypothermia."

"Viable," he admits.

I think about the female passengers on the snowmobiles. "What if there's something else going on? Something . . . I don't know, bigger? What if Rachel figured it out and became a threat?"

"Something like what?"

"I don't know. But there's *something* going on. We have Amish men on snowmobiles. Foreign women being held against their will. Assault. Allegations of sexual abuse. Drugs. That's not to mention the level of intimidation."

"That place is beginning to sound more like a damn cult than an Amish settlement," he grumbles.

It was an offhand statement. But something pings in my head at the usage of a word that hadn't yet occurred to me. "You're right," I say slowly.

"Oh, shit," he mutters.

"It fits." I'm still trying to settle the word in my head. *Cult.* "If he's controlling people through intimidation . . ." I think about Abe and Mary Gingerich. Laura Hershberger at The Calico Country Store. The ugly allegations against Schrock. "One of the things that struck me right away is the level of devotion to Schrock. Some of these people speak of him as if he's God. And yet those same people are careful about what they say."

"They're afraid of him."

I remind him of the Amish man in the kitchen at The Dutch Kitchen and for the first time Mary's level of paranoia makes sense. "He was *listening*. Probably reporting back to Schrock. That's why they cut off Abe's finger."

"Kate, I'm no expert, but there's a specific criteria used to identify cults. Let me get with Betancourt. See if we can get an expert involved." He sighs unhappily. "So what's next?"

206

"I want to talk to Rachel's best friend. Marie Weaver. So far she's been pretty hostile. I want to try again. I think there's something there. Mary Gingerich's daughter told me Marie had been locked in the chicken coop."

"Weaver works at Huston's Restaurant afternoons, so you might catch her there." He rattles off an address.

I write it down. "I'm going to approach Rebecca Beiler, too. She's not happy with Schrock, so maybe she'll open up or tell me what happened with her finger."

"She and her husband live on a dairy farm south of Roaring Springs." Computer keys click and then he confirms the address I already have.

"I've yet to meet the parents of Rachel Esh, but I'll keep trying."

"They're not real forthcoming."

"Interestingly, there's a young woman living with Schrock. She just had a baby, so I don't know how available she is. If I can get her alone, I'll talk to her, too."

"I guess the bishop isn't too concerned about appearances."

"He should be," I tell him. "People are talking."

"What else?"

I pause, wanting to get the words right because I'm afraid they may be met with resistance. "I want to talk to Schrock again."

"Kate . . . maybe you ought to steer clear for a while."

"When you're Amish and there's a problem, you go to the bishop. I've got good reason. I was accosted by two Amish men in the middle of the night. If I don't take that to him, he'll have reason to be suspicious."

"Chief . . ." A heavy sigh hisses over the line. "Look, I gotta be honest here. I don't like the idea."

"All I have to do is tell him what happened. Quick in and out."

When he says nothing, I add, "You know what they say about keeping your enemies close."

He doesn't laugh. "You need to coordinate the visit with me. That means call me before you go in. And you call me the minute you leave. You got that?"

"I got it."

"In the interim, I'll run Yoder and Smucker through some of the databases and see if anything pops."

"Thanks, Dan. I'll keep pushing forward on my end."

"Don't push too hard, Chief. Sounds to me like these sons of bitches are starting to push back."

CHAPTER 18

That place is beginning to sound more like a damn cult than an Amish settlement . . .

Suggs's words ring hard in my ears as I disconnect. For a moment, I stand there trying to get my head around the notion—and the ramifications. My experience with cults is nil. In fact, I've not worked a single case that involved cult activity. My only knowledge stems from a workshop I attended during a statewide chiefs-of-police conference in Columbus a few years ago. One of the things that stuck with me in the course of that conference are the red flags law enforcement uses to identify a cult and differentiate it from a legitimate religious sect. At the moment, I can only recall two: Untoward secrecy. And coercion.

It's a chilling and disturbing possibility that changes everything. It's the reason I haven't been able to get my head around the case in terms of motive, means and operandi. A cult is the one scenario that makes all of the jagged pieces of the puzzle fall together.

Huston's Restaurant is located on the east end of town, not far from the highway. A steely sky spits snow pellets as I park the scooter bike in a space that's out of sight from the street. The restaurant is housed in an old Victorian home in a neighborhood that was once residential but rezoned for commercial businesses. The interior is warm and dark and smells of fried fish and onions. Lots of wood. Rustic fixtures. Windows covered with wooden shutters that let in little in the way of light. I walk directly to the counter where a young man of about twenty stands at the cash register looking bored. He doesn't greet me.

"I'd like a cheeseburger to go," I tell him.

He looks me up and down, taking in my dress, and smirks. "Would you like a buggy with that?" He barks out a laugh. More laughter comes from the kitchen behind him. "I mean, a drink?"

Rolling my eyes, I dig a few bills from my pocket and set them on the counter. "Just the burger."

He makes change and then turns his back to me. I watch as he passes my order form through the window to the kitchen in the rear.

"Is Marie around?" I ask.

"Marie?" He looks at me a bit more closely, as if wondering why I'd want to speak with her. "I think she's on break. Out back."

Nodding, I head for the door.

I find her behind the restaurant, using the wood fencing surrounding the Dumpster to protect her from the wind. She's bundled in a black puffy coat, a fuzzy scarf pulled over her *kapp*, smoking a cigarette.

"Marie?" I call out as I approach.

She turns. In the light from the street lamp, I see eyes laced with attitude just south of bad. Freckled nose and full lips the color of watermelon. At the moment those lips are twisted into a sour expression that's part annoyance, part looking-for-a-fight and I might just do.

"I'm Kate. We met at worship." I stop a few feet from her, aware that she's annoyed by my presence.

"I remember. What do you want?"

I smile, more amused than irritated by her rudeness. "I was getting some dinner and saw you out here smoking. I thought I'd stop by and see how you're doing."

"As you can see . ." She makes a sweeping gesture from herself to the restaurant. "I'm meeting all the right people and making all the right connections."

"Hey, it's a job. More than what some people have." Reaching into my coat, I pull out a five dollar bill and offer it to her. "Can I bum a smoke?"

She offers a slow, appreciative grin. "For five bucks?" Snapping up the bill, she digs a pack of Marlboro Reds from her coat pocket, shakes out two and passes them to me along with a lighter. "Knock your socks off."

"Thanks." I drop one in my pocket, light the other, drawing in the smoke deeply. "Here's to breaking the rules."

She looks at me with a little less disdain as I return the lighter to her and I realize my I'm-a-rule-breaker-too tactic is working. "No one comes out here?" I ask.

"Too cold."

"Smoking was against the rules back at my church district in Ohio. The men and boys could get away with it, but not the women."

"That's the Amish for you," she mutters. "Equality for all."

"I'm assuming it's against the rules here, too."

"What's *not* against the rules here?" She rolls her eyes.

"I hear the bishop doles out some pretty serious punishment."

She looks at the ground, blows out smoke. "I wouldn't know."

We smoke in silence for a moment, then I ask. "I heard you got into trouble."

"Don't believe everything you hear. In case you haven't noticed, the Amish are a bunch of gossips."

"Anna Gingerich told me you got locked in a chicken coop."

"Anna's a retard." She sucks hard on the cigarette. "Makes up stories."

"My bishop in Ohio—" I pause to correct myself, making up the story as I go—scrambling to keep her talking, get her to trust me, like me, open up. "My *former* bishop in Ohio locked a man in a wood shed for two days once."

"What'd he do? Forget to wear his hat?"

I hesitate, look away, then meet her gaze. "Someone saw him . . . you know, with a horse."

She tries to appear nonchalant, but doesn't quite pull it off. Her eyes widen and she looks like she just bit into something sour. "That's sick."

"Yes, it is." I give a nod of satisfaction. "The bishop was hard on him, but he deserved it. He never did it again." I look at her. "I can't imagine what you might've done to warrant such a severe punishment."

"I sure didn't fuck a horse." She's trying to shock me. When it doesn't work she says, "You're weird."

I inhale smoke, enjoying the nicotine buzz more than I should. "I'm just trying to understand how things are done."

"Yeah, I can tell." Her expression turns annoyed. "What are you doing here, anyway? I mean, in Roaring Springs?"

"I told you. I moved here from O—."

"I got that part of it. But why?" She hefts a laugh. "No one comes here. It sucks here."

"My husband died. I needed . . . a change. I wanted to—"

"Take a walk among the wicked?" She offers a nasty grin.

"I was looking for . . . something else."

"Yeah, well, be careful where you look around here because you may not like what you find."

"What do you mean?"

"In case you haven't noticed, Bishop Schrock is strict to the extreme.

212

If he likes you, you're in. If he doesn't, you're screwed. I guess you'll figure it out soon enough."

I look away, draw on the cigarette. "Maybe I already have."

She cocks her head, her eyes narrowing on mine. Inwardly, I smile; finally, I have her undivided attention. She's fully engaged, as if she's been invited into some exclusive private club and gets to hang out with the beautiful people. She wants the scoop. She wants to know what I did to deserve it. This is *the thing* I can share that might prompt her to share something in return.

"What did he do to you?" she asks.

I tell her about the two men on snowmobiles throwing me into the chicken coop. "That's why I asked you about it. It scared me."

"What did you do to deserve *that*?"

I shrug. "I'd rather not say."

She seems to accept that. "You'd better be careful."

"I plan to." I hit the cigarette again. "You don't like him much, do you?"

She lowers the cigarette and gives me a hard, hostile look. "What are you going to do? Report back to him and tell him what I said?"

"I'm not going to tell anyone anything." I tilt my head, holding her gaze. "Why would you think that?"

"I don't know you. You're not my best bud. As far as I know you're a spy."

"A *spy*?" Spoken aloud the word sounds absurd and I let fly with a laugh. "What does that mean?"

She looks at me as if I'm a dim-witted child. "You think that's funny? How do you think he knows so much? He has people watching everyone."

"Bishop Schrock?" I offer another laugh, unapologetic, at her expense. "No offense, but that sounds paranoid."

"Let me tell you something Kate-from-Ohio: It pays to be paranoid around here."

"If that's the case, why does everyone speak so highly of him?"

She gives me a withering look. "Because they're scared shitless."

"Are you afraid of him?"

"I'm not afraid of anyone," she fires back.

"Even after what happened to Rachel?"

Her eyes skate away from mine, blinking, as if she doesn't know what to say. She recovers quickly. Dropping the cigarette on the ground, she crushes it with her sneaker. "I gotta get back to work."

"Wait and I'll walk in with you."

"Fuck off."

She brushes past me and stalks inside without looking back.

Marie is nowhere in sight when I pick up my sandwich at the counter. I go to a corner booth and eat it without pleasure, all the while my mind running through the odd conversation.

He has people watching everyone.

It pays to be paranoid around here.

Sheriff Suggs's words echo the entire time. *That place is beginning to sound more like a damn cult . . .*

It's evident I'm not going to get anywhere with her tonight. At least she knows who I am. She knows I'm a fellow rule breaker. While those two things don't exactly make us kindred spirits, she knows the door is open if she wants to talk.

I finish the sandwich and head for the ladies room. Inside a stall, I pull out my cell phone, call up a map app and punch in the address for Rebecca and Levi Beiler. They live a few miles south of Roaring Springs. If I hurry, I'll make it before dark.

I'm loathe to go back outside and into the cold, but I don't have a choice. Pulling on my gloves and wrapping my scarf around my head and neck, I go through the door and get on the scooter. I'm losing daylight, so I set a brisk pace, traveling back through town where the lights of The Dutch Kitchen glow with warm light. The Calico Country Store windows are darkened, but I can just make out the pretty window display and, thinking of the time I spent there earlier, I'm warmed.

Main Street forks at the east end of town. I go right and set a fast pace toward Bear Creek Road. Despite temperatures in the twenties, I break a sweat beneath my layers of clothing. Two miles into the trip, I shake the scarf from my head. Another mile down the road and I catch a whiff of cattle and manure. I round a curve and the dairy farm comes into view. The two-story brick house sits atop a hill. A split rail fence surrounds a large yard crowded with blue spruce. Despite the lack of formal landscaping, the abundant trees and rustic fence make the old house a pretty sight to behold.

I turn into the long lane and muscle the scooter bike through snow. A big white barn stands tall behind the house. In the side pen, a dozen or so Holstein cattle stare at me through the fence rails, bawling. The big sliding door stands partially open and I wonder if it's feeding time. Maybe a good chance to catch Rebecca alone inside.

Leaning the scooter behind a hay wagon loaded with loose timothy, I follow the sidewalk around to the front door and take the steps to the porch. The daylight is waning, the cloud cover ushering in dusk earlier than usual. There's no lantern light inside and I hope I haven't missed them.

A dusting of snow covers the porch. No footprints, just the paw prints where a cat walked. Two old-fashioned, shell-backed chairs with a plain wooden table between them. Someone left a mug with an inch or so of coffee inside that's now frozen solid. I cross to the door and rap the wood with my knuckles, then turn to take in the view, listening for footsteps. The wind whispers through the boughs of the spruce trees. At the foot of the hill, a sparrow chatters from atop a fence post. It's peaceful and pretty here, the perfect place to sit and look out over the land.

When no one comes to the door, I knock again. Vaguely, I wonder if the couple is in the barn, feeding the stock. I'm on my way to the steps to check when I glance through the window to my right. Black curtains cover the glass, but there's a gap where one of the panels has caught on something and is pulled away. A closer look reveals the curtain rod has come loose from the wall. Odd that someone would leave it like that . . .

Bending, I peer through the gap. Something on the floor snags my attention. At first glance I think it's a dog, lying on a rug. As my eyes adjust to the semi darkness I discern a hand against the wood plank floor. A burst of alarm in my gut. Instinctively, I reach for my radio, but it's not there.

"Shit. *Shit.*"

The first thought that strikes my brain is that someone has had a heart attack or succumbed to carbon monoxide poisoning. The latter scenario is all too common in the winter months, when people use kerosene space heaters. If the heater isn't properly vented, carbon monoxide can reach dangerous levels and cause unconsciousness and death.

"Mr. and Mrs. Beiler!" I slap the window with my open palm, then move to the door, striking it with the heel of my hand. "Rebecca! It's Kate Miller! Open the door!"

I try the knob, but it's locked. I rush to one of the shell-backed chairs, pick it up and smash the window. The sound of breaking glass seems deafening in the silence.

"Mr. and Mrs. Beiler! Is everyone okay?"

Even as I call out, I drag the chair along the bottom of the window to knock out the remaining shards. Simultaneously, I yank the phone from my pocket and hit the speed dial for Suggs.

Before he can even utter his name, I shout, "I'm at the Beiler farm. I got one person down. Maybe CO poisoning. I see a space heater."

"I'll get an ambulance out there. They alive?"

"No one's moving." Inside, an Amish female lies on her side in front of the sofa. I can see the legs of a male near a doorway. "Two down, Dan. I'm going in."

"Shit. Go. I'm on my way."

Then I'm through the window, rushing toward the fallen woman. Too dark to see. An unpleasant smell I don't want to name. Thinking of carbon monoxide, I dart to the door, flip the bolt lock, yank it open. Light and cold air flood the room. I cross to the woman and kneel.

"Rebecca." I set my hand on her shoulder. "Are you okay? Can you hear me?"

I know immediately I'm too late. The feel of her skin, even through my gloves, isn't right. Hard. Lifeless. Like frozen meat.

Gently, I push her onto her back. A wet sound against the wood floor. Blood on her chest. Face ghastly pale. Blue lips gaping. Flesh pinkish-blue on the right side of her face. Not bruised, but the beginning of livor mortis.

Not enough light to tell if she's been shot or stabbed, but it's a devastating wound. I scramble back, nearly trip on the foot stool, catch my balance just in time.

Lifting my skirt, I yank the .22 Mini Mag from the holster, spin to face the kitchen doorway.

I don't think there's anyone there, but the last thing any cop wants to do is walk into a scene to help someone and get shot because she didn't clear the place. I'm not taking any chances.

"Who's there!" I shout. "Get out here! Keep your hands where I can see them! Do it now!"

The house is dead silent.

No one there.

Craning my head right, I glance at the male. He's lying in the kitchen doorway. Toes up. He's wearing work boots. Trousers. My hands and legs shake as I cross to him. He's face up. One eye open and staring. The other at half mast. A black hole for a mouth. Shattered teeth. Perfect half circle of blood around his head, stark against the floor. A shotgun lies next to him, the muzzle a few inches from his head.

At first glance this looks like a murder-suicide situation. Levi shot his wife, then turned the gun on himself. But one of the golden rules of any investigation is to never take anything at face value.

I step back, keenly aware that I've contaminated the scene. My face is hot, my back covered with sweat. I dial Suggs as I head toward the door.

"They're dead," I say when he picks up.

"Aw, man. How—"

"Dan, they've been shot—"

"*What?*"

"There's a shotgun on the floor. It looks like a murder suicide. But . . . I don't know."

"You see anyone?" Even over the phone I hear the groan of his cruiser's engine, telling me he's rushing to the scene.

"No. I haven't looked around, but I don't think there's anyone else here."

"You okay?"

"Yup." It's a lie. It's disturbing as hell to walk into something like this. By the time I go through the door I'm shaking so violently I can barely hold the cell. "I hear sirens."

"Look, this is kind of an unusual situation. I mean with your cover and all. I don't know what the protocol is, but it might be a good idea for you to get out of there. I'll get an official statement from you later."

"I've left tracks. Contaminated the scene."

"I'll take care of it. Just get out of there. I'll call you as soon as I know something."

"All right."

I flee the scene and don't look back.

Two hours pass before Suggs calls with an update. I've been pacing the living room relentlessly since arriving back, a dozen scenarios running through my mind. None of them are good. By the time my cell rings, my patience has grown thin.

"I got Frank on the line with us," Suggs begins. "You there, Frank?"

"I'm here."

I don't bother with a greeting. "What happened to them?"

"I just left the scene," Suggs tells me. "Medical examiner is there. It looks like both suffered fatal gunshot wounds. My undersheriff is overseeing things."

"I got an investigator with the state police out there, too, Chief Burkholder," Betancourt adds. "Along with a crime scene unit."

"What's your take on this?" I ask.

"It has all the hallmarks of a murder-suicide," Suggs tells me. "Looks like the husband accosted his wife in the living room and shot her once in the chest at close range. He then went to the kitchen, put the barrel in his mouth, and pulled the trigger."

I think of Rebecca and I can't believe something like this would happen to her. "Have you notified next of kin?" I ask. "Talked to family members?"

"We're still trying to find them." Suggs sighs. "No luck yet."

"Last I heard, their son, Andy Beiler, his wife, and their two teenage girls moved to Shipshewana, Indiana," I tell them. "The grandson went to Missouri to live with an elderly couple."

"We got that," Betancourt says. "We're looking. Nothing yet."

"What were you doing out at the Beiler farm, anyway?" Betancourt asks.

"I went to talk to Rebecca." Quickly, I summarize my conversation with Laura Hershberger. "She told me Rebecca's three grandchildren were taken in and 'counseled' by Schrock. Laura wouldn't go into detail, but intimated that some kind of abuse occurred while the kids were at Schrock's farm."

"Dan briefed me on that," Betancourt says. "Did she mean sexual abuse?"

"I don't know." I tell him about my encounter with Schrock. "That would be my guess."

"I ran the grandson's name through every database I could think of and I got nada."

"Not even an ID card?" I ask.

"I checked Missouri, Indiana, and New York," Betancourt replies. "Nothing."

"Odd for someone to go off the radar so completely," I say. "Even an Amish person." I think about that and something unsettling pings in my brain. "Unless he's not in any of those places."

"What are you getting at?" Suggs asks.

"Maybe Andy Beiler and his wife didn't go to Shipshewana. Maybe her grandson wasn't sent to Missouri. Maybe Rebecca was fed a lie to cover up something else."

"Something like what?" Betancourt asks.

No one replies, but they know what I'm thinking.

Suggs finally says it. "You think they're *dead*?"

"I think it's something we need to consider," I reply. "Maybe the bit about them fleeing in the middle of the night is the story Schrock's putting out."

"I'll double down," Betancourt grumbles. "If the three grand-children and their parents are anywhere to be found, we'll find them."

I'm still thinking about Rebecca and Levi Beiler. "The timing of this is suspect as hell."

"You're not buying into the murder-suicide scenario," Betancourt says.

"Rebecca Beiler was an opinionated and vocal woman," I tell him. "She was upset about her grandchildren being sent away. Her son and daughter-in-law moving away. She was no fan of Eli Schrock and she'd been speaking out against him."

Suggs mutters a curse.

"You think Schrock is responsible for this?" Betancourt asks.

"If Schrock is running some kind of cult, if there are kids—teen-agers—being abused, he's got a lot to hide and even more at stake if he's found out," I tell him. "What if Schrock got wind of Rebecca speaking out against him? Badmouthing him? What if she'd become a threat?"

"You think Schrock went over to their place, shot them, and made it look like a murder-suicide?" I don't miss the doubt in Betancourt's voice.

"I don't think he pulled the trigger," I reply, "but I think it's possi-ble he had someone do it for him."

"The two men who accosted you," Suggs says.

I nod. "That would be my guess."

"If that's the case, this changes everything," Suggs says.

"You comfortable staying with the assignment, Chief Burkholder?" Betancourt asks.

"For now," I tell him. "I've made some headway establishing myself in the community. I've met a lot of people. They know who I am. I'd hate to throw that away."

"In light of recent events, I'd feel a lot better if you checked in twice a day instead of once," Betancourt says.

"I agree," Suggs echoes.

"Not a problem," I tell them.

"In case you're not reading between the lines here, Chief, that means watch your ass," Suggs says.

"You can count on it."

CHAPTER 19

Nights in the trailer are the worst; they're dark and cold and seemingly endless, each of those things amplified by the resurgence of my old friend insomnia. Ever present in the back of my mind is the reality that the front door may not keep out those who would do me harm. That I'm alone and without backup if I need it.

It's during those long hours between dusk and dawn that I can't shut down my thoughts. I can't seem to get my head around this case. While my knowledge of the Amish culture, the understanding of what it means to be Amish, has been a tremendous benefit, it has also, in some ways, been a handicap. For the first time I realize the one thing that made me perfect for this assignment—the reason I was chosen—is the same reason this case has been so difficult: my Amish roots.

No single group of people can be lumped together and neatly categorized. But I've always seen the Amish as fundamentally good. Not perfect, but moral and benevolent. It's those preconceived notions that have tainted my judgment and blinded me to the darker possibilities.

In the course of infiltrating this community, I've opened a door I thought was closed, inadvertently ushering in the ghosts of my past. I re-entered a life I thought I'd left behind forever. Kate Burkholder, perpetual outsider, shunned by those I love, looked down upon—pitied, even—by a community I'd once been part of. It comes as a shock to realize that even after all these years, there's still a part of me that's conflicted.

I've stepped into the shoes of the woman I might have been had fate not intervened in and changed everything. While there were plenty of things I hated about being Amish, there were just as many aspects of the plain life I loved—and that I missed desperately when I left. This week has illuminated the truth: that I've not fully come to terms.

It's one A.M. and I'm on the sofa, huddled beneath a blanket in a futile attempt to stay warm. On the table in front of me is a mug of tepid tea, my .38 revolver, my .22 mini Mag , the pepper spray, and my cell. What a collection. If my mood wasn't so dark, I might've laughed.

I want to call Tomasetti, but I know he's probably sleeping. I should be, too; tomorrow promises to be a busy, stressful day, and I need to be on my toes. I tell myself I don't want to wake him. But I'm honest enough to admit that's not the only reason I haven't picked up the phone. I know if I tell him about the deaths of Rebecca and Levi Beiler, he'll ask me to call it quits. Ending this assignment would probably be the prudent thing to do at this point. The problem is, I'm not always a prudent person, particularly when it comes to my job.

I don't want to walk away from this. Not when there's a dead teenage girl, an entire family missing, and now a middle-aged Amish couple gone, too. Maybe it's my ego talking, the part of me that likes to win no holds barred, but I know in my gut that if anyone can get to the bottom of it, it's me. The problem is convincing the man I love to support a decision that's as flawed as I am.

Tomasetti knows me. He knows how my mind works. He knows, better than anyone, that I'm driven and imperfect. That sometimes I try too hard and can be a sore loser. He knows that when I sink my teeth into a case, I can't let it go, sometimes to my own detriment. He understands all those things. And yet he loves me anyway.

I pick up my phone and speed dial his cell because I know he keeps it on the night table beside our bed. He picks up on the second ring. "Yep."

"I'm sorry to wake you."

I hear rustling on the other end and I picture him sitting up, leaning over to flip on the lamp. "Is everything okay?"

"Everything's fine." My first lie.

"Okay."

I'm gripping the phone hard. I can hear my heart beating in my ears. The wind tearing around the trailer outside. A piece of the skirting flapping. "I miss you," I tell him.

"You, too." Another pause. I sense his mind working. He's trying to figure out why I've called him so late.

"Everything's not so great," I say.

"Maybe you should tell me what's going on."

"I will, but I need you to shut up and listen without interrupting."

A moment's hesitation and then, "All right."

Taking a deep breath, I lay out everything, good and bad—the two men, the chicken coop incident, my encounter with Schrock, and the deaths of Rebecca and Levi Beiler. "Tomasetti, Schrock isn't an Amish bishop. For him, this has nothing to do with religion. He's running a cult. He's taking advantage of these people, deceiving them, controlling them through intimidation, threats and physical violence."

"Are you on his radar?"

"I don't think so."

He makes a sound low in his throat. He's got a pretty good bullshit detector, and he's not buying it. If he knew what Schrock had done, he'd blow his stack . . .

"Goddamn it, Kate."

"Don't ask me to quit."

"Why the hell not?"

"Because I can't."

"Kate—"

"I'm tired of walking on eggshells around you when it comes to my job. I'm tired of lying because I can't tell the truth. I'm tired of hiding things from you. Keeping things from you because you can't handle it. It's . . . stupid and dishonest and I need for us to be honest. I need *you*. I need to be able to talk to you."

"You can talk to me," he growls. "You know that."

"How can I when you worry? When I know it hurts you? I know what it does to you and I hate it."

The silence that ensues is thick with tension. It's so quiet I can hear his breathing. The wind pressing against the windows.

"Look, Kate, I'm going to be honest with you," he says tightly. "I don't like you being up there on your own. You have no backup. No transportation. Very little in the way of communication. You can dress that up however you like, but it's a dangerous situation. If something goes wrong—"

"It already has," I cut in. "A lot of things have gone wrong. In case you weren't listening, I handled it. I'm okay."

He makes a sound of frustration. "You're not bulletproof."

"I'm a cop, and I'm doing my job. Maybe you should have a little more faith in my capabilities—"

"Being a good cop isn't always enough."

We fall silent. Closing my eyes, I wish we could reconcile this moldering pool of fear and worry that's plagued us nearly from the start of our relationship.

"You're right," I tell him. "Being a good cop, being careful and fol-

226

lowing the rules isn't always enough. Cops still get hurt. Sometimes they die. Welcome to law enforcement."

He makes a sound of annoyance.

I don't stop. "I know you're worried about me and I'm sorry for that. But I can't stop being a cop. It's what I do. It's who I am."

"I get it," he growls.

"I don't think you do. Tomasetti, it's not going to change. If we're going to get past this, you have to trust me. You have to trust my judgment and my abilities."

"I do. All of that."

"Then show me. Have faith in me. Let me know you have my back on this."

"I've got your back. Always. You know that."

"I'm afraid," I whisper. "I haven't been able to tell you that. This has been difficult and you're part of that. I need to be able to talk to you and know you're not going to lay into me and add yet another layer of turmoil to this pile of chaos I'm trying to work through."

After an interminable silence, he whispers my name, softly and with affection. "I'm sorry."

Tears burn my eyes, but I blink them back. "I needed to hear that. I needed to hear your voice."

"Usually, that's the one thing people *don't* want to hear."

I laugh. He doesn't join me, but it clears some of the tension.

"So what do Suggs and Betancourt have to say about all this?" he asks after a moment.

"They want me to hang tight."

"I'm sure you had nothing to do with that."

"I'll be checking in twice a day from here on."

"That's good."

"I'm getting close to some of these people. Decent Amish people

227

who need to be able to live their lives without the threat of violence. Sooner or later, someone is going to talk to me, and Schrock is going to take a fall."

He takes a deep breath. "At the risk of sounding like an overbearing son of a bitch . . . you know some of these cults can be dangerous."

"I know."

"When I was with the Cleveland Division of Police, I worked a homicide case involving a cult."

"Tell me."

"These cult leaders prey on people looking for something. The lost. The vulnerable. They offer security and friendship and a place to belong. They give people what they think they need. Tell them what they need to hear. Once they're in, they're isolated, indoctrinated, and brainwashed, and then it's all about dominance and power. Most of the time it's difficult, if not impossible, to leave."

I think about Rebecca and Levi Beiler lying dead on the floor. I think of Abe Gingerich's missing finger and the time I spent in the chicken coop, and I shiver.

"Are you sleeping?" he asks.

"I'll sleep better tonight."

"So . . . we're good?"

"We're good." A sense of warmth pours over me. "I just . . . I wanted you to know what was going on. I want you to know I'm being careful and Suggs and Betancourt are on top of things."

"Be safe," he says.

"I will. I'll let you get back to sleep."

"I love you," he tells me.

"Same goes."

The lines goes dead.

When the tears come, I don't bother to wipe them away.

•   •   •

I'm jogged awake by the sound of pounding. Adrenaline burns like mercury through my midsection as I swivel from the bed and set my feet on the floor. I reach down, grab the .38 off the table next to my bed. Cram the phone into the pocket of my sweatpants. The .22 and pepper spray in the other. Pounding sounds again, hard enough to shake the door. *Sons of bitches*, I think. Then I'm moving down the hall, my revolver leading the way, my temper bringing up the rear.

I step into the living room, sidle right toward the window and lift the curtain half an inch with my finger. In the meager light of a hazy half moon, I see a figure standing on the deck, a couple of feet from the door. Not the men I'd expected, but a diminutive female silhouette. It could be a trap; they could have anticipated my being prepared and sent a decoy.

Silently, I walk to the door, lower the .38 to my side. "Who's there?" I call out.

"Your favorite Amish girl."

Marie Weaver. "You alone?"

"Just me and the coyotes."

Pulling the chair from beneath the knob, I disengage the bolt lock, twist the knob, and open the door a few inches. "You'd better not be lying to me," I say, my eyes sweeping the area behind her and around the trailer. There's no one there.

"You're kind of paranoid, aren't you?" She looks intrigued by my fulsome caution.

"Shut up and keep your hands where I can see them."

"Sheesh." Sighing, she yanks her hands from her pockets. "What do you think I'm going to do? Rob you?"

"Or worse." I give her a hard look. "What do you want?"

Cocking her head, she looks at me a little more closely. "You don't act like a normal Amish woman."

I motion toward her clothes. "Same goes."

She's shivering beneath a Walmart puffy coat. No hat. No gloves or scarf. Her cheeks and the tip of her nose are red from the cold. Why is she here?

"You want to come in for a minute?" I ask, calming down.

"I didn't come here to stand on your porch and freeze my ass off."

Taking a final look beyond her, I step back. I smell cigarette smoke and strawberry shampoo as she pushes past me. I motion toward the kitchen table. "Sit down."

Frowning, she obeys. I've still got my hand on the butt of the .38 in my sweatpants' pocket, out of sight. Not a good place for it, so I take a few steps back and snag my coat off the sofa where I left it. Placing the revolver on the sofa, I slide into the coat, then put the gun in my pocket.

Crossing to the bar that separates the kitchen from the living area, I pick up a book of matches and light the lantern. I go to the kitchen and put a match to the lantern on the kitchen table, turning up the wick for maximum light. Keeping one eye on the girl, I check the clock on the wall. Three A.M.

She looks like a kid sitting there, shivering, probably half lit on beer, her leg jiggling a hundred miles an hour. Tufts of hair stick out of her *kapp*. She's got dirty hands. I remind myself this girl is only sixteen years old. Troubled. Vulnerable. The perfect victim for a cult.

"You want something hot to drink?" I ask. "To warm up?"

"Some whiskey would hit the spot."

"Fresh out." I go to the stove, run water into the kettle for two cups, and set it over the flame. "What are you doing out so late all by yourself?"

She lifts a shoulder, lets it drop. "Just hanging."

230

"With who?"

"No one in particular."

"Uh huh." I snag two mugs from the cupboard, set them on the counter. "Your parents know you're out?"

"No."

She lifts her hand, picks at a hangnail. Her fingernails are painted green and chipped at the tips. For the first time I notice she's wearing jeans. A red sweater. A cheap pair of boots that don't look very warm. The hems of her pants are wet. She's been out in the cold and snow for quite some time.

The kettle begins to whistle, so I pour water over teabags, set one of the mugs in front of her, and, carrying my own mug, take the chair across from her.

"What's going on?" I ask. "Why are you here?"

The girl is shivering so hard she spills a little bit of her tea on the table and, without apologizing for the spill, slurps loudly.

My curiosity grows while I wait, but I opt to give her a few minutes before questioning her.

"I think they killed her," she whispers without looking at me.

My heart bumps hard against my chest. I know to whom she's referring, but I ask anyway. "Rachel Esh?"

She nods. "She was my best friend. She didn't deserve what happened. I miss her." She closes her eyes for a moment. "I'm scared because I think they want me gone, too."

"Who?" I ask.

"Schrock. The people he surrounds himself with."

"How do you know this?"

"It's complicated."

"We have all night."

She digs into her pocket. Simultaneously, I reach into mine, set my

231

hand on the pistol. Marie pulls out a pack of Marlboro Reds and lights up without asking permission. I consider taking it away from her and tossing it out, but I want her talking so I let her light up.

"Rachel was staying with Schrock when she died," she says after a moment.

"I thought she was living with Mary and Abe Gingerich."

She looks away, then back at me. "Her parents didn't like her wild ways. They were afraid she was on the fast track to hell. You know, the drinking and staying out." Her mouth twists, but she doesn't quite manage a smile. "They didn't like me. Mary Gingerich stepped up to help." She shrugs. "It didn't work out there, either. Someone told the bishop. He took Rachel in to counsel."

Counsel. Something goes tight in my chest. How I've grown to hate that word.

"How long had she been living with Schrock?"

"Three weeks."

"What makes you think he had something to do with her death?"

"I just . . . Everyone thinks Schrock is some kind of fucking messiah or something. He's not. He's . . ." She sighs, frustrated because she can't seem to find the words. "Rachel was my first friend here in Roaring Springs. We've known each other since we were ten years old. When we were twelve, Schrock started . . . paying attention to us."

"Paying attention to you how?"

"He started inviting us to his house. For hot chocolate or pie. He gave us chores in his barn, mucking stalls or whatnot, and paid us. He let us ride his horses. We got to see the new filly born. Stuff like that. You know, innocent like. I mean, he'd preach sometimes. Read the bible. He was always quoting Jacob Ammann."

I know from my school days that Ammann was an Anabaptist leader from the mid-1700s and the namesake of the Amish religious movement.

She pauses to blow on the tea and then sips. "Last summer, he invited Rachel to a party at the barn at the rear of his property."

"What kind of party?"

Her mouth twists. "I wasn't invited, but she told me about it. She said there was music and beer. Yoder and Smucker were there. Other people she didn't know. I guess it got kind of wild, but Rachel thought it was exciting and fun. It was her first, but not her last."

Marie doesn't notice when the ash on her cigarette falls to the tabletop. I wait.

"Anyway, Schrock liked Rachel after that so she got invited again. And again. In the beginning, she was into it. She was part of it. She liked being included. I was always a little jealous."

"What happened?"

Her brows knit. "After a few of those parties she stopped talking about it. Stopped telling me stuff. When I asked, she'd just bite my head off."

"Any idea why?"

"I dunno. But I knew it wasn't good. She wasn't happy." She puffs absently on the cigarette. "A few days before she died, she was acting all weird, like she was going to tell me something. We were going to meet . . . like we did sometimes at night. She died before . . ."

I sip the tea, give myself a moment to digest this sudden flood of information. "What do you think happened?"

"The last time I saw her, we were drinking and she started talking about it. She told me she did things she wasn't proud of and she started crying. I didn't know what to say and all of a sudden those parties didn't sound so great."

The words creep over me, like the stench of garbage left to rot in the sun. "Was Rachel there against her will?"

"No." She shakes her head. "I mean, not at first. But . . . the last couple of weeks she was different. Like it wasn't fun for her anymore. She was stressed about something."

"Any idea what it was?"

Marie shakes her head.

"Did she have a boyfriend?" I ask.

"She was tight with Jacob Yoder."

"Anyone else?"

Her eyes flick away from mine and then back. "Maybe."

"She told you that?"

"Not really. But Rachel wasn't very good at keeping secrets. She was . . . honest and real. Didn't play games. Didn't lie like everyone else. I think she was involved with someone. I think that's what she was going to tell me."

"I thought she was tight with Jacob Yoder."

She thinks about that for a moment. "It was a different kind of tight. I mean, Rachel and Jacob knew each other since they were kids. They played together and as they grew up they just sort of became girlfriend and boyfriend. Everyone always thought they'd get married. I know she loved him. But this . . . other guy just came in and swooped her off her feet."

"What guy?"

"I don't know."

I think about that in terms of motive. "Did she tell Jacob?"

"Rachel didn't tell anyone. She didn't even officially break up with him. They stayed friends, but I think things changed between them. He wanted more; she wanted less. It happened quick. She stopped spending time with him. I think she was crazy for this other guy."

"How did Jacob take it?"

"He wasn't happy."

"Unhappy enough to do something about it?"

She shakes her head. "Jacob can be an ass. I mean, you saw the way he was acting on Sunday. But he'd never hurt Rachel. He was crazy about her. After she . . . died, he just changed. Starting with the drinking and acting like a jerk."

I nod, but Jacob Yoder has just graduated to the top of my suspect list. Right below Schrock.

"Rachel didn't die out there by herself. She was too smart to get caught out in a snowstorm unaware." She puffs hard on the cigarette, blows out the smoke between tight lips. "I'm scared."

I go to the stove, pick up the kettle, and refill her cup. "Did you tell your parents?"

"They wouldn't understand. They think Schrock is like a one-way ticket to heaven or something."

"Do you think you're in danger?"

She lifts her shoulder and lets it drop. "I don't know. Maybe."

"Why didn't you go to the police?"

"That would go over well." She says the words with far too much cynicism for a girl her age. "Probably get me put in a foster home or something awful like that."

"Marie, I'll do what I can to keep you safe. But you have to be honest with me and tell me everything."

"Yeah, right." She looks down at her hand where the hangnail has started to bleed. "I don't even know why I'm telling you all this. You can't do anything. You probably don't even care."

"I care," I tell her. "And I'm a good listener."

She drops the cigarette into her tea and it sizzles out. "So was Rachel, and look what happened to her."

We sit in silence for a few minutes, wrapped in our thoughts. There's no way I can let this girl walk away. Not if she's in danger. If she leaves and something happens . . .

I'm trying to figure out how to handle the situation without blowing my cover when she speaks.

"There's nothing you can do," she says.

"I can help you."

"No one can help. He runs things and he's got everyone behind him." She laughs. "Or scared of him."

"Why did you come here tonight?"

Shrugging, she offers a penitent smile. "I guess I liked the way you stood up to those guys at worship. Like you were some badass and going to take them apart all by yourself. No one's ever done anything like that for me before."

"Let me look into all of this," I tell her. "In the interim . . . will you do me a favor?"

"Oh, brother . . ."

"Let me walk you home."

"You sure you want to be seen with me?" But her relief is palpable.

"It's three thirty A.M. and twenty degrees outside. No one's going to see us." I say the words lightly, but her expression tells me she doesn't believe the time or temperature is relevant. "Your parents find you gone and they'll be worried. You shouldn't do that to them."

"They're sleeping. I went out the window." Rising, she starts toward the door. "I've done it before and they never even know."

"Something happens to you and they'll know."

She nods. "Okay."

I grab my scarf and step into my boots. "One more thing."

She reaches the door and turns in time for me to see her roll her eyes.

"Lay low and let me handle this," I say.

"You're not going to involve the cops, are you?"

"Not yet. But if someone hurt Rachel, they'll need to get involved at some point." I hand her my gloves. "Might be the only way to stop Schrock."

When both of us are bundled up, I open the door and we step into the night.

CHAPTER 20

Murder is big news in a small town. Make it a murder-suicide with an Amish twist and the story goes viral—at least in terms of the grapevine. It's ten A.M. and I'm sitting at the sewing table at The Calico Country Store. A subdued Laura Hershberger sits across from me, staring into a cup of coffee that's long since gone cold. There are no customers in the store, but I'm thankful for the time alone with her.

"I can't believe they're gone."

It's the third time she's uttered the words. I don't look at her this time, just let her say what she needs to say. I stare down into my coffee, feeling more than is prudent for someone in my position, but that's the human heart for you.

"For goodness' sake, she was here just yesterday." Shaking her head, she presses a hand against her mouth. "How could this happen? Why didn't she give us a sign or *something*. Maybe one of us could have helped."

"Was Levi depressed?" I ask after a moment.

"I don't know." She raises her gaze to mine. "You know how the Amish are. We don't talk about such things." She presses her lips together. "For better or for worse."

I hold her gaze. "Was he distraught about his children and grand-children leaving?"

"Of course he was, but this?" She shudders. "I don't understand. He was so kind. Is it possible? Could he have done such a thing?"

"Did you know him well?" I ask.

Her mouth twists into a poor imitation of a smile. "I've known Levi as long as I knew Rebecca. He was quiet. Hardworking. A good man. Gentle. And devout." She takes a breath and releases it slowly. "He was the first one in line to help when a neighbor needed it. The last to ask when he needed it himself." Lowering her head, she rubs her temples with her fingers. "What he did . . . and taking her with him . . . it goes against everything the Amish believe in."

"Maybe he didn't do it," I tell her.

Her head snaps up and she looks at me as if the thought hadn't occurred to her. "But the newspaper . . . and the police are saying . . ."

"They're still investigating. I don't think it's been determined yet."

"If not Levi, then who?" She scoffs at the notion. "Who would do such a thing and why?"

"Did they have any problems with anyone? Neighbors? Family?"

Her brows go together. "Everyone loved Rebecca and Levi."

The cowbell on the door interrupts. I turn to see Naomi, Ada, and Lena walk in, carrying their sewing bags. Laura and I get to our feet. The women are midway to us when Lena bursts into tears.

Laura crosses to her, arms open. "Come here, baby."

Lena falls into her embrace. "We had harsh words," she sobs, "and now she's gone."

"Shush," Laura coos. "Rebecca never met an argument she didn't like."

"She was full of forgiveness," Naomi adds.

"And a little bit of vinegar," Ada puts in.

For most Amish, grief is expressed quietly and in private. But the Amish are human, and there are times when emotions run high and public displays can't be helped.

"I was going to make it right today," Lena says.

I didn't know Rebecca well, having only met her once. But whether I knew her or not, she deserved the chance to live her life. And as the grief pours off these women, I feel that same sadness welling inside me.

Naomi goes to the coffee pot and returns with two cups, shoves one of them at Lena. "Rebecca thought of you as her own daughter."

"She enjoyed a lively spar, too," Laura says.

"Never had to wonder where you stood with her," Ada adds. "Just look at how she talked about the bishop."

Seeing an opening, I pick up my own cup of coffee and casually ask, "Speaking of the bishop, I'm surprised Levi didn't reach out to him. Especially if he was distraught. . . ."

Naomi nods. "I wish he had."

Lena pulls away from Laura and takes her cup. "Bishop Schrock would have guided them through the darkness."

"Did Rebecca and Levi have family?" I ask. When Laura shoots me a warning look, I add. "Sometimes if you're going through a rough spot, it's your family who pull you out."

The women exchange glances and suddenly it dawns on me that Laura isn't the only one who knows Rebecca's family is gone. Either Rebecca confided in someone else, or people simply noticed they were gone.

"I heard her son and daughter-in-law left," Naomi says in a low voice.

All eyes sweep to Naomi. "Took the two girls with them," she says. "That's all I know."

"Why did they leave?" I ask.

"I suppose no one rightly knows," Naomi replies.

Laura motions toward the sewing table where the quilt they'd been working on waits. We take our chairs. Rebecca's is conspicuously empty.

Lena lowers herself into the chair, scooting it away from the table to make room for her belly. "What about her grandson?"

Ada picks up her needle, threads it and begins to stitch. "Rebecca told me Bishop Schrock sent her grandson away to help an elderly couple who'd lost their family in a buggy accident. Never understood why he did that."

"I knew about it," Laura admits. "She told me last summer. Evidently, the couple was in their eighties. They lost their family in a buggy accident and had no one to take care of them. Andy was on *Rumspringa* and had gotten into trouble a few times. The bishop saw it as a way to help that old couple—and help Andy at the same time."

Ada lifts her chin. "Didn't help Rebecca or Levi much, did it?"

It's a heavy topic for a sewing circle, but sometimes tragedy has a way of loosening tongues. I take advantage of the opportunity to try to find out what else they know. "What kind of trouble did her grandson get into?" I ask.

"The bishop caught him with a radio in his buggy," Ada tells me.

"He was sent away for *that*?" I keep my eyes on my sewing.

"The bishop took Andy in for counsel," Ada says. "Next thing I know he's gone."

"What exactly does the bishop's counseling entail?" I'm feigning interest in my stitching, but it's not easy and in my peripheral vision, I see the other women look my way.

"Just a good talking to, I imagine," Lena says. "Bishop Schrock is good with the young folks that way."

241

Ada pulls her thread through the fabric with a little too much force. "Nothing good came of any of it, if you ask me."

"Sometimes you make sacrifices to help others," Lena says gently.

I steer the subject back to Rebecca's missing family. "Did Rebecca hear from her grandson after he was sent away?"

"Rebecca wrote him, of course," Ada says. "Don't think she heard back, though."

Naomi huffs. "He should have, but you know how those young men are sometimes."

Lena offers a sad smile. "Maybe he's courting a pretty Amish girl about now."

The smiles that follow are subdued and thoughtful.

"Rebecca would have liked that idea." Ada sighs. "I'm sure going to miss her."

The afternoon at the quilt shop was a bust, at least in terms of garnering new information about the fate of Rebecca's family. Ada is particularly displeased with Schrock and the only one willing to speak out against him. The others are either too frightened—or devoted. Tomorrow, I'll try to get Ada alone and see what else she has to say about the bishop.

I stow the scooter bike in the shed, watching the windows and keeping an eye on the ground for tracks. I let myself into the trailer and without removing my coat, I call Suggs. "I'm going over to Schrock's farm."

"Shit, Kate." The sheriff doesn't sound pleased to hear from me. "You don't beat around the bush, do you?"

I tell him about my conversation with Marie Weaver last night. "She told me Rachel Esh lived at Schrock's place for three weeks."

"First I've heard of that." He pauses, thoughtful. "Is this Weaver girl credible?"

"I think so," I tell him. "She's scared. Probably on Schrock's radar."

"That's not good. At this point she may be the closest thing we have to a witness," he says.

"She sneaks out at night and runs around all hours. Doesn't have much in the way of supervision. Maybe you could give CPS a heads up and have them pick her up."

"Sounds like the right thing to do," he says. "We can sort it out later with the parents."

The solution isn't ideal; Marie sure as hell isn't going to like it, but there's no other way for us to guarantee her safety.

"About Schrock," I say. "I just want to go out to his farm and take a look around."

"Yeah, and I want to lose sixty pounds."

"He won't know I'm there, Dan. Just a quick in and out, and no one will be the wiser." I pause, getting my words in order, formulating my argument. "It's a huge property with several buildings. I want to know what he does out there when he thinks no one's looking."

"You know if you see something, we won't be able to use it against him. There's this little glitch called a warrant."

"I'm aware—"

"What the hell are you going to do if someone catches you on the property?"

"It's dark," I say firmly. "There's a lot of cover. If something unexpected happens, I'll play innocent. Tell them I took a wrong turn. Got off the trail. Got lost."

"I don't like it."

"Dan, there's a young woman with a new baby out there."

He falls silent for a moment and then says, "You don't pull any punches, do you?"

"Not when I'm right."

"You going to go right now?"

"Yep."

"All right." He heaves an unhappy sigh. "You got one hour. If you don't call, I'm going to drive out there, hunt you down and drag you out myself."

I'm about to pop off a smartass reply, but he hangs up on me.

Ten minutes later I'm out the door and walking west on Swamp Creek Road. The snow has stopped, but it's brutally cold. The sky is overcast, but the clouds are thin enough for a hazy moon to light my way.

An hour isn't much time when I've half a mile to travel on foot just to get there, so I take advantage of the absence of traffic and jog. If a car or buggy happens by, I'll duck into the woods until it passes.

By the time I reach the turnoff for Schrock's farm, I'm out of breath. Keeping in mind that he has at least one dog, I start down the lane, staying alert, keeping an eye on my surroundings. But the place is seemingly deserted. I pass by the barn where worship was held. On Sunday, it was a pleasant place filled with Amish families, singing, and frolicking children. Tonight, the darkened windows watch me like menacing eyes as I pass.

A few hundred yards in and Schrock's house looms into view. The downstairs windows glow yellow with lantern light. The upstairs windows are dark. The scent of wood smoke laces the air, and I wonder if he's inside, sitting next to the fire, reading *Martyrs Mirror*. I wonder if Esther and her new baby are with him. I wonder if they're safe.

The sound of a horse's snort jerks my attention to the two buggies parked outside the barn. I hadn't noticed them upon my approach.

Slinking into the cover of the trees, I skirt the house and move closer to the barn. The sliding door is open. A yellow slash of lantern light bleeds out. Evidently, Schrock has visitors and they're in the barn.

It's a two-story bank barn with a stone foundation and a dirt ramp that leads to the sliding door. The second-level windows are dark, the loft door closed.

A sound resembling the pop of a BB gun startles me. I look over my shoulder, but quickly realize it's coming from inside the barn. My feet are silent against the snow as I wind through the trees. I'm close enough to hear voices now. Men speaking Pennsylvania Dutch and engaged in an animated conversation. I'm about twenty feet from the barn with my back against a tree when I realize the exchange is not a friendly one. Another *pop!* snaps through the air. This time it's followed by a yelp. Not a BB gun, I realize. Something else . . .

I stand there for a moment, listening, wondering if I can get close enough to see what's going on without being seen. I'll have to traverse ten or twelve yards of open ground with no cover. No trees. Not even a fence.

I work my way through the trees to the rear of the barn. Thankfully, there are no cattle or horses. Out of the line of sight of the front door, I leave the cover of the trees and cross to the barn. Upon reaching it, I press my back against the foundation and sidle toward the front of the building. I struggle to control my breathing, but my heart is pounding. If someone walks out of the barn and comes around to the side, I'll have some explaining to do.

I reach the front of the barn and peer around the corner. There's no one there. Nothing has changed. To my left the two horses and buggies still stand idle. The sliding door is open, light slanting out. The men are still arguing. I can't be sure, but it sounds as if someone is crying—or in distress.

An instant of hesitation and then I'm around the corner. My back scrapes against the siding as I edge toward the door. I duck beneath a window, light spilling onto the snow-covered ground to my left. I reach the door and pause to listen. For the first time I recognize Schrock's voice. He's berating someone for some serious offense involving a woman *ime familye weg.* Pregnant.

Pressing myself hard against the wood, I peek around the jamb. Jacob Yoder and Jonas Smucker stand with their backs to me. Eli Schrock stands a few feet away from them, his back to me as well. A fourth man whose face I can't see stands with his back to them, his hands braced against the wall. At first glance, I think he's wearing a white T-shirt mottled with rust-colored paint, then I realize his back is bare, his flesh striped with welts.

Abruptly, Schrock draws back. For the first time I notice the buggy whip in his hand. He brings it down hard on the man's bare back. "*Gottlos!*" Ungodly.

A scream tears from the man's throat. His body goes rigid. His hands clench like claws against the wood. For an instant, I think he's bound. Shock rattles through me when I realize he's not.

"Oftentimes pain is the only way to cast out the devil." Schrock slams the whip against the man's lower back. Leather pops sickeningly against flesh.

Yoder watches dispassionately, unfazed by the scene playing out before him. But I don't miss the signs of discomfort in Smucker's body language. He flinches each time the leather smacks against the man's skin, averting his eyes, shifting his weight from one foot to the other. Still, he does nothing to stop it.

The whip falls again. The man's body jolts, his hands scrabbling against the wood. A terrible groan bubbles up from his throat.

"*Aybrechah!*" Schrock shouts. Adulterer. "What would you do if Jesus came to your house today?"

The man begins to cry. "*Bekeahra.*" Repent.

Shrock swings the whip, brings it down hard. "Repent ye therefore, and be converted, that your sins may be blotted out, when the times of refreshing shall come from the presence of the Lord!"

The man's legs buckle. He goes to his knees, his nails scraping the wall all the way to the floor. He bends at the waist. At some point he's wet his pants, the stain spreading nearly down to his knees. Dear God . . .

Schrock steps back, shakes himself as if waking from a nightmare. The buggy whip falls to the ground. Abruptly, he turns. I lurch back. For a horrifying instant, I think he spotted me. But his voice is level and calm as he addresses Smucker and Yoder.

"Take our brother to the house. Clean his wounds. Send him home to his wife."

I don't wait to hear more. Quickly, I back away, ducking to avoid being seen through the window. I glance down at my tracks. *Shit.* No way to cover them, and I curse my carelessness. I reach the corner of the barn, turn and run as fast as I can across the open area. Relief surges when I reach the cover of the trees. Only when I'm deeply ensconced in the shadows do I stop and look back.

Yoder and Smucker are on either side of the man, helping him toward the house. Eli Schrock stands outside the barn door, looking in my direction. There's no way he can see me. It's fully dark; I'm twenty yards away, tucked into the shadows of a thousand trees. Still, a chill passes through me at the sight of him.

I can just make out his face and in the instant before he turns and starts toward the house, I think I see him smile.

• • •

I'm breathless when I arrive back at the trailer. I'm midway up the steps, anxious to tell Suggs what I just witnessed, when I spot the note taped to the door. My first thought is that my landlord Mrs. Bowman stopped by, tried to let herself inside only to realize I'd changed the locks. I pluck the note from the door and read.

Wer visa voahret fer in busch an mitt-nacht.

If you want to know the truth, go to the woods at midnight.

The hair on the back of my neck prickles. Turning, I scan the area in front of the property, but there's no one there. No fresh tracks. Someone must have put it on my door shortly after I left for Schrock's place. . . .

I look down at the note. It's a plain white piece of paper about four inches square, torn on two sides. No identifiable markings or print.

"Which woods?" I mutter.

It could be a prank—or a trap. There's only one way to find out. Holding the note by one corner in case I need to send it to Suggs for fingerprints, I let myself in to the trailer and lock the door.

As usual, the place is cold as an icebox. Tossing the note on the kitchen table, I go to the stove and turn on a couple of burners for heat, and set the kettle on for tea. I don't bother removing my coat as I tug the phone from my pocket and call Suggs.

He answers on the first ring. "Everything okay?"

"I'm fine." Quickly, I summarize the scene in Eli Schrock's barn. "I've never seen anything like it in my life."

"Just when I thought nothing could surprise me." He makes a sound that's part groan, part sigh. "How badly was he injured?"

"They marked him up badly. He was conscious, but he could barely walk." I consider that a moment. "Dan, if Schrock hadn't stopped when he did, the guy could have gone into shock or worse."

"Did you recognize him?"

"No. But he's Amish. Forty years old. Had a full beard, so he's married."

"You witness Schrock beating him?"

"Yes."

He pauses. "That's it. We're pulling you out. Get your things packed."

"We still don't know who—if anyone—was involved in Rachel Esh's death. And we still don't know what the hell's going on over there at Schrock's place."

"We've got him on felony assault. I want you out of there so that's going to have to do."

"It's not enough."

"Kate, damn it—"

"Give me until morning."

He says nothing.

"If you call it now," I tell him, "all this will have been for nothing."

"Felony assault—"

"I was there without a warrant. A defense lawyer will tear that to shreds and you know it."

He sighs and I sense him calming down, getting ready to acquiesce.

"There's more." Quickly, I tell him about the note. "Give me an hour to check it out. When I get back, I'll pack and you can pick me up in the morning."

"Any idea who might've left the note?"

"No, but it wasn't Schrock. It wasn't Yoder or Smucker. I had eyes on them."

"Could be a trap."

"Or a break in the case," I tell him. "Someone knows what's going on and wants it to end."

For a moment, neither of us speaks. Finally, I say, "I thought I'd bundle up and hang out in the woods north of the trailer for a while. See what happens."

"You know there aren't many roads up that way. Not a whole lot of anything except trees. If something goes wrong and we need to get there quick . . ." He makes a tight, unhappy sound. "Look, the only way I'll give you my blessing on this is if I can park a deputy off that two track that runs north off Swamp Creek Road. There's a little turn-around that goes into the woods."

"I know it," I tell him. "It's about a quarter mile down the road from Schrock's place."

"You comfortable with that?"

"You're not worried about me, are you?"

He's not amused. "Just do me a favor and call me half an hour before you walk up there. Don't stay any longer than an hour, and call me the instant you get back to the trailer."

"You got it."

"And keep the damn letter so I can send it to the lab."

CHAPTER 21

The thing about undercover work is that instead of laying low and trying to stay out of trouble, you basically walk around with your stick
and jab it into every beehive you can find just to see what flies out.
Tomasetti would tell me I'm a natural. The problem is, those beestings
can hurt. If they swarm, they can kill you.

The aerial photos tell me the woods north of the trailer encompass
hundreds of acres of rolling hills, ravines, and the occasional creek.
Since the note didn't specify the exact location where I would discover
this mysterious truth—if it indeed exists—I decide to head straight
north a quarter mile or so. I'll follow Suggs's instructions and give it
an hour.

At eleven thirty P.M. I'm bundled in long underwear, two pair of
socks, my dress, cardigan, and barn coat. I slide the .22 into its holster beneath my skirt, over the long underwear for easy access. The
pepper spray goes in my coat pocket, the mini Maglite flashlight in
the other.

Standing at the door, I call Suggs. "I'm heading out."

"Be safe and call me in an hour, or before if you need to."

"Roger that."

I disconnect and tuck the cell into my pocket. Wrapping a scarf around my head and neck, I pull on my Walmart gloves. A quick glance through the window tells me it's dark and I can't see shit. And, of course, it's snowing like the dickens.

Locking the door behind me, I descend the steps and set out. It's twenty degrees with a wind chill in the single digits. The snow on the ground reflects just enough light for me to avoid any close encounters with the trees, but it does little to light my way. I consider using the flashlight, but it would make me visible to anyone else out here, so I nix the idea.

I push myself into a brisk pace, swinging my arms to stay warm. I head due north, in the general direction of the area where I saw the men on snowmobiles. Occasionally I stop to make note of landmarks and listen for the whine of engines, but the only sound is the whisper of wind through the trees and my boots squeaking against the snow.

It takes me ten minutes to reach my destination. The tracks are long gone—covered by new snow—but I recognize the area. I decide to hunker down for a while and see what happens.

Glancing around for cover, I spy a copse of trees twenty yards to my right. In the darkness, the thicket at the base looks like a tangle of black, fragile bones. The last thing I want to do is spend the next hour sitting in snow; I'm not exactly dressed for extreme weather. But it's the best seat in the house, so I cross to the trees, break through the brush, and use my boots to tamp down the scrub. When I've made enough room, I kneel. I can just see over the top of the brush in a 360 degree circle. Not perfect, but it'll do.

It doesn't take long for me to realize it's going to be a long hour. My face and hands and feet are already cold. The physical exertion of the walk kept me warm earlier. Now, motionless and with the wind bearing down, I'm getting seriously cold. Within twenty minutes, I'm shivering. I'm thinking about calling it a night, wishing I'd thought to buy chemical hand warmers, when the whine of an engine interrupts.

I get to my knees and peer over the top of the brush. No one in sight, but the sound is growing louder. Definitely from a snowmobile, possibly two, and coming toward me. A minute later, I spot the flicker of headlights. The first machine emerges from the trees and glides to a stop twenty yards from where I sit. Male driver. No passenger. Same green and white helmet as one of the men I saw two nights ago.

A second snow machine pulls up beside the first. Male driver. No passenger. I recognize the snowmobile. Blue and white Polaris. What the hell are they up to?

The men dismount and remove their helmets. Next comes the ski masks. I recognize them instantly. Jacob Yoder and Jonas Smucker. Casually, they lean against their snowmobiles as if setting in for a wait. Yoder reaches into the pocket of his snowsuit, pulls out a pack of cigarettes and lights up. He passes it to Smucker, who does the same. When they're both smoking, Yoder presents a flask and takes a long pull. For several minutes, the two men pass the flask back and forth. They're talking and laughing, but I'm too far away to discern what they're saying.

I'm wondering how all this relates to the note, pondering who might've left it and why, when I hear the approach of yet another snowmobile. Through the scrub, I see the machine materialize from the woods to the east. Male driver. No passenger. I'm trying to make out the type of machine, searching for a license plate, when the headlights play over me. For an instant, I'm blinded. Ducking, I crouch more deeply into the brush.

The headlight flicks off and the man shuts down the engine. Removing his helmet, he sets it on the seat, peels off his ski mask. I don't recognize him. White male. Mid-twenties. Dark hair. Medium build.

Even from this distance I can see he doesn't have the "bowl" haircut representative of so many Amish men. This guy doesn't get his hair cut at home. He's English. Interesting.

The three men converge. The newcomer looks agitated, gesturing animatedly and looking around. Yoder and Smucker don't look happy. Voices are raised. Shouting, Yoder shoves the newcomer. The other man reels backward. For a moment I think they're going to fight. Then the third man stalks to his snowmobile, yanks the ski mask over his head, and puts on his helmet. He mounts the snow machine. The engine fires. Shouting something at Smucker and Yoder, he peels out, showering them with snow, and then disappears into the woods in the same direction from which he came.

"Fuck you!" Yoder kicks snow in his direction. "Stupid pussy!"

Rushing now, the men don their masks and helmets and speed away in the opposite direction, toward Schrock's farm.

I hold my position until the sound of the engines fade completely. Finally, shivering and stiff, I rise and leave the copse of trees. I cross to the place where the men congregated. There's nothing there except the track marks and a couple of cigarette butts.

What did I just witness? Three friends out for a midnight snowmobile ride? Did they simply get into an argument over something inconsequential? If that's the case, why did someone leave me a note? Is there more to it? More to come? Ever present in the back of my mind is the fact that Rachel Esh's body was found less than a quarter mile away.

Pulling the phone from my pocket, I hit the speed dial for Suggs.

He answers on the first ring. "You okay?"

"I'm in the woods a quarter mile north of my trailer." I tell him about Yoder and Smucker, the third man, and the argument between them. "I couldn't get the plate number. Dan, I think Smucker and

Yoder are headed toward Schrock's place. There's something going on and I think it's happening tonight. A quick look-see and I'm out of there. If things get dicey, I'll back off."

"Hmmm." He's not convinced, but doesn't call me on it. "I got a deputy parked out on that two track so if you get into any shit, he's just a few minutes away."

"I appreciate it."

"Be careful, and if the cold becomes a problem, let me know and we'll pick you up."

"Roger that."

Tucking the cell into my pocket, I check the time—one A.M.—and start off at a jog. Light snow is still falling, but the cloud cover has thinned. Misty moonlight silvers the tree branches and makes the track shoe marks visible and easy to follow. Within minutes, the physical exertion warms my core, staving off the shivers and helping to ease the ache in my hands and feet. I jog until I'm out of breath and slow to a brisk walk.

Around me the trees thicken. The snowfall tapers off, and when the moonlight beams down, the world transforms into an ethereal place of scampering shadows and snow that sparkles like diamond sand. I'm fifteen minutes into my hike when I hear music. I stop and listen for the source or the sound of a snowmobile engine, but there's no one there. I walk another two hundred yards before I see the flicker of light coming through the trees. I slow down, wary now, doing my best to not make any noise.

I visualize the aerial map; I'm on Schrock land now. His house is a mile or so southwest of where I stand. Highway 30 is due west. The Trout River State Forest lies to the north. Beyond is the Canadian border.

So where the hell is the music coming from?

I continue on another fifty yards. To my right the land slopes steeply. If my sense of direction is correct and memory serves me, I think the Little Trout River lies to the northeast. I pick my way around a rocky outcropping and duck beneath low branches. The music is louder now. An old Led Zeppelin song I haven't heard for years. The haunting pulse of Jimmy Page's guitar echoes off a thousand trees. Ahead, light beckons. There's some kind of structure a hundred yards away. I wonder if I've walked up on one of Schrock's late-night parties.

As I draw closer, I realize it's an old barn. Paint long since gone. Tin roof with several sheets peeling and curled. A fire blazes in a stone fire pit, light flickering against a concrete silo that leans at a precarious angle. Another building has already collapsed to a heap—the source of the firewood no doubt. Beyond is a tumbling frame house that's long since been abandoned. Part of the roof has caved in, the remainder a swayback patchwork of splintered planks and tin shingles. The lone window stares at me like a black eye socket.

Two snowmobiles are parked outside the barn, but no one's in sight. I'm too far away to see footprints, but golden light spills out through the big sliding door, telling me someone's inside.

I recall seeing the roof of the old barn when I looked at the aerial maps. It's part of the original homestead and is probably close to a hundred years old. Suggs had seemed confident none of the old outbuildings were in use. Evidently, he hadn't looked closely enough.

So what the hell are two Amish guys doing out here on Schrock's land at one o'clock in the morning? The first answer that enters my head is drugs. Are they using the barn to manufacture meth? Store marijuana? Either scenario would explain the late night snowmobile traffic. Perhaps even the presence of the two women I saw them with. But why did someone leave me that note? I can't help but wonder if maybe Rachel Esh stumbled upon this place, same as me, and saw something she shouldn't have. . . .

It's too cold for me to stick around much longer. The last thing I need is frostbitten fingers or toes. But I want to know what's inside the barn. If I swing south and make my way through the trees, I'll have a semi-decent view of the interior through the door.

I veer left, away from the tracks I'd been following, and, using the trees as cover, I make my way closer. I've only gone a few yards when the drone of an engine sounds behind me. Instinctively, I drop to my knees. Light flickers off the trees around me. I glance over my shoulder and see a single headlight glinting through the trees just ten yards away. Hunkering down, I crawl to a rock the size of a shopping cart and peer around it.

The snowmobile zooms past, so close I can smell the exhaust fumes. It's the same snowmobile I saw earlier. Only this time the driver has a passenger. I get to my knees and watch as he parks next to the other machines.

The passenger is female. I almost can't believe my eyes when I notice her dress. She's bundled up in a man's coat, but it doesn't quite cover her skirt and boots. She's Amish. What the hell is she doing out here with these men? The man slides off the machine, unfastens the strap of his helmet, and hurls it twenty feet. Bending to his passenger, he shouts something I can't hear. Using both hands he shoves her off the seat.

The woman lands on her back, but quickly jumps to her feet. The man approaches her, yelling. She unfastens her helmet and swings it at him. He deflects the blow, yanks it from her grasp and flings it to the ground.

Movement at the barn door draws my attention. I glance over to see Yoder and Smucker emerge. Still wearing their snowsuits. No ski masks. The music blares. Even forty yards away, I can hear every note of Lynryd Skynyrd's "Freebird."

The two Amish men approach the newcomer. Friendlier now. A happy reunion. They talk for a few minutes, laughing and gesturing. Yoder pulls out the flask and presents it to the third man. He tips his head back and takes a long pull. The woman leans against the snowmobile a few yards away, arms crossed, watching them.

After a few minutes, the newcomer approaches her and offers the flask. The woman turns away. Laughter erupts from Smucker and Yoder. The third man stalks to the passenger, grasps her *kapp* at her nape and yanks her head back. The woman shoves him. The man stumbles back, but he doesn't let go of her. Holding her head between his hands, he swings her around, takes her to the ground and climbs on top of her. The woman fights him, slapping at his face with both hands, but her efforts are ineffective. Pinning her arms with his knees, he presses his palm against her forehead, upends the flask, and pours into her mouth.

Disgust rises inside me, followed by a dark tide of dread because I know this isn't going to end well. I'm going to have to intervene, which means I'm not going to be able to maintain my cover.

Is this is what someone wanted me to see?

A few feet away, Yoder circles the people on the ground like some referee, pointing and laughing every time the woman takes a shot at her attacker. Smucker stands near the fire pit, watching.

Pack mentality, I think. It's not the first time I've seen it, especially when it comes to young males and bad behavior. They egg each other on, emboldened by their peers, each taking it one step further.

I have no idea if the woman is here of her own accord or if she was brought against her will. Whatever the case, she's being assaulted and the situation is getting ugly. I'm well aware that scenarios like this aren't always as they appear. It never ceases to amaze me the kinds of behavior some women tolerate. How many times have I taken a domestic dispute call only to have the victim defend her abuser and somehow the police become the villains?

The man rises, looks over his shoulder at Smucker, and shouts. Still on the ground, the woman rolls away, scrambles to her feet, and runs. Yoder and the third man go after her. A dozen strides and Yoder tackles her to the ground. The other man falls to his knees beside them. Her scream raises the hair on my arms. The man draws back and punches her in the abdomen.

Never taking my eyes from them, I work pull out my phone and hit the speed dial for Suggs. Simultaneously, I jam my hand beneath my skirt, yank the .22 from its holster.

The sheriff answers with a gruff, "Yeah."

"I'm on Schrock's property," I whisper. "The old barn a mile northwest of my trailer. Yoder and Smucker and a third unidentified male are assaulting a woman. I need backup."

"I'll get that deputy over there now. I'm heading out there, too. How far are you from the Schrock house?"

"Not sure. A mile maybe."

"Give me ten minutes."

The woman doesn't have ten minutes. I watch as Smucker and the unidentified male drag her through the snow and into the barn. "Expedite," I tell him. "Dan, I'm going to have to intervene—"

"Do what you gotta do. Be careful. I'll be there as soon as I can."

I drop the phone into my pocket, pull back the hammer on the .22. I hold my position until all of them have gone inside. Every sense on high alert, I leave the cover of the trees and approach the barn. I listen for voices, but the only thing I can hear is the music.

I reach the barn, sidle to the open door, and peer inside. The interior is large and well lit. A hard-packed dirt floor leads to a raised wooden floor at the rear. At its base, an aisle tees left and right. Wood steps lead to the loft. There's no one in sight.

A few feet away from me, a horse-drawn disc harrow is shoved against the wall. I strain to hear anything that will tell me their location, but the music drowns out all other sound.

This is no ordinary barn. There are no farm animals. No feedbags or hay. It's Amish owned and yet there's electricity. It's heated. The interior is clean and well used—no dust or cobwebs. The windows are intact—not a single broken pane. What *is* this place, and what's it being used for?

Stepping inside, I walk toward the back and reach the place where the aisle tees left and right. I pause to listen, frustrated because I can't hear shit. The aisle to my left is dark. I can just make out the fronts of old horse stalls. The aisle to my right is dimly lit. I see an open door and, beyond, three additional doors, all of which are closed. Shiny new padlocks hang from old-fashioned hinge hasps. All locks are engaged. At the end of the hall, a fifth door stands ajar. Bright light slants into the aisle. For the first time I hear voices and laughter over the music.

Moving quickly, I dash to the first door. It's actually a narrow stairway that leads to an upper floor. I go to the second door and peer through the small diamond-shaped window. I see a cot. A water bottle atop a small table. A toilet and sink. Clothes scattered on the wood plank floor. It looks like a jail cell . . .

I go to the next window and the next. The three rooms are set up identically and similarly appointed. Who's staying here and why are the doors locked from the *outside*? The possibilities send a chill up my spine.

Making sure the aisle is clear, I back away, never taking my eyes from the door at the end, expecting at any moment for someone to come through. All I have to do is get out and stay out of sight until Suggs's deputy arrives. He should be here any time now. I take another step back. Too late, I spot the woman standing in the open doorway to my right. Adrenaline burns through my midsection. She's looking at me as if I'm some dangerous animal that's wandered in, looking for meat.

In an instant, I take in her appearance. My height. Twenty years old. Dark hair. Dark eyes. Pale skin. Pretty. The thing that stands out most is the overt terror on her face.

I press my index finger to my lips. "I'm here to help you," I whisper.

For an instant I think I've blown it; she's doesn't know English and she's going to scream. I'll be found out and all hell will break loose. Instead, she glances toward the room where the men are, then motions to the stairway behind her.

"Come with me."

CHAPTER 22

I follow the woman up the stairs. At the top we go through a door and into a good-size room that had once been a hayloft. A small table and two chairs are set against the wall to my right. I see a bed in the corner. A large-screen TV. A space heater. A set of drawers. Farther, another door where I can just make out the white porcelain of a sink.

There's no lock on the door. "Are we safe here?" I ask.

She shakes her head. "The men will come soon," she replies, not getting too close, watching me cautiously.

"I need to lock the door. Keep them out. How do you lock it?"

"I'm not allowed."

Edgy with adrenaline, I stride to the table, pull out the chair, and wedge it beneath the doorknob. If someone tries to get in, it won't keep them out. But it will buy me some time.

"What's your name?" I ask.

"Alina," she tells me. "Marchenko."

I indicate the room and all of its contents. "What is this place?" I ask. "What's going on here?"

"They brought me here. This is where I live." She looks me up and down, taking in my Amish dress. "You are new?"

I have no idea what means by that. I go to the door and listen. No one there. Yet.

She follows me. "You are police?"

"No." I try to tone down some of the intensity in my voice. It's not easy because I'm scared. I know it's only a matter of time before someone comes up those steps.

The woman stares at the .22 in my hand. It's scaring her, I realize; she looks like she's about to bolt, so I lift my skirt and holster it. "I'm not going to hurt you," I tell her. "Do you understand?"

She nods.

"I need you to tell me what's going on here." I motion toward the door. "We don't have much time."

She nods. "This is where they keep us when we first come in from Canada."

I can tell from her accent this woman isn't Canadian. "Where are you from?"

"Odessa."

"Odessa?"

"Ukraine. I'm . . . looking for a job. To start a new life. I have visa." But her eyes flick down and to the right. She's lying. At the moment, it doesn't matter.

"Are you being held here against your will?" I ask.

"No, I just have to . . . you know, pay before I can go." She shrugs. "If they find husband for me, that would be good because then he pay."

"Who brought you here?"

"Ivan."

"What's his last name?"

"All I know is that he's American and promised us he would take care of our papers. I meet him in Donetsk last year when the tanks rolled through. Everyone was afraid and he was promising some of the women new lives in Canada and the U.S. Wealthy husbands. Jobs. We got on the marriage list. A few weeks later they put me on the boat. Gave me the papers. Sofiya was supposed to be on the next boat, but she never came."

I stare at her, trying to get my head around this new direction in the case. Her story raises more questions than it answers. I don't know what to make of it; I'm not even sure I believe her. But if she's telling the truth—if women are being smuggled into the U.S. from eastern Europe and "married off" for money—the situation is more explosive than anyone imagined.

"How long have you been here?" I ask.

She lifts a shoulder, lets it drop. "Six weeks."

"How many of you are here?"

"Five at first. But then two left." She shrugs. "Husbands or jobs. I don't know."

"They were staying in the rooms downstairs?" I ask.

"I think they're waiting for their papers."

"Who else is involved? What are their names?"

"Jacob and Jonas." She looks down at her hands. "They come here, to my room sometimes."

"Who else?"

"The elder. I don't know his name, but we call him *Dido*." Her mouth twists into a parody of a smile. "It means grandfather in Ukrainian."

I wonder if she's talking about Eli Schrock. She's young enough to think of him as an elder. . . .

Turning away, I pull out my cell and call Suggs. I'm at the door, listening for footsteps when he picks up.

"Eli Schrock, Jacob Yoder, and Jonas Smucker are smuggling people into the U.S. and Canada," I say without preamble.

264

"*What*? Smuggling? Are you—"

"I'm at the old barn a mile or so from Schrock's place. The deputy isn't here yet. Dan, you need to get out here. I need help."

"I'm at Schrock's house now. No one's answering the door. You okay?"

"For now." I'm vaguely aware of the woman trying to get my attention. I hold up a finger, letting her know I need to finish my call. "Yoder and Smucker and another unidentified male are downstairs. I don't know if they're armed. If they find me here . . . I'm outnumbered."

"Shit. Look, just . . . hang tight. Stay out of sight. Keep yourself safe. I'll get someone over there pronto."

"Roger that."

I drop the phone into my coat pocket. When I turn back to the woman she raises her hands and backs away. "*Nemaye politsiyi. Nemaye politsiyi!*"

"Calm down and be quiet." I snap the words as I go to the door, press my ear against it and listen for footsteps.

She follows me to the door. "The police are bad. They already know about us."

"The police aren't bad here—"

"Yes! He comes here, to my room, all the time!"

I turn to her, a chill scraping up my spine. "What? Which police?"

"The big man with red hair. He knows," she whispers. "He looks the other way."

Sheriff Dan Suggs is a large man with red hair. My intellect, my sense of loyalty, rejects the idea. Dan Suggs has been the consummate professional; he's been helpful and accommodating, even protective. I don't know how reliable this woman is; I don't know if she's victim or perpetrator or somewhere in between.

"He comes to my room," she hisses. "He tells me safe passage isn't free. That I have to pay. Believe me, he makes me pay."

I stare at her, my heart pounding. Doubt is a punch between the eyes. Is it possible Suggs is involved? But if that's the case, why in the name of God would he let the investigation go so far?

Using my cell, I go to the Franklin County Sheriff's department website and pull up a photo of Sheriff Dan Suggs. "Is this him?"

She narrows her eyes, nods. "That's him."

If she's telling the truth, backup isn't coming. There is no deputy parked nearby. I'm on my own. If the men downstairs don't already know I'm here, they will soon . . .

I hit the speed dial for Betancourt. He growls his last name. Sleeping. I don't bother identifying myself. "I need backup. I'm at Schrock's place. I need the state police. Expedite."

"What's going on? Where's Suggs? Burkholder, he can get a deputy out there faster than—"

"Suggs is involved," I say. "Whatever's going on here in Roaring Springs, he's part of it."

"*What?*" he says crossly. "What the hell are you talking about?"

"Eli Schrock, Jonas Smucker, and Jacob Yoder are smuggling people through Canada into the U.S."

"*Human smuggling*? For God's sake, how do you know that? When did this come about?"

"Just now. I have a witness."

The woman is standing a few feet away, her hand over her mouth, her eyes wide. I lower my voice. "She identified Suggs. There are people being held here, locked in rooms. Get someone out here now."

"All right. I'm on it. You're at Schrock's place?"

"An old barn a mile north of the house. Hurry."

He curses exorbitantly. "Where's Suggs?"

"I don't know. But he knows I'm here."

"I'll get him on the horn. Stay away from him until we get this straightened out."

I start to respond but he hangs up.

Dropping my phone in my pocket, I look around for some way to secure the door. "Do you have any nails? Tools? Something we can use to jam the door?"

She rushes to the table beside her bed and comes back with a small package of half-inch brads, offers it to me.

"Too small." I cross to the bed. It's a full size. Heavy, but not so much that we can't shove it against the door. It won't keep anyone out, but it'll slow them down.

"Help me move it," I say to the woman.

We're sliding the bed across the floor when a woman's scream rends the air.

We stop and look at each other. "Who is that?" I ask.

"They brought her yesterday. The plain girl. They always . . . you know. The new ones."

I go to the door, press my ear against it, listen. No sound of anyone approaching. No voices. I crack open the door and peer out. The stairwell is empty. I hear voices downstairs. Male laughter. The unknown female crying.

I turn my attention to the woman. "He's assaulting her?"

She nods. "They won't hurt her. She's money to them."

Another scream sounds. A hysterical outpouring of outrage, a visceral sound of pain. Her cries are met with ridicule.

It would be foolhardy for me to intervene. I'm outnumbered three to one—four to one if I include Suggs in the equation. I don't know if the men are armed. I have no idea where Suggs is or how long it will be before real backup arrives. All of that said, there's no way in hell I can do nothing while a vicious crime takes place scant feet away.

I turn to Alina. "I want you to drag the bed over here and shove it against the door. Do you understand?"

She looks alarmed. "You can't go down there. They'll—"

"No, they won't." I step onto the landing, then look back at the woman. "Don't let anyone in. The good police are on the way."

Lifting my skirt, I unholster the .22 and start down the stairs. I wish for my .38. Not only does it have six shots, as opposed to five, it's got a lot more stopping power.

At the base of the stairs, I peer around the corner into the main area. The barn door stands open, undisturbed. No movement. The same as I left it. I can hear the woman wailing over the blare of the music. One of the men is taunting her. I know better than to let that get inside my head or let my emotions get involved. But I know what that kind of violence does to a person, and I make an effort to dial it back.

I step into the hall and go right. Straight ahead, the door is still ajar. Pressing my back to the wall, I edge toward it, ducking at each window I pass in case someone's locked inside and they start making noise. I reach the door. Using my fingers, I push it open a few inches and look inside.

Straight ahead I see a folding table. Playing cards, a bag of chips, and several beer bottles sit on top. A flat-screen TV is mounted on the wall to my right. A pornographic movie plays on the screen in vivid color. Music blares from a sleek sound system stacked on a shelf unit. A newish sofa, end table, and lamp. Clothes strewn on the floor. There are no weapons in sight.

I look left. I see a man on a bed. His back is bare, his lower half covered by a blanket. I can only see the side of his face. Black hair. Scruffy beard. The woman lies motionless beneath him. Bloodied lip. Misery on her face.

A door near the bed swings open. I slink back, but not before I see Jacob Yoder emerge from what looks like a bathroom. No need for me to be worried he'll see me; his attention is riveted on the man and woman in the bed. He's wearing trousers, unfastened and unzipped. No shirt. Wiry arms. Skinny white chest. His face is flushed.

There's no sign of Smucker. I take a step back, trying to figure out how best to handle this when I hear a minute sound behind me. I spin to see Smucker coming down the aisle. His eyes meet mine and go wide. His mouth opens. For an instant, time stands still.

His gaze flicks to the pistol at my side. "What the fuck?"

I bring up the .22, aim center mass. "I'm a cop," I hiss. "Get your fucking hands up. Face the wall. Now." I say all of it quietly enough so the other two men can't hear.

I don't see a weapon, but that doesn't mean he's not armed. It sure as hell doesn't mean he's not dangerous. I don't like the close quarters of the hall. I'm ever aware that two more men are scant feet away on the other side of the door.

"Cop?" But he raises his hands. "Shit. Okay. Whatever you say."

"Put your hands against the wall. Your face, too. Do it now."

Watching me, moving slowly, he obeys. "What the hell is this?"

"Shut up." Keeping as much distance between us as possible, the .22 trained on his back, I sidle past him.

I walk backward toward the open area. Smucker watches me, his cheek pressed against the wall. I wonder if Betancourt got to Suggs, if the state police are en route. I sense movement behind me. I swing around, catch a glimpse of Suggs an instant before his fist slams into my face. Pain explodes in my nose. The force of the blow buckles my knees, sends me reeling backward. As I go down, I see intent in his eyes. The blue steel of a revolver in his hand and I think: *You fucked up, Burkholder.*

An instant before I hit the floor, something slams into my head from behind. Stars fly in my peripheral vision. I look up, see Smucker bending toward me, teeth clenched, arms reaching. I bring up the .22 and fire blind.

Smucker screams and staggers backward. Red blooms on his coat sleeve. He looks down at the tear, goose down sticking out, blood soaked. He grasps his arm with is uninjured hand. "You shot me, you bitch!"

"Get that fucking gun!" Suggs kicks my wrist, but I don't drop the .22.

The door bangs against the wall. I glance up to see Yoder rush out, a rifle in his hands. Eyes locked on me. Mouth twisted into a snarl. "What's going on?" he shouts.

I shift the pistol, fire at him. My shot goes wide, takes a chunk of wood out of the door. Suggs comes down on top of me like a truck-load of bricks. The crushing force of his weight smacks the breath from my lungs. Grasping my wrist, he slams my hand against the floor. Pain zings up my arm. I lose my grip on the .22. It skitters across the floor and strikes the wall.

I'm thrashing, trying to wriggle out from beneath Suggs when Smucker draws back and drives a steel-toed boot into my ribs. White-hot pain streaks across my rib cage and lights up my spine. An undignified sound rips from my throat. I throw a single ineffective punch. A second kick lands in my temple. My head is knocked violently sideways. Stars scatter and my vision dims. For several seconds, I lay there, dazed and gasping. I'm aware of Suggs rising. The men speaking words my brain can't quite process.

I see Jacob Yoder looking down at me, his eyes alight with satisfaction, and then the world fades to black.

CHAPTER 23

I open my eyes to bright light. I'm lying on my back. The kiss of snow-flakes against my face. I'm aware of snow beneath me. Cold all around. My head pounding with every rapid-fire beat of my heart. Knife-sharp pain on the left side of my rib cage.

I shift slightly, moaning as another layer of pain wraps around my chest. A quick physical inventory tells me I have broken ribs. My hands are bound in front of me. I roll onto my side and glance down to see they tied me using my scarf. The memory of how I arrived at this unfortunate situation floods my brain following quickly by the realization that I'm in serious trouble.

Raising my head, I look around. I'm on the ground outside the barn's sliding door. Light rains down from a spotlight mounted above the door. I've no idea how I got here or how long I was unconscious. Dan Suggs stands over me in his khaki pants and sheriff's department parka, looking out over the woods, a flask in his hand.

"What the hell are you doing?" I ask, my voice thick and rough.

He looks down at me. "I'm sorry it came to this, Chief. I like you. I really do. You're a good cop. Too goddamn good, probably."

"Dan, come on. What are you *doing*? You're a cop, for God's sake. You don't have to take this any further."

"Already gone too far." He looks away and for a moment I think he's going to actually cry. "Jesus Christ, I'm in deep."

"It's not too late to stop this. I'll help you. Betancourt will, too."

"You know what the kicker is, Chief?" His laugh is a terrible sound, like the tearing of flesh. "It wasn't even about the money."

"Then what?"

"Oldest reason in the book. Any time I wanted it. Day or night. All I had to do was come here and climb on. It was like a drug and I was a junkie. Pathetic, huh?"

"Why did you let things go so far?" I ask. "I mean with the investigation? You knew how it would end."

"That fucking Betancourt called me at the last minute, after Walker had his heart attack. You were here in a matter of days." His laugh is an ugly, coarse sound. "If I'd gone to Schrock, he would have killed you. That would have been a clusterfuck." He lifts a meaty shoulder, lets it drop. "I never thought you'd get this far. Figured I could control you. Keep a tight rein." He frowns at me. "But you were like a dog with a bone. The harder I pushed to get you out of here, the harder you pushed back to stay.

"Hell, I knew it would end one day. Always figured if things blew up, I could put all of it on Schrock. Or put a bullet in him. I got a lot of shit on him." He swigs from the flask. "You beat me."

Lifting my head, I look around. Beyond the aura of light, it's still dark. The three snowmobiles are parked in the same spot, twenty feet away. I look around for my cell, but it's nowhere in sight. No sign of the .22. Where the hell are the state police Betancourt promised to send?

"Look, Kate, I'm fucking sorry, but this isn't going to end well for you." He sighs. "I don't think it's going to end well for either of us."

I work the fabric at my wrists, but it's wrapped tightly around both wrists, run between them, and knotted. "What are you going to do?"

"The boys are going to take you across the border to a lake, cut a hole in the ice, and . . ." He shakes his head and lifts the flask. "I'm sorry."

He kneels, grunting as if it's painful. Setting his hand against the back of my head, he helps me to a sitting position and brings the flask to my lips. "Here you go."

I sip, buying time. The taste of the whiskey makes me shudder.

His eyes are red-rimmed and bloodshot. His nose is running, snot shiny on his upper lip. He doesn't seem to notice. "It'll make all this a little easier for you."

"I appreciate that."

My voice is calm, but fear is a beast rampaging inside me, pacing and clawing and tearing me up from the inside out. Where are the state police? Why aren't they here yet? Did Betancourt realize the situation was urgent?

"Frank Betancourt knows," I say after a moment. "About you."

He looks down at me, studying me intently. "You're lying."

"He knows you're part of it. I told him. Dan, it's over. Give it up while you still can."

Smucker and Yoder emerge from the barn. There's blood on Smucker's coat where I shot him. I look at it, meet his gaze, and force a smile. He starts toward me, cursing, but Suggs stops him. "Go get the other woman. Tie her up. Bring her down."

"Alina?" Yoder casts him a mutinous look.

"She ran her mouth to a cop, idiot." Suggs gestures at me. "She saw this one's face. You gotta get rid of her, too."

Neither man looks happy about it, but they go back inside.

Suggs sighs and looks down at me. He offers the flask, but I shake my head. He takes another long pull.

"Tell me one thing," I say.

"Guess I owe you that much."

"What happened to Rachel Esh?" I ask.

He looks away, wipes his mouth with his hand. "Damn stupid kid. She knew too much. Tried to run."

"She didn't die out in the snowstorm all by herself, did she?"

"No, she didn't."

"Who?"

His eyes fill with tears. Plucking off a glove, he rubs them hard with his fingers. "Goddamn this is a mess."

"What happened to her?"

Sniffing a runny nose, he turns his head and spits in the snow. "Let's go inside." He takes my arm and hauls me to my feet. "Come on. Up and at 'em."

For an instant my head spins, but I shake it off. Something heavy in my coat pocket, brushing against my hip. *The pepper spray.* I can't believe they didn't find it. I feel Suggs's eyes on me and I pray he can't read my thoughts. *Keep him talking.* I say the first thing that comes to mind. "How did she die?"

A quiver runs through him. He stops our forward progression and looks at me, his expression angry, as if I've overstepped some invisible line of decorum. "I figure that's the last thing I want to talk about." He nudges me toward the barn door. "Move."

I do as I'm told. "I'm scared."

"Nothing I can do about that now."

We go through the door. His right hand grips my left bicep. He's so close I can hear his breathing. I feign a stumble and twist right. Jamming both hands in my pocket, I yank out the pepper spray. He releases my arm, reaches for his pistol. I spin toward him. The revolver coming up. But he's not fast enough. I spray his face. High velocity, right in his eyes.

He tries to bat my hand away, but the burn kicks in. His hands fly to his eyes. An animalistic roar tears from his throat. His knees hit the ground. Coughs rack his body. I spray again, get the side of his face. Sputtering, he swings at me, but I dance back and he misses. I look around for his weapon. It's on the ground. Too close to him for me to reach. I need my hands free first.

I dart right to the disking implement, drop to my knees, and use the rim of the plowshare to saw at the fabric binding my wrists. The pain in my ribs screams with every movement, but I don't stop. I don't slow down. I scour at a frantic pace. Back and forth. Back and forth. My breaths rushing in and out as the pain hacks like an ax against my ribs.

Comeon. Comeon. Comeon. The words are a scream inside my head.

Four feet away, Suggs coughs and spits, digging into his eyes with his fingers. I'm about to give up on the binds and make a run for it when the fabric gives way. Hands free, I rise and start toward Suggs and his .38.

He turns devil-red eyes on me. Nose and eyes streaming. Tears and snot dripping off his chin. "You fucking—"

I hit him with the spray again.

Spinning, I sprint through the door and into the night.

I run to the snowmobiles, checking for keys as I pass. Nothing there. Damn. Damn. *Damn.* Pouring on the speed, I lope toward the cover of the trees and the path that brought me here, think better of it, and swerve right. I'm running full out when I enter the woods. There's just enough moonlight for me to make out the trunks as I whiz past. I try to keep an eye on the ground, watch for fallen logs, rocks or holes or anything else that might send me tumbling. But all I see is a blur of white.

Behind me, I hear shouting. Suggs. The rev of a snowmobile engine. Yoder and Smucker are coming after me.

I'm in no shape to run. The pain in my side is intense and growing worse as my breathing begins to labor. I'm in good physical condition, but I won't be able to keep this up for long. My only hope is that the rough terrain and dense trees will slow them down. Had I stayed on the path, they'd already be on top of me.

The land slopes abruptly. My feet tangle and I nearly go down, but manage to maintain my balance. I slow my pace, ignore the pain, keep moving. I'm running parallel with the path I used to get here. The same path the snowmobilers use. If I stay on course, I should be able to find my way back to the trailer, my cell—and my .38.

A second snowmobile engine fires. Fainter now because I've descended a hill and put some distance between us. I barrel down an incline, skidding over rocks slick with snow, nearly falling a second time. There's a stream at the base of the hill, frozen and snow covered except where the water runs fast. Slowing, I glance both ways, looking for the best place to cross. I dash right, round a boulder and step onto the ice. Three strides and I'm across. The opposite bank is steep, so I use my hands and climb.

Headlights glint off the trees in front of me. I glance back to see one of the machines approaching fast. *Too close.* Panic flares hot in my chest. I veer right, pick up speed. Every breath is an agony now. I'm not going to last.

The high-pitched rev of an engine sounds behind me. I look over my shoulder, see the second snowmobile nose down in the creek. The driver misjudged and tried to cross where the bank dropped off too steeply.

The second machine is still in business, less than thirty yards away, weaving between trees, gaining fast. I slide on a fallen branch covered with snow, go to my knees. I scramble to my feet, crash through heavy brush, barely avoiding a low-slung branch. I duck left, pain screaming in my side.

At the crest of the hill I slow, look around to get my bearings. I'm a scant half mile from the trailer. I run at a reckless speed, downhill now. Branches grab at my coat and scratch at my face like claws. I push through the boughs of a massive spruce. Round an outcropping of rock. I'm ever aware of the rise and fall of the engine as the driver makes his way over and around obstacles. Headlights glint on the trees ahead of me, moving up and down as he flies over bumpy terrain.

Arms flailing, I fly over a fallen log and then I'm at the bottom of the hill. A path of sorts runs left and right. The trailer is straight ahead, so I cross the path, back into the trees, go down a short incline. That's when I realize I've reached a lake, snow covered and blending into the land. I've walked here, I realize. Straight across the lake is the shortest distance to my trailer. I'm debating whether to go around or cross the ice when the snowmobile bursts from the trees a few yards away.

I start across the lake at run, the snow giving me some traction on the ice. Hovering in the back of my mind is the thought that if my pursuer is armed, I'm a sitting duck. I have zero cover and nowhere to hide. My only hope is that the machine is too heavy to venture onto the ice.

A quick glance over my shoulder. A small thrill goes through me when I see the machine stopped at the bank. The driver stands on the ice, watching me. I wonder why he's not coming after me. The thought flits though my brain, leaving a streak of uneasiness in its wake.

I've nearly reached the opposite shore when the ice groans beneath my feet. A chill runs through my body. I spent many a day on the ice when I was a kid; I know what that sound means. The ice is unstable, too thin to sustain my weight, or else there's a pressure ridge.

I slow, sliding my feet across the surface to more evenly distribute my weight and lessen the force of impact. I keep my eyes on the surface, looking for water coming up over the snow. Even with the moonlight, it's difficult to see.

"It's gonna break!" comes Yoder's voice from behind me.

I don't stop.

"I'm not going to fish you out!" he calls to me, his voice amicable. "Come on back here and we'll forget about all this."

I continue toward the bank, cautiously, sliding one foot in front of the other. The opposite shore is twenty yards away. Almost there. I glance behind me. I can just make out the hulking form of the snow-mobile, but the driver is nowhere in sight.

Where the hell did he go?

The back of my neck prickles. I focus on the shore, moving faster now, like a speed skater, covering the distance as quickly as possible. I'm nearly there when water sloshes over my boot. I slide my other foot forward. The sole of my boot bumps over a large ridge in the ice.

A loud *creak!* echoes across the surface. I know I'm going into the water an instant before the ice breaks open beneath me. A giant mouth swallowing me whole. I spread my arms to break the fall, but the momentum sucks me down, forcing my arms over my head. My coat rides up, trapping my arms.

The cold shocks my brain, paralyzes my body. My lungs contract. I gasp and inhale water. Chest too tight to cough. The world goes silent and black. Water in my mouth. In my eyes. My ears. Panic descends.

I struggle mindlessly against the tangle of my coat. My fist strikes ice and for a terrible moment I think I've been swept under. I kick my feet. My boots hinder me but I don't stop. Somehow my coat rights itself. An instant later my face breaks the surface.

I spew water, coughing and retching. The cold burns my skin like fire. My face dips below the surface again. I tamp down panic, kick harder. My face scrapes ice and emerges. Reaching out, I grasp the edge of the ice. It breaks off in my hands. I make another wild grab. It holds this time and I cling to it.

It takes precious seconds for my brain to kick in. I try to remember my cold-water rescue training. I roll onto my back. Night sky overhead. Clouds rushing past a hazy moon. I'm shivering so violently I can barely maintain my grip on the ice. I know my strength won't last long.

The opening through which I fell is about three feet in diameter. I raise my right leg, try to get my foot out of the water and onto the ice, but my boots are too heavy, filled with water. I can't reach down, so I use my foot to remove the other boot.

My strength is waning at an alarming rate. If I'm going to survive, I have to get out of the water. Turning, I locate my tracks, the last place where the ice was strong enough to support me. Sliding my arms across the surface of the ice, I kick my feet as fast and hard as I can. I'm hampered by my single remaining boot, but it can't be helped. Kicking, kicking, I claw at the ice. An animal trapped and fighting for its life. Slowly, my feet rise so that I'm belly down and nearly horizontal.

Then my chest is on the ice's surface. I reach out, hands scrabbling, sliding, fingers digging in. A flurry of kicks and I'm facedown on the ice, wet hair in my eyes. Violent shivers rack my body. I don't have the strength to get up. Even if I could, the risk of falling through a second time is too great. Instead, I do the only thing I can—roll.

A few feet from shore, I get to my hands and knees and crawl. Frozen cattails scratch my face, but my skin is numb. I don't stop until I'm on solid ground, where the bank slopes steeply up. I collapse, coughing and choking. I rest my head against the snow. My hands and legs are numb. Oddly, I'm no longer cold. My thoughts slog through a brain filled with cotton.

I think I hear the engine of a snowmobile. There's nothing I can do about it. I'm physically spent. I know if I close my eyes I'll tumble into a waiting darkness.

But the darkness scares me. I don't want to die here. I want to see Tomasetti again. I want to see my team of officers back in Painters Mill. Glock and Mona and Pickles. I want to sit at the table in my old farmhouse and listen to the rain pound the roof. I want to stand on the dock of the pond and look out over the water with the man I love.

Rolling onto my side, I push myself upright. I get my knees under me and crawl to the top of the bank. My hands are in the snow, but I don't feel the cold. Unsteadily, I get to my feet.

Swaying like a drunk, I put one foot in front of the other. One foot bare. The other sloshing in a boot. I'm so uncoordinated I go to my knees twice before reaching the woods. Once I enter the trees, my mind shuts down. I don't think about anything except putting one foot in front of the other. I'm a machine. Left foot. Right foot. Stay upright. Keep moving. I hear the snowmobile, but I feel no fear. The only thing that matters is one more step. Reaching the trailer. Survival.

By the time I emerge from the woods, I'm staggering. My hair and the hem of my dress are frozen. The whine of an engine sounds scant yards away. I see the glint of headlights against the trees. Choking back sobs, I make my way around the end of the trailer, stumble to the stairs, crawl up them using my hands. The snowmobile skids to a stop twenty feet away. The driver cuts the engine. Out of the corner of my eye, I see him dismount and start toward me.

"I got you now," he says. "Fucking ran me all over hell and back."

Yoder. Getting closer. Feet crunching through snow.

Somehow I get the key into the lock. Then I'm inside, slam the door behind me. I'm about to throw the lock when the door explodes open. A scream pours from my throat. I lurch across the living room, down the hall, into the bedroom. Footsteps thud against the floor.

"Come here, you bitch!" But he laughs.

I reach the bed, go to my knees, jam my hands beneath the mattress. I can barely feel the .38. I clutch it, spin, thrust it at Yoder's silhouette as he comes down the hall.

"Police officer. I got a gun." I try to shout the words, but they come out as puffs of air. "Stop. *Stop.*"

He doesn't stop.

I fire and miss. Cursing, he ducks sideways, keeps on coming. I have no grip. No aim. Little strength in my hand. I fire four more times. Yoder yelps and goes down three feet from where I'm huddled on the floor against the bed. He's facedown. Still moving, scrabbling toward me. Hands reaching. I fire the final round. He jolts and goes still.

Swiveling, I jam my hand beneath the mattress, yank my cell phone from its nest. I'm trying to dial Betancourt when pounding sounds at the front door. If it's Suggs or Smucker I'm done. I have nothing left.

Betancourt picks up with a harried, "Where are you?"

"My trailer," I pant. "I'm down. *Hurry.*"

He says something, but I don't hear. I drop the cell without disconnecting and pick up the .38 even though the cylinder is empty.

"New York State Police! Chief Burkholder!" comes a male voice. "Kate Burkholder! New York State Police! Are you there?"

The trailer rocks as someone comes inside.

The .38 clatters to the floor. I sag against the bed, put my face in my hands. It's not until I speak that I realize I'm crying. "I'm here," I say. "I'm here."

A man wearing a navy parka with the iconic flat-brimmed trooper hat stops at the end of the hall. I catch a glimpse of his sidearm in hand an instant before he blinds me with his flashlight.

"You Burkholder?" he asks.

"Yes."

Lowering his head slightly, he speaks into his shoulder mike. "I'm ten seventy-five Burkholder." He lets dispatch know he's made contact with me as he approaches. "Ten fifty-two," he adds, requesting an ambulance. "I got an officer down. I repeat, officer down."

CHAPTER 24

One of my most vivid memories of the police academy was the day the instructor brought in a retired vice detective who proceeded to tell us it's usually the easy cases that kill you. That case you swagger into with a shit-eating grin on your face because you think it's going to be a cakewalk. Those are the cases, he told us, where in the end you'll probably end up getting your ass handed to you.

We got a good laugh out of that. Some old dude with an eye patch and a limp. What did a dinosaur like him know about law enforcement today? Turned out he knew plenty because in addition to the eye patch and limp, he also had a dead partner. He'd worked undercover narcotics for seven years. He'd infiltrated a dangerous cartel and become one of them—until the day he was found out. The cartel had tortured him nearly to death with a cattle prod and roofing nails. He wasn't quite so cocky the day they airlifted him to the hospital with the assignment left unfinished.

I spent the night in the ER at Alice Hyde Medical Center in Malone, where I was treated for hypothermia and frostbite. When I arrived, my core body temperature was 94.3 degrees Fahrenheit. Over a period of six hours, it was raised back to normal by heated blankets, warm fluids, and an IV. An X-ray revealed I had sustained two cracked ribs. A CT scan showed no evidence of a concussion, but I had a headache and didn't argue when they gave me painkillers. By dawn, I'd had enough and asked to be checked out. They wanted to keep me for observation, but I'm no fan of hospitals. By the time Betancourt arrived with my street clothes, I was showered and ready to go.

I'd called Tomasetti from the ambulance. He took the news of the end of the assignment in stride and without a single I-told-you-so. The news of my impending trip to the hospital not so well. He didn't rant or overreact, which he's been known to do on occasion, at least when it comes to me. It was the quiet, creeping fear I discerned in his voice that scared me. That hurt me. I hated doing that to him.

"You don't have to drive all the way up here," I told him.

"I've always wanted to see Plattsburgh in January," he returned.

I laughed a little too hard.

Tomasetti must have heard something in my voice, because he asked, "Are you all right?"

"Aside from the hypothermia, a couple cracked ribs, and superficial frostbite, I'm fine." We both know that's not what he meant, but he lets it pass. Ground that can be covered later.

I was really thinking that I was fortunate to be alive and we were both lucky he wasn't driving up here to claim my body.

"Don't go anywhere," he told me. "I'll be there in a few hours."

It's one P.M. and I'm occupying a visitor chair in Frank Betancourt's office at the state police Troop B station in Plattsburgh, an hour's drive from Roaring Springs. Earlier, he sat with me in one of the interview rooms with a laptop and pumped me full of hot coffee while I completed a seven-page report relaying the events that transpired overnight in the woods and on Schrock's compound. It was a slow process, made worse by the bandage wrapped around my pinky and ring fingers to protect my frostbite-damaged skin. If Betancourt noticed my shaking hands, he didn't show it. But he hasn't let me out of his sight for more than a few minutes at a time.

Last night, the ER folks kept me pretty busy at the hospital. Hypothermia and frostbite are common in upstate New York this time of year. Hunters and other outdoor enthusiasts mostly. The male nurse who took care of me had a wicked sense of humor, which I appreciated. This afternoon, I'm mostly recovered physically. The painkillers make me loopy, but they help with the cracked ribs and lingering headache, so I keep them handy. I'm doing well psychologically. It's only when I'm alone that my mind drags me back to my wild run through the woods, the whine of the snowmobile engines, and the time I spent in the water, fighting for my life.

Betancourt pops back into his office a little too often, each time looking at me with shoddily concealed concern in his expression and some lame excuse for needing to talk to me.

"I'm still okay," I mutter, hoping I manage the frown I was going for.

"I didn't ask." He grins unconvincingly. "Just FYI, I've been instructed to stay with you."

I roll my eyes. "I should have figured he'd call you."

"So you two are . . ." He lets the sentence dangle.

"Yep."

He clears his throat. "We'll just pretend we didn't have this conversation."

I grin. "What conversation?"

He sobers as he slides into the chair at his desk. "I thought you should know, Chief. I just got word from the hospital. Dan Suggs is dead."

It's the first bit of new information I've received about the case since I've been here; Betancourt has kept me sequestered in his office since I arrived, obviously wanting to keep me focused on my statement. The news is a shock and I'm not exactly sure how to process it. "How?"

"I guess he knew how things were going to go down. Drove out to his favorite fishing lake. Put his thirty-eight in his mouth and pulled the trigger."

"I never suspected him." I don't mention the fact that I'd enjoyed working with him. I'd trusted him. I'd actually *liked* him.

"No one did. Dan had been a cop for going on thirty years. He was highly respected. Not a mark on his record. Happily married. Who would've thought he was involved in something like that?"

I recall our strange last moments together. The way Suggs had looked at me when he told me they were going to kill me. I'd seen regret in his eyes. But whatever regret he'd been feeling wasn't powerful enough to stop it. It hadn't been enough for him to spare my life. Dan Suggs might've been sucked into the operation for reasons understood fully only by him. But he was still a dirty cop.

"What about Schrock?" I ask.

"Taken into custody without incident."

"Yoder? Smucker?"

"Yoder's in the hospital. Critical, but he's going to make it." He grimaces. "We didn't get Smucker. We think he took the snow machine and crossed into Canada. We've alerted the border patrol and the local authorities up there. Chances are he'll seek medical attention for that gunshot wound. We'll get him."

I agree. Even a flesh wound is serious. Smucker's no criminal mastermind. With no one to tell him what to do, he won't last. That's not to say he isn't an extremely dangerous individual, an animal caught up in the flight or fight instinct. I know when law enforcement catches up with him, he'll go down hard.

"What about the other people out at the compound?" I'm not sure when we began referring to Schrock's farm as "the compound" but that's what it is now.

"We got the warrant shortly after you were brought in. State police and St. Lawrence deputies are out there now, searching the place. Chances are there will be more arrests; Schrock and Yoder and Smucker didn't do this by themselves." He sighs. "They found three females locked in that old barn. We've run into some language issues. We think some of the women are Ukrainian. We've got a translator on the way."

"They were smuggling people into the U.S. from Canada?"

"Smuggling and possibly trafficking. Some of these women were promised husbands. Evidently, Schrock and his pals made contact with men via the Internet. The men basically paid cash for these women, either to marry or prostitute them. We confiscated four laptops. Going to take a while to sift through all of it, but preliminarily, it looks like Schrock took in illegals and other vulnerable individuals, people down on their luck or homeless, and kept them at the compound. An unknown individual in Canada was sending people down to Schrock. Smucker and Yoder would smuggle them into the country using snowmobiles at night. Most were women, but we believe there may have been children involved, too."

"Somehow, it always makes it worse when kids are involved," I say.

"Whatever the case, multiple individuals were being held against their will. Most were subjected to physical abuse and sexual assault while they were here."

"What about the Amish kids living at the compound?" I ask.

"We've got social workers out there. I'm assuming most of them will be placed with foster parents until we can figure out what else was going on out there. Interviews are happening today and will probably continue the next couple of weeks."

288

I nod, wondering what they'll find. If the kids will talk. How much they know. If the parents will cooperate.

Betancourt studies me a moment. "What's your take on the Amish connection to all of this, Chief?"

"I think all this began with Schrock," I tell him. "He's a predator and a sociopath. His views are extreme. I'm guessing, but he was probably ousted from his former community because the leaders there realized what he is. He came to New York. Designated himself bishop. He used his charisma to bring people in. Amish who were disgruntled with their own church districts. He took in those who'd been excommunicated. The lost and unwanted. People looking for something. He controlled them through intimidation and violence." I shrug. "In essence he was running a cult. When someone displeased him, he punished them. Or did away with them."

"Suggs knew about the Esh girl?," Betancourt says with a good bit of anger.

"Interestingly, when I asked Suggs about her, all he would tell me is that she'd become a threat. I don't know how or why. He said she tried to run away." I shake my head, remembering Suggs's bizarre reaction. "I suspect they caught her and let her die in the cold."

"Any idea who?"

I shake my head. "Maybe Schrock will be able to shed some light."

"So far the son of a bitch isn't talking," he growls. "We're probably not going to get a handle on the scope of this thing for a while, Chief." Leaning back in his chair, he contemplates me. I can tell by his expression there's more and it's not good. "Call came in from Franklin County twenty minutes ago. They found some graves on that hill by the barn."

Something inside me sinks. "How many?"

He shrugs. "They're trying to get a forensic anthropologist out there now. I guess one of the deputies uncovered some bones. He started looking around and sure enough, he found more. He's pretty sure they're human. We'll get a better picture of things in the hours to come."

I think about Rebecca's family. Her missing son and daughter-in-law. Her missing grandchildren. Schrock is a murderous son of a bitch. So much pain. So many lives destroyed, and for what?

Tomasetti arrives forty-five minutes later. Betancourt rises to greet him and the two men shake hands. "Chief Burkholder and I were just finishing up the debriefing."

"Good timing on my part," Tomasetti says. He's trying to play it cool, but he hasn't taken his eyes off me since he entered the room. "I hear you guys broke the case wide open."

"It was bigger than any of us imagined." Betancourt grimaces. "Dan Suggs was involved. Shot and killed himself sometime last night."

"Sad for his family."

"Chief Burkholder had a few dicey moments. I was just thanking her for sticking with it and making the sacrifices she did. We appreciate it."

A brief silence ensues. Betancourt makes a big deal of looking at his watch. "I've got a meeting to get to." He raises his hand. "Take care, Agent Tomasetti."

We watch Betancourt go through the door and close it behind him. I'm still sitting in the visitor chair. Tomasetti is standing next to the desk. He looks at me and says, "Ten to one there's no meeting."

"He sort of figured things out. I mean, about us."

"Probably didn't help that I called him six times," he admits. "Asked him to keep an eye on you."

Then I'm out of the chair. Tomasetti steps toward me, raw emotion flashing on his face before he can tuck it away. I fall against him. His arms wrap around me and pull me close. I take in his scent and the feel of his body against mine, and I'm overwhelmed with the knowledge of how things could have turned out. I'm about to thank him for coming, let him know how happy I am to see him, but his mouth comes down on mine. The words leave my head and I forget about everything except kissing him back.

After a full minute, he eases me to arm's length and looks me over. "You're in pain."

It's not a question, so I nod and tell him about my cracked ribs.

He sighs. "You scared the hell out of me."

"I know. I'm sorry. I didn't mean to scare you."

"You never do."

He's looking at me closely, running his hands up and down my arms as if making sure I'm really there. That I'm not going to slip away. "You look shaken up."

"I guess I am."

"That's honest."

"My new policy, remember?"

"Betancourt told me what happened. Kate, for God's sake, you were nearly killed."

" 'Nearly' being the key word in that statement."

Growling low in his throat, he faces me more squarely, takes both of my hands in his and squeezes gently. "I don't want to be the guy getting a phone call in the middle of the night, telling me the person I love was killed in the line of duty."

"No one knew what was happening out at that compound. No one could have foreseen things turning out the way they did."

"That's the thing, Kate. No cop eats his bowl of Cheerios in the morning and then leaves the house expecting to get shot in the course of his first traffic stop. It just happens."

"Had you been in my shoes, you would have done the same thing."

He starts to argue the point, but I raise my hand and press two fingers against his lips. "*Shhh*. I'm here. I'm okay. It's over."

Taking my hand from his mouth, he turns it over in his and brushes his lips across my knuckles. "What am I going to do with you?"

"For starters, you can take me home."

CHAPTER 25

An hour later, Tomasetti and I are in my Explorer eastbound on State Route 11 traveling toward Roaring Springs. Unbeknownst to me, he'd rented a car in Wooster, made the nine-hour trip in seven, and returned the rental car in Plattsburgh, so we could drive my vehicle back to Painters Mill.

I'm thankful because I didn't get much sleep last night; I've been running on caffeine and adrenaline most of the day. Now that those two things are waning, I'm starting to relax. The case is over, I can leave Roaring Springs, and I'm ridiculously happy Tomasetti is here to drive me home.

I must have dozed because when I open my eyes we're idling through downtown Roaring Springs. It's nearly four P.M. and the downtown area is, as usual, deserted.

Tomasetti glances over at me and takes my hand. "I figured you'd sleep."

I sit up straighter, give his hand a squeeze. "Didn't want to miss seeing this place in the rearview mirror."

It's a true statement. But the heart is a fickle thing. When I see the sign for The Calico Country Store, an emotion I can't quite identify jumps inside me. I find myself thinking of Laura Hershberger and her homey little shop and for the first time it occurs to me that not all of my time spent here was unpleasant.

I glance over at Tomasetti. "Are you game for a cup of coffee?"

He knows it's not coffee I'm craving, but he doesn't ask and angles the Explorer into a parking space.

"This is the shop where I met the Amish women," I tell him.

"Ah . . . the quilt shop where you passed off someone else's work as your own."

"Thanks for reminding me of that."

But we grin at each other as we disembark.

Snow flutters down from a pale sky as we cross the sidewalk. Tomasetti opens the door for me. The cowbell jingles cheerily as we walk inside. The aromas of hazelnut coffee and cinnamon rolls welcome us. The shop is quiet; a single customer picks through the jams and jellies at the far wall. The Mennonite girl at the cash register looks up from her romance novel and smiles.

An uncomfortable pang sounds in my chest. While I don't necessarily want to be here, I know this is the last time I'll walk through that door. The last time I'll see these women I've come to care about. The last time I'll come so close to being the woman I might've been had I remained Amish. While I'm happy with who I am, there's an odd sense of loss in there somewhere.

Our shoes are muted against the plank floor as we start toward the back. There's no chatter of female conversation this afternoon. No sound of laughter. Not even the sharp tone of a lively debate. News travels fast in the Amish community; more than likely, the women have heard what happened at Schrock's compound last night and they're still absorbing the shock of it. I imagine the day has been rife with emotion as they deal with the ensuing disbelief and disappointment.

Pleasure flickers high in my chest when I see the women sitting at the sewing table—Laura Hershberger, Lena, Naomi, and Ada—and I'm glad I took the time to bid my Amish friends farewell.

My chair, of course, is vacant. Someone has placed a stuffed teddy bear on Rebecca's. The lovely tulip basket pattern quilt is spread out on the table before them, all hands busy with the requisite seven stitches per inch.

"Hello, ladies," I say to them. "*Wie geth's alleweil?*" How goes it now?

"Kate! Oh my goodness!" Laura takes the time to finish a stitch before looking up. "We've been wondering—" Her words end abruptly as she takes my measure: Jeans. Leather knee boots. Black puffy coat. Purple scarf.

Slowly, she rises. "*Kate?*"

Naomi does a double take, a sound of surprise escapes her. "Oh!"

Lena seems to be frozen in her chair, eyes wide, her hand pressed protectively over her belly. "*Was der is kshicht?*" What's happening?

"We heard you were caught up in all that mess at the bishop's farm," Laura says.

"The police wouldn't tell us anything," Ada puts in.

"The story in *The Bridge* said there were bad goings on out at Bishop Schrock's barn," Naomi adds in a subdued voice.

"That the sheriff was killed," Lena puts in.

"Can't hardly believe any of it." Laura crosses to me and throws her arms around me. "I'm glad you're okay. We've been worried."

"Me too. Thank you." I hug her back. She smells like lavender soap and I let my arms linger around her a beat too long. "I couldn't leave without . . ." I'm not sure how to finish the sentence so I let the words trail.

"What is this?" Naomi gestures at my clothes. "You're leaving the plain life?"

"I haven't been Amish for a long time," I tell her.

The four women fall silent.

"I don't understand," Laura says.

"I'm a police officer." I give them the condensed version of my assignment. "After Rachel Esh died, the local police became worried about the children. There were a lot of rumors. I traveled here from Ohio to see if I could find out what was going on."

"I've never heard of such a thing," Lena says when I'm finished.

Laura shushes her. "So you're not Kate Miller from Ohio . . ."

"I'm Chief of Police Kate Burkholder from Painters Mill."

Laura blinks as if trying to absorb all of it. "It must have been very difficult for you."

"It was," I tell her. "You made it a little easier."

Her eyes go soft. "I still can't believe it. I mean, everything that happened at the farm. We put our faith in him."

Naomi shakes her head. "I suppose we all knew something wasn't right."

"Especially Rebecca," Ada adds.

"We didn't want to think the worst about the bishop," Lena puts in.

"We should have," Laura interjects.

"Eli Schrock is no bishop," I tell them. "Not even close."

"We trusted him," Lena says. "We believed in him. Looked to him for guidance."

"He lied to you," I tell them. "He betrayed you. All of you."

"The elders are to have a meeting tonight," Naomi informs me.

"Abe Gingerich has already been in touch with the bishop in Conewango Valley," Laura adds. "They're sending their deacon and one of their preachers. I suppose we'll be nominating a new bishop."

"A new beginning," I say.

A lull settles and Laura tosses a speculative look at Tomasetti. "You're a policeman, too?"

Stepping forward, he extends his hand to her. "Agent Tomasetti, ma'am. Nice to meet you."

Laura nods and turns her attention back to me. "What you did. Coming here. Alone. It was a very brave thing to do, Kate Miller."

"Burkholder," I correct her.

She grins. "No offense, but I liked you better as Kate Miller."

The laughter that follows is subdued.

"You can renew the lease on your shop now," I tell Laura.

"I'm happy I won't have to close it," she replies, looking pleased. "Sad about the other things. But such is life."

"When a door closes, a window opens," Naomi says.

Across the table, Lena winces, gives a small gasp. All heads turn her way.

"Sorry," she says, looking embarrassed. "Just Braxton-Hicks."

"Braxton-Hicks?" Naomi gives her a puzzled look. "Who's that?"

Lena chuckles.

Laura sets her hand on Naomi's. "Just the little one making himself known."

I look at Lena. "Will you be using a midwife?"

She shakes her head. "We don't have a midwife."

"I thought Mary Gingerich was a midwife," Naomi says absently.

Something pings in my brain. "Mary's a midwife?" I ask.

"Before she came to Roaring Springs," Laura tells me. "She was a midwife in Cambria County, Pennsylvania."

Mary Gingerich was a midwife.

"In any case," I tell them, "I didn't want to leave without saying good-bye to my Amish friends."

We exchange our final good-byes and hugs. I wish Lena luck with her baby and Laura with the shop. Then Tomasetti and I are on the sidewalk. I stop midway to the Explorer and look at him.

"I didn't know Mary Gingerich was a midwife," I say.

His gaze sharpens on mine. "You're thinking about the Esh girl."

I nod. "I'm not sure it matters now, but according to the ME, she'd been recently pregnant and may have had a home abortion."

"You think Gingerich might have performed the abortion?"

"I think it's worth asking about." I motion toward the storefront of The Dutch Kitchen. "She's a waitress there. Want to walk with me?"

"Probably not a good idea for me to let you out of my sight at this point." But he smiles.

The Dutch Kitchen is nearly deserted this afternoon. The only customer is a middle-aged man wearing khaki pants and a JCPenney shirt and tie who taps on an iPad and sips coffee in one of the booths. The aromas of French fries and coffee float on the warm air as we make our way to the counter. Mary Gingerich is there, scrubbing the sink with a good bit of vigor. I glance toward the pass-through, but the Amish man who'd been there last time I was here is nowhere in sight.

"Be with you in a—" Straightening, Mary cuts the words short and stares at me with unabashed shock. "Kate?"

"Hi, Mary." I climb onto a stool. I don't reach for the coffee cup turned upside down in front of me. "How are you today? How's Abe?"

Her eyes flick over my street clothes and then sweep over to Tomasetti and back to me. "But . . . what . . . I don't understand."

I tell her the same thing I told Laura and the other women. "Eli Schrock's in jail facing an array of charges. Sheriff Suggs is dead."

"*Mein Gott.*" She presses her hand against her stomach, takes a step back. "I heard something happened out there last night. I knew it was bad, but . . . I don't know what to say."

"You don't have to be afraid of him anymore," I tell her. "You and Abe are safe now."

I'm aware of Tomasetti sliding onto the stool beside me. His attention divided between me and Mary.

"So you're not Amish?" she asks, trying to regain her composure.

"Not for a long time."

"I can't believe Bishop Schrock was doing the things they said. I can't believe he's . . . in jail. An Amish *bishop*."

"He's no bishop, Mary. He never was. He's a predator. Maybe worse. Now that he's locked up, no more intimidation. No more threats or hurting people. No more lies."

"So many things have happened." She makes a sound of pure emotion, fighting tears. "Bad things."

"I know. It's over." I give her a moment. "Mary, I need to ask you some questions and I need you to be honest with me."

"Questions about what?"

"Rachel Esh."

"Rachel . . ." She looks down at the soapy sponge in her hand. "She was such a sweet girl. A *good* girl. She was so kind to my Anna."

"I know you were a midwife in Cambria County, Pennsylvania," I say.

Her gaze jerks to mine. I see knowledge in her eyes; she knows where I'm going with this. Fresh tears shimmer in their depths.

"You know Rachel had recently been with child before she died," I tell her.

She glances past me at the lone customer, as if wishing he'd call her over and ask for something. But he hasn't moved from his place in the booth or taken his eyes off the iPad.

When Mary finally speaks, her voice is so low I have to lean closer to hear. "Rachel and Marie were such pretty little girls. Sweet and funny and . . . exuberant." She closes her eyes for a moment. "It broke my heart when Schrock took notice of them.

"Rachel was still a child. She'd just turned fifteen." Pressing her hand to her chest, she lowers her voice. "A few weeks . . . after. She came to me one night, crying. Hysterical because she was *ime familye weg*." In the family way.

"Schrock was the father?" I ask.

Mary looks away, drops the sponge in the sink. A shudder runs through her. She shakes her head. "Not Schrock."

"Who?"

She lowers her voice. "The policeman. The big man with red hair." *Suggs.*

For the first time, the sheriff's suicide makes sense. "He molested a fifteen-year-old girl."

"Yes."

I have no way of knowing exactly what happened. Suggs told me he was involved because of the sex. I wonder if Schrock knew about the sheriff's weakness and offered up Rachel Esh to keep Suggs happy. To keep the sheriff quiet. But I know sometimes lines can be blurred.

I look at Mary. "Why did Rachel come to you?"

"She was going to run away. I offered to help her. So I gave her money, helped her plan it."

"What else?"

Mary closes her eyes tightly. Tears squeeze between her lashes. "She didn't want the baby. She asked me to . . . make it go away. She knew I used to be a midwife. I knew how to make her bleed."

"You aborted the pregnancy?"

She nods. "She wasn't so far along, you know. Just a few weeks. I thought it would be like a regular monthly episode for her." She shrugs. "She was young enough so that she'd forget the pain of what we'd done and move on with her life. I wanted her to be happy. I wanted her to be away from here. Away from Schrock and Suggs and the rest of them.

"She left the next morning and I never saw her sweet face again." She puts her hand over her mouth to smother a sob.

Next to me, Tomasetti takes my hand and squeezes. I don't look at him; I can't. All of those gnarly parallels between Rachel Esh—and me—hover too close to the surface. The circumstances are different, but too much is the same. I was lucky; I got to live my life. Rachel didn't.

Reaching into my pocket, I remove Frank Betancourt's card and slide it across the counter. "When you're ready, you need to call him and tell him what happened."

She looks down at the card as if it's on fire. "Am I in trouble with the law?"

I struggle to find the right words. I meet Mary's gaze and hold it. "Detective Betancourt is mainly going to want to know everything Rachel told you about Dan Suggs. The rest is up to you."

CHAPTER 26

When I was nine years old and grumbling about some chore I'd been tasked with by my *mamm*, my *grossmuder* made a statement I never forgot: Appreciation has the power to transform the mundane into something beautiful. At the time, I was too young to understand the wisdom of those words. It wasn't until decades later that I realized my *grossmuder* was as wise as she was astute and very much unappreciated by her nine-year-old granddaughter.

It's late afternoon and I'm sitting at my beat-up desk in my cramped little office, trying to ignore the cold draft wafting down from the window that looks out over downtown Painters Mill. The once-vibrant fiddle leaf fig plant my team of officers gave me for my birthday last summer is as dried and brown as a cornstalk. The old steel file cabinet next to the door looks as if it's been run through a car crusher and hastily refurbished. I won't even get into the paint on the walls—or the lack thereof.

I love every imperfect inch of this place. Through the open door, I can hear my dispatchers cutting up with my officers. Glock and Skid debating a topic that shouldn't be discussed in mixed company. Pickles grousing about a motorist that sped through the elementary school crosswalk this afternoon. Mona's talking about how things will be done when she's a cop—a possibility that might just become a reality one of these days. I don't have to look to know there's more than likely a good bit of flirting going on as well.

I listen, smiling, and a sense of belonging and pride swells in my chest. Not for the first time since finishing my assignment in Roaring Springs, I count my blessings.

I'm putting the finishing touches on my notes for our weekly meeting when my third shift dispatcher, Mona, sticks her head in my office. "Gang's all here, Chief."

"Thanks, Mona. I'll be right there."

"Oh, and you have a visitor."

I look up from my notes to see Tomasetti standing slightly behind her in the hall, Mr. Professional dressed to the hilt in a slate gray suit and the paisley tie I bought him for Father's Day last year. We've never made it official, but I suspect just about everyone here at the station knows we're a couple. We don't discuss it, and he doesn't visit me here often. But that's one of the things about small town life: keeping secrets, especially big ones, is nearly impossible.

Behind him, Mona grins like an idiot. Slipping into my chief of police persona, I make eye contact with her. She loses the smile, but gives me a thumbs up, then melts back into the hall.

"Sorry to interrupt right before your meeting," he says as he enters my office.

"It's okay," I tell him. "Going to be a short one." I glance out the window. "Looks like we're in for some snow and I wanted to get everyone out of here early."

"You're such a hard ass."

"I do my best."

I turn my attention to the good-size cardboard box tucked beneath his arm. He sets it on my desk. "I had to drive into town so I thought I'd bring this by."

"What is it?"

"Not sure." He extracts a pocketknife from his slacks. "From Roaring Springs."

I look at the return address and something warm quivers in my chest. "The Calico Country Store."

He cuts the boxing tape seal and pries open the box. We peer inside. A pretty handmade card on top. Something wrapped in white paper.

Tomasetti plucks out the card and hands it to me. "Never liked the card part when I was a kid."

I grin at him. "You were probably too anxious to get to the good stuff."

We both know the good stuff is inside the card.

Dear Kate,

I hope this letter finds you well. Our sewing circle is meeting five days a week now. (So much gossip to cover, especially since we're about to nominate a new bishop!) We've been working hard here at the shop and taking on new sewing projects, one of which is a crib quilt for Lena's baby, which will be coming any day now. We finished the tulip basket quilt we were working on while you were here. We decided we should send it to you, since you couldn't make a quilt to save your life. Ha! (I think Rebecca would have agreed!)

> Wishing you all things good and God bless!
> Laura, Ada, Naomi, and Lena

I read the card a second time, smiling, while Tomasetti pulls out the quilt.

"Nice of them to mention your quilting skills," he mutters as he peels away the protective paper. "Looks like a king." He raises his brows Groucho Marx style. "I guess they knew you'd be sharing it with someone?"

"Don't ever underestimate the judicious nature of Amish women," I tell him. "One look at you and they knew we're sleeping together."

"I have a whole new respect for them."

I run my hands over the fabric, taking in the intricate stitching, the beautiful patchwork of colors, and I can't help but think of the strong, capable hands that created it.

"It's an heirloom." I bring the quilt to my face and breath in deeply, not surprised when it smells of lavender and cinnamon and for an instant, I'm transported to that homey little shop on Main Street.

"It's the only thing I miss about being Amish," I whisper.

"The quilting?"

I elbow him in the ribs. "Being part of . . . something. The camaraderie. The friendship. Especially among the women. They don't have easy lives."

"It's nice." Wrapping his hands around my upper arms, he turns me to face him. "I'm assuming those are tears of happiness."

I feel a quick wash of embarrassment. The heat of a blush. "Not a great way to start a meeting with my officers."

"They might think you're human if you're not careful."

I choke out a laugh. Pulling away from him, I set the card on the corner of my desk where I can see it. Together, we begin folding the quilt and tucking it back into the box.

"Going to look nice in our bedroom," I say.

"*You* look nice in our bedroom."

We look at each other and smile. "I'll be home in a couple hours."

"See you then, Chief."